AF267356

SENSING YOU

SENSING SERIES 1

J.M. ADELE

SENSING YOU

Copyright © 2016 J.M. Adele

All Rights Reserved

Edited by Eeva Lancaster
Cover design by Tall Story Designs
Proofed by Fiona Dreaming
Formatting by Book Flare Publishers

Print Edition
ISBN: 978-0-9944516-6-8

Titles by J.M.

Coming Home Series

Shattered Home
Remembering Home
Finding Home
Leaving Home (TBA)
Coming Home (TBA)

Sensing Series

Sensing You
Convincing You
Indulging You (TBA)

Bloodlust Series

Ashes & Dust
Ember & Flame
Bone & Blood (TBA)

To my EB.
As I released this book into the world,
you had to leave us.
For sixteen years, you saw me through
all sorts of sorrow and joy.
You brought me comfort just by being.
Thank you.
I'll be seeing you.

Disclaimer

The following story contains scenes that may be of a disturbing nature to those sensitive to triggers. Please do not proceed if you feel you may be at risk of emotional or psychological harm in doing so.

Please reach out for support should you need any. You don't have to suffer alone.

Contents

Aussie Glossary

Agro - Aggression

Bogan - An uncouth person

Chippie - Carpenter

Dacks - Pants

Glove Box - Glove compartment/ Jockey Box

Goldy - The Gold Coast in Queensland, Australia

Grub - Food

Knackered - Exhausted

Op Shop - Thrift store

Pulling someone's leg - Teasing them.

Ranga - Redhead

Rocky - Rockhampton, Queensland, Australia

Shirt-front - to push your chest into another person's. Usually an aggressive move

Sneakers - Running shoes

Sparrow's fart - Before dawn

Squiz - A glance or a look

Taking the piss - Having a laugh

The box - Television

Tucker - Food

Uni - University

Ute - Utility vehicle/ Pickup truck. A car with a tray on the back for hauling loads

Prologue

My mind wandered to that place where my dreams flee, replaced with vaporous intruders and penetrating horrors. My body twitched and jerked, struggling to find consciousness as the misty form of a woman drifted into my room.

Not again.

She wore a floral, summer dress. One strap was torn and hung loose from her shoulder, and dark bruises circled her neck. Reaching out her hand, she wrapped it around my foot. My body stilled. Inside my chest, my heart froze while my stomach threatened to prolapse. She pulled on my foot, imploring me to listen. I knew she couldn't really drag me away, but I felt the icy touch, the drag of her fingers on my terrified flesh. I wondered if I would somehow disappear. My hands reached desperately for the pillow.

"Stop," I pleaded.

"You have to help me. You have to stop him."

My whimpers turned into sobs. "Please … g-go away."

I felt another presence. Heard the shaky rumble of his voice as he told the lady to leave.

"Daddy," I whispered, relieved. He smiled at me with sad eyes.

But the spirit refused to budge.

"I'm sorry, honey bunch. I love you," my father's voice whispered, heavy with regret.

The wretched fingers of loss clawed their way into my chest, pulling apart my ribcage as if just learning of his death.

I dropped the pillow, and reached out to him. "Nooo! Daddy!" My screams were useless. He was gone.

Wrenching my sweat-soaked body upright, my throat ached as the scream continued to escape the depths of my chest. I pressed my lips together to cut off the sound, but that only lasted a second. My mouth opened wide again as I gasped for much needed air.

A hammering sound filled the room. My muddled brain mistook it for the pulse in my ears, but it was the beating of a fist on my bedroom door.

"SHUT UP!" My housemate screeched as she continued to pound.

I was definitely awake now. My hand circled my throat. I needed to check for myself if my screams had stopped. *Yup. All good.* "Yeah, keep your skin on!" I tried to shout back, but my voice came out hoarse.

"Fucking freak," she mumbled before I heard the shuffle of her feet on the tiles.

Again, frozen fingers grasped my toes and pulled. I snapped my foot back, leaving her hand suspended and empty. I watched my stubborn, unwanted visitor through narrowed eyes, and a whole lot of false bravado.

"He's coming. He's going to take another."

"Okay got it. You can go now. You're not wanted here. *Leave.*" My voice was low, but firm.

Her face went blank, and her hand dropped from its raised position. The holographic image of her faded, but the chill running up and down my body remained.

I liked to think I could run from this, but there's no hiding from things unbound to time or matter. My stupid sixth sense was telling me the proverbial shit was going to hit the proverbial fan … soon.

Fuck my life.

Chapter
1

Brad—Six Months Ago

Screaming sirens and the roar of engines pierced the pre-dawn tranquillity. Red and blue flashing lights blocked my view and I could see a motorcycle cop gesturing for me to pull over. *Ah, fuck.* Dropping through the gears, I eased off my bike's throttle, and pulled over behind the bacon.

The cop kicked out his stand and casually strolled over, flipping the cover of his ticket book before looking at me. "Morning, sir. Could you please dismount and turn off your engine?"

I did as he said. My headlight died, just like my chance of getting home without getting caught by the pigs.

"Any reason why you're not wearing a helmet?"

I'm fucked.

Truth is, I didn't want to wear the fucking thing like a good little boy. I just wanted to feel the wind in my hair, and hide behind a bandana like an outlaw.

"It was stolen while I was taking a piss."

His bland expression flattened by a fraction. The guy had clearly heard every sort of bullshit excuse from every kind of nut job. "Did you realise you were speeding around the bend back there?"

"Nuh. What speed was I doing, *cunt*-stable?" He ignored my jibe and started jotting down my licence plate on his ticket book. "Don't you guys have an app for that now?" His pen paused for a millisecond before he continued to write the government a cheque for an obscene amount of my money.

"I'm going to need your driver's licence. Have you been drinking tonight?" He narrowed his eyes, obviously unamused. His look told me that he'd like to add the word 'dickhead' to his question.

I shook my head. Even though I did have a drink late last night, technically, I haven't had anything today. He tested me anyway and I just scraped in under the limit.

I've got nothing against the pigs. They've got a shitty job, and we're all buggered without them. I was just being a petulant little shit because my care factor was in the negative. I *wanted* to stir up trouble. I *wanted* the adrenaline rush of skirting the edge of danger. Riding the winding roads of Mount Glorious in the early hours of a

Saturday morning had felt like a good plan. If I happened to take a corner too wide and launched into sweet oblivion, well, I'd crack one last smile before my exit. If my face remembered what to do. There was nobody home to answer the door anyway, if the cops came knocking. So, what would it matter?

He handed my licence back with the ticket, explaining my offences, and the consequences that came with them. Five hundred and ten dollars and four demerit points later, I still felt no remorse. As I stood there with my arms folded and legs apart, I felt the adrenaline continue to pump through my veins, feeding the anger that thrived in my shrivelled heart. I was pissed that I didn't just slide off the edge of the mountain. Now, I was stuck waiting for a cop car to take me to the nearest train station.

I didn't want to go back to that house. I didn't want to go back to living the nightmare I've been forced to endure. I did not fucking deserve to live at all.

————

Ronnie—Present Day

Rhythmic breaths screamed through my lungs. As my feet hit the pavement, shocks ricocheted up my body. I was sharing the dawn light with a handful of diehards, braving the onslaught in order to flog our bodies into a state of fitness, discipline and beauty, or in my case—numbness. This torture was as necessary to me as breathing. Sometimes I run twice a day, even more when I'm not working. It was a feeling I revelled in. The pulsing of muscle, the surging of blood and endorphins, the sting of fatigue and lactic acid … it's my bliss.

I lifted the collar of my singlet to wipe the sweat from my neck as I passed another runner. If there's one thing I didn't like about running, it was the sweat. The feeling of it trickling down my neck was particularly offensive. It reminded me too much of … unwanted visitors. They're never too far away. As inescapable to me as the need to take a dump, and about as pleasant.

My arms and legs continued to pump as I turned my head to gaze across the brown, Brisbane River, watching the city wake up. Vehicles either scurried home for the day, or started out early on the Riverside Expressway. Cranes perched themselves on infantile skyscrapers, stretching their necks, ready to cast their lines for the next piece of the puzzle. I couldn't hear anything but the thumping of rock music through my earbuds, though, and that's just the way I liked it. But I could smell the river, and the overlay of wet clay on the humid breeze.

I swivelled my head back around just in time to notice an ibis scavenging for treasures left over from last night's social scene in South Bank. Heaving my body up, I leaped over the bird, spinning in mid-air so that I landed facing the direction I'd come from. It opened its long black beak, giving me the stink eye and probably squawking at me. Not that I could hear it. I was tempted to give it the finger. I was tempted to give anything the finger, if it got too close.

My head jerked up at some movement behind Featherbrain. A young woman stood applauding with a huge grin on her face. *Smart arse.* I resisted the urge to bow and flip *her* the bird. Turning back, I pushed my aviators up the bridge of my nose, pulled down the shade of my baseball cap, and yanked two handfuls of my long, brown hair to tighten my ponytail. It flapped against my back as I ran, acting like a blanket in the sticky heat.

My peripheral vision registered that I'd gained a companion. The young woman had started running beside me. She was actually keeping pace, so I picked it up a notch. She kicked it up a gear, too.

Smart arse.

I flicked my eyes sideways to get a better look at her. Wearing bright blue shorts and a loose yellow tank with the words 'MADE LAST CENTURY' embroidered across the chest, she barely reached my shoulders. *Wait a minute.* Her chest wasn't rising and falling from breathing hard, only from the swing of her arms … and she looked a bit hazy around the edges. She stopped moving her legs and turned sideways, but her body continued to move along with me.

Oh. She's a spirit.

I slowed down again. She had an advantage over me. Smart Arse was unavoidable. As I passed the Wheel of Brisbane lying in wait for its first volunteer, I wondered who she was with so I could tell them to put a leash on.

As if they'd believe me.

"Gonna be a beautiful day," she yelled with enthusiasm as she jogged beside me. I wanted to smack it out of her.

I continued to ignore her and sped up again. Not many people could keep up with me once I got going. I really should do a fun run or two. Hmm, running in a crowd. How horrific. I suppressed a shudder.

"You are super fit, aren't you? How often do you run?"

I pointed to my ear buds and shook my head, mouthing, "I can't hear you." Punching the volume up, the music beat against my eardrums like my head was between two clashing cymbals. When she reached over to take out my ear bud, I stumbled to a stop, grabbing at the cord.

Damn, she knew how to move things.

"Hey!" I yelled before thinking.

"Would you stop for two minutes, Elektra?"

"Pfft! Elektra. Good one. Too bad I don't carry a Sai or you'd be a goner." I hissed the words under my breath while fiddling with my earphones.

"I've been watching you for weeks. I really need to talk to you," her pretty eyes pleaded.

She looked young; late teens, maybe early twenties. Her family must've been devastated that she was taken so young. Reluctantly, I softened towards her, but only a little.

"Okay. Just a tip. If you're trying to make a friend, it's probably best not to admit that you've been stalking the person, first."

"Lol," she said with a smirk and a lift of the eyebrow, flicking her bronze ponytail back over her shoulder.

"Oh God, she speaks in text." I snorted and turned back to the path. She followed my lead. *Great.* My shoulders slumped as I let out a sigh. "If you really need to talk to me, you're going to have to run."

I turned off the music and tucked the ear buds into the pocket of my running shorts, before I took off at a jog. Everything felt thinner, my skin, my clothes, the oxygen content in the air. I had the irrational urge to duck for cover in the garden. But I pulled the brim of my hat lower instead.

"Cute shorts. Where'd you get 'em?"

With an exaggerated eye roll, I answered, "The Op Shop."

"Ooh, I used to love op shopping," she sighed.

That was unexpected. She looked a bit too pampered for the second-hand-shop scene.

The whoosh of air from being overtaken by the exercise crowd grated on my personal space. It was one of my pet hates. I ground my teeth and chewed on the flesh of my cheek, wiping the trickling sweat off my brow.

"Are you going to get to the point any time soon? I have to get ready for work." My lips barely moved. I was so good at it; I could do a side gig as a ventriloquist.

"Okay, okay. I need you to find my brother and give him a message for me," she half mumbled.

My jaw and hands clenched in unison. I'd heard some version of this question for as long as I could remember.

I need you to tell my kids I love them and I'm okay.

Tell my son I buried five thousand dollars in the backyard, in a Milo tin.

My wife doesn't know I had a son.

I didn't want anything to do with anyone's family bullshit.

"Can't you find him yourself? You can walk through walls, you know."

"I haven't lost him, obviously. He's just ignoring me because I did something stupid."

"Like die?" I glanced at her and watched her face fall as the words left my mouth. I wanted to suck them back in and crunch them until they were dust. Swinging my gaze back to the path, I resurrected my hard exterior. I couldn't let her get to me. I wanted to keep my sanity. "Can't help you," I said curtly, omitting the word 'sorry' on purpose.

"Wait! Hear me out, " she pleaded.

"No."

"Oh, come on, you're starting to sound like your flatmate."

My head whipped around and my feet faltered. "Stop stalking me!"

"I'm sorry, but I've seen you around on campus, and my brother starts his degree there this week." She twisted her hands together before dropping them back to her sides. "What if I told you your life is about to change for the better because of me?"

Change? No, I didn't like the sound of that at all. I wiped my hands on my shorts, erasing any trace of panic as I rolled my eyes. "Unless you can tell me the lotto numbers, I'm not interested."

"I'm going to save your life," she said soberly.

Her expression made me pause, turning my thoughts back to the dream, and the visitor I had this morning. I wiped my hands again as the chill returned to my foot, winding its way up my leg. My heart rate sped out of control. I did jumps on the spot, jiggling my shoulders to dislodge the bad juju.

"Look, whatever you've heard about me is rubbish. Yes, I can see you. No, I'm not a PI. Seriously, how do you think I'd be able to reach out to a complete stranger with the opener, 'Your dead sister sent me?' I'm just not interested, and I'm afraid your time is up. So … good luck with that." I stabbed my ear buds back into my ears.

Looking around to get my bearings, I saw that we'd reached the Maritime Museum, and the end of the path. I turned west so I could head back to my car. The tension in my shoulders worked its way up my neck. What a shit start to the day.

After two steps, I ploughed into a solid object and landed hard on my arse. I was on the ground with my legs splayed out in front, while my arms were braced behind me, the skin on my palms being sanded down to the flesh beneath.

"Shit! Are you all right?"

The gruff bark was alarmingly close. I wanted to scurry away like a crab. I tried to push myself up with my hands, but it was like trying to touch fire. The pain in my backside screamed, 'GET THE HELL OFF!'

I rolled over onto my knees and elbows, hearing the unmistakable sound of guffaws coming from my petite, little stalker, as she enjoyed my predicament. *Smart arse.* Rolling from side to side with her knees curled up to her chest, she was lost in a fit of laughter. A scowl took up residence on my face, and right about then, I realised that I was showing my best side to the obstacle in question. I dared a glance over my shoulder. *Yep.* From under the brim of his cap, I distinctly saw a mouth twisted to the side trying its damnedest not to smirk.

"Can I help you up?" The amusement in his voice was obvious.

I turned my face back to the ground. "No, you've done enough." *He's only trying to help, it's not his fault.*

Don't be a bitch. "Thanks," I added, screwing my nose up at the word.

"Your hands are bleeding." His big body knelt beside me, engulfing me in his energy. It spun around him like a vortex, beckoning me into its core.

Whoa. That pushed my red, panic button and the alarms in my head blared. I needed to wipe my palms, and not only because of the blood. The inside of my cheek took the brunt of my anxiety instead.

"Yup … got that. Thanks, Sherlock. I have tissues in my pocket. You can go." *In case you missed the sarcasm, you have been dismissed, mister!*

"You fell really hard. Just let me help you up so I can see if you're able to walk back to wherever you're going, or if I have to call a cab."

He sounded like he was trying not to laugh. *Bastard.* I was growling on the inside. *Why isn't he taking the hint?* I was pretty sure I'd bruised, if not broken, my tail bone.

It. Fucking. Hurt.

The rubberneckers were starting to congregate. I looked up for a second and saw a couple of sweaty, middle-aged men leering at my backside. Their lewd thoughts slithered along my skin like a hundred leeches looking for a meal. I shuddered, and I found myself embracing the stranger's energy like a shield.

With a resigned sigh, I nodded my head. He wrapped his hand around my arm, infusing my skin with a feeling of safety, and a wave of anticipation. Like everything was going to be okay if we remained in contact. I'd never felt at peace with anyone, besides my granny. A stranger's touch usually, triggered a sick feeling in my stomach. As though some of their negative energy had seeped into me, infusing me with their worries and pain.

I didn't like the message my body was sending me in response to his touch. He pulled me gently to my feet, but didn't let go of my arm. Annoyed, I tilted my face up to glare at him, and give a curt 'thank you'. But the retort dissolved on my tongue. Thick, dark, bronze eyebrows were cranked low over grey eyes that bored into me. They completely sucked me in, removing me from the world … removing me from my pain. I wanted to slump in relief, but I was frozen. I never wanted to stop looking at his beautiful face. My eyes flitted around his features. The rusty stubble over freckled skin, shiny with sweat. A scar over one eyebrow, denying space to any hair that might want to take up residence. Pale, pink lips. His top lip was slightly thinner than his bottom lip, with more freckles splattering their surface.

He gave me a small smile, somehow breaking through the wall I hid behind. I must've looked like a stunned guppy fish, standing there with eyes wide, mouth wide, and forgetting that I was trying to shake my arm free.

You will spend the rest of your life with this man.

The knowledge hit me from somewhere unknown, imprinting in my long-term memory. Like an ice-filled bath, that realisation snapped me back to a very cold reality.

Oh, Shit. I'm out of here.

I yanked my arm out of his grip. "You know what? I think I'll be fine. Thanks for the massive bruise. Bye." My words ran together into an incoherent jumble.

I turned gingerly and waddled away, wincing not only from the pain, but from my foreboding premonition. Even though I was hobbling away at a snail's pace, he didn't come after me or say anything more. But I felt his concern dragging at me.

I couldn't help myself. I glanced back and saw him, arms tensed by his side. His mouth was set in a tight line as he frowned, and his eyes were locked on mine. I had no doubt that he felt whatever this was, too.

Christ! Did the temperature just go up ten degrees? Forget butterflies, that look was like a punch to the gut. I wondered if I'd ever get my breath back.

Chapter

2

Brad

Fuck, fuck, fuck! I just shirt-fronted the Amazonian Gazelle. That's one way to make myself memorable, I s'pose. I watched her hobble away. Even limping, she was graceful. And, those legs … those legs were a fucking dream. I wanted them wrapped around me. Dirty bastard. I smacked my hand against the back of my head for allowing my thoughts to sink into the gutter.

I'd seen her before. She always had her head down when she ran, like she was being chased by the devil. Until today, she'd kept her face hidden behind the hat and glasses. Freed of the barriers, I was struck by the kind of beauty she presented. Eyes almost black, with long thick lashes. Chicks had to stick on falsies if they wanted eyelashes like that. She had an exotic beauty no man could resist. The way her body moved was mesmerizing. Her deep brown, curly hair flowed out through the back of her cap, swinging from side to side as she ran. Yeah, I wanted to see her hair on my pillow, but it was more than that.

She intrigued me. I'd passed her on the path, as she was mucking around with her earbuds and muttering to herself. Strange behaviour for anyone, I guess. I wanted to know what was going on in that head of hers, as much as I wanted to bury my face in her skin, her hair and in the heaven between her legs.

Must be time to head home. I was losing my grip on reality.

Standing in my bathroom, I stripped out of my sweaty clothes, and dumped them in the corner somewhere near the hamper. I adjusted the spray to cold, hoping for lukewarm water, at least. The middle of summer didn't offer much reprieve from hellfire temperatures. You'd think I'd be used to it since I grew up on the Capricorn Coast. But, today, the heat made me think of sweat and long legs, dark hair, and brown skin. It was no good. She was inside my head. I couldn't stop my brain from going there. My body couldn't help but respond to my thoughts. She was beyond gorgeous.

I couldn't believe I'd knocked her on her arse. I'd nearly choked when she got up on her elbows and knees, waving it at me.

I pushed my arousal down until it hurt, needing to punish myself for my lack of control. I was such a sick bastard. She didn't like me touching her. And why would she? I was no one to her. Well, now I was the guy that probably fractured her tailbone. *Awesome*. That thought effectively got rid of my boner.

I squirted some soap onto a washer and roughly dragged it over my skin as further punishment. Doing the same with the towel, before walking back to my room, naked. I purposely avoided looking at the photos on the hallway wall because I was already feeling like shit. I should take them down to make it easier on myself, but I didn't want to. I wanted to torture myself. I made myself look at those photos every morning to remind me of how I'd failed. How I didn't want to fail again.

Exactly like I'd just done. Again.

Bloody pathetic. I had this stupid feeling that I needed to get to know this woman, maybe protect her or some shit. Don't ask me why, I have no fucking idea. The thought just came to me and embedded itself in my brain. I was crazy for a woman I'd never met, until now. She was the only one that lit my darkness and I didn't even know her. I doubted she'd want to stop and talk to me in the future … and that thought just made me want to go and have a bottle of bourbon.

Today was a bad day. I started to lose hope again. Sitting on the edge of my bed with my elbows on my knees and my head in my hands, I desperately tried to ignore the emptiness of the house. The emptiness of my soul. My thoughts shifted to figuring out how to fill it.

Adrenaline or alcohol, what'll it be?

And the winner was … alcohol.

Throwing on a singlet and shorts, I headed to the kitchen. The sooner I got to that bourbon, the better. The feel of the burn as I poured it down my throat, and the sweet, dulling of the senses. To get rid of the loneliness, normally I thought of her, focusing on becoming a man worthy of someone like her. Now, I just thought of her limping as fast as she could to get away from me.

I just fucked up my chances.

——

Ronnie

The relief I felt when I got out of the car, and off my butt, was tremendous. An animalistic keening escaped the confines of my chest as the pinch of pain receded. I knew the bone was broken. I felt the sickening click vibrate up my spine when I sat in the driver's seat. Luckily, the trip from South Bank to the suburb of West End—where I rented a room—was short.

The flat was on the fifth floor; exactly halfway up the modern, charcoal coloured, concrete structure. I skipped the stairs and headed for the elevator. My keys jingled as I hastily unlocked the door. The throb of pain in my backside was intensifying. I just wanted to take painkillers, have a shower, and curl up with an ice pack strapped to my rear end.

Two steps into the wrought iron and glass themed living room, and the smells of leather polish and glass cleaner assaulted my senses, adding a headache to my repertoire of aches and pains.

"I was hoping you'd forget your way home," my flatmate, Felicity, snapped from the leather lounge. Her laptop sat open as she read what looked like an online tutorial for one of her law classes. She was following in her daddy's footsteps.

Something I hope I never do.

"I'm good with directions. Sucks to be you, huh?" I left her in the lounge, and limped along to my room.

Her snide voice followed me. "What happened to you? Did your suicide attempt fail?"

My shoulders stiffened and my feet faltered a step. The annoyance I felt from the stellar start to my day had just upgraded to downright pissed.

Without sparing a glance in her direction, I shot out my retort, "I've just had the best marathon sex session of my life. If you're able to walk after sex, then you're not doing it right." I looked back at her over my shoulder. Felicity's mouth was wide open, and disgust twisted wrinkles into her face. "Never mind, Flick. Someone will take pity on you, someday." Her face paled as her mouth snapped shut.

I retreated behind my bedroom door, feeling marginally better, and disgusted in myself at the same time. I'd been cruel.

It was necessary.

The wonderful smell of lavender assailed my senses. A flimsy wooden door and the smell I grew up with, these were the only two things I found comforting about this room. I missed the feeling of belonging somewhere. Being able to come home, and throw your feet up on the couch because it was yours. Having someone to offload all your crap to, because you knew they'd return the favour. That person had always been my granny.

When she broke her hip a couple of years ago, she felt it was time to move into a retirement unit, where nurses were available at the push of a buzzer. I knew I couldn't look after her, and still keep a full-time job. And I needed to work to help pay the bills. It was the best thing for her, but it was the beginning of a spiral of shit for me. I didn't want to be selfish or needy, but I was devastated to lose my home. Being separated from my only family caused a fault line in my foundations that I didn't know how to patch.

I thought this room was the answer to my prayers. A bargain price for quality accommodations. She'd probably had to drop the price due to the bitch factor.

The sunlight filtered in through the window above my queen-sized bed, reflecting off the almost white walls. Moving to the bedside table, I took a couple of painkillers, and switched on my lava lamp. I found them so mesmerizing. And Flicker hated it, so I loved it.

Placing my gear on the chest of drawers, I reached into one of the drawers to grab some underwear. My hands paused before finding their prize. Things had moved. She'd been through my things again. My eyebrows slammed down. What the fuck was she looking for among my knickers and bras? Drugs? Money? Incriminating evidence? It wasn't as if she could borrow my clothes, she's half my height and twice my girth. I hated living like this. I couldn't trust her to leave my stuff alone. If I thought seeing dead people was going to send me off the deep end, I clearly didn't account for this single, white female.

I grabbed what I needed, and headed down the hallway to the bathroom. The skin on my back prickled with the force of daggers that flew from Flick's eyes. I really needed those painkillers to kick in. Ten minutes and I could be out the door again to get some breakfast before work. No way was I going to use the kitchen with her staring me down.

In the shower, I hung my head and let the warm water help soothe the pain as the medicine did its thing. I let out a deep sigh into the towel, before I turned my back to the mirror, twisting around so I could inspect the damage. A big purple bruise had started to form on my tail bone. It looked like I wouldn't be sitting down much today.

I dried myself quickly, and dressed for work. With sore hands and no time, I didn't bother with hair or make-up. Instead, I made sure I'd packed up everything. I didn't want to get comfortable here, or give her an excuse to complain about my stuff cluttering up her space. I was like a ghost. *Ironic.* Nobody knew I lived here, unless they looked in my cupboards.

With my arms loaded, I opened the door, jerking at the sight of Felicity waiting like a lioness about to pounce. My towel slipped off my shoulder, falling to the floor.

"I hope you're going to pick that up," she spat at me.

I cleared my throat to refrain from swearing at her. "What is it, Flick?"

"Don't call me that, it's so juvenile."

Yeah, it suits you.

I bent down to get my towel, gaining an eye full of fake toenails. *Ugh.* Standing back up to face the wrath pouring off her, I quirked my eyebrow, waiting for the tirade.

Her baby-blue eyes narrowed at my insolence. She had the 'unimpressed face' down pat. It was a shame she didn't realise how it twisted her pretty features. She took a big breath, and crossed her arms over her designer blouse. "I'm having a party for all my friends tonight. You're not invited. Don't bother coming back after work." With a satisfied smirk, she turned on her heel and walked back to her laptop, toe nails clicking on the tiles.

Un-fucking-believable. The pounding in my head returned, amplified. This was becoming a weekly occurrence. I wasn't allowed in my own home. Because it wasn't *really* my home. It was just a place to crash. I just knew I would be coming back to a toilet and sink filled with vomit, and I'd probably have to burn my sheets.

Good times. Good times.

———

I pulled up to the driveway of Granny's retirement unit, just as Errol, her neighbour from two doors down, wrestled with the security door, while trying to balance himself against his walking frame. Over his shoulder, a frail looking lady in a nightie wore a look of disgust on her face. As if Errol had just done the unthinkable, and taken a dump in the rose bushes.

I moved to his side. "Good evening, Errol. How are you?" He spun his head around, stopping abruptly before his eyes reached mine, wincing in pain.

"Argh! Put my neck out, damn it."

The lady in the nightie shoved her finger towards his face. "Serves you right, you old coot!"

Ooh, she was ropable.

I ignored her. "Oh no, you poor thing. Here, let me help you get the door shut and I'll walk you back home." I tried soothing him, knowing full well that he hadn't been leaving, but was trying to get into the unit. I could see Granny peering through the crack in the curtains.

"I was just coming to visit your sweet grandma, hoping to get a slice of her famous cheesecake, but she didn't answer the door."

The old woman grew even more agitated after that statement. "She won't answer the door if she knows what's good for her. You always did think you were 'in-like-Flynn' there, didn't you, Errol? You should be ashamed of the way you carry on like the milkman!" She shook her fists in anger as she delivered her verbal spray.

I peeled Errol's gnarled hand from the door handle, and gently wrapped it around his walker. "I think she's at her reading group tonight. She asked if I could get some supplies and drop them off for her." The lie tripped off my tongue, unheeded. Luckily, I had a bag of groceries in my hand. I brought something every time I came because I visited so often, but he didn't need to know that.

I turned him around and headed back to his unit, glancing over my shoulder to throw a wink at Granny. Deep lines bracketed her mouth as she focused on the old woman. I recognised her now as Mrs McGuffey, from the unit next door between Errol's and Granny's. She didn't look healthy, at all. I looked back at Granny. Lowering her eyes, she gently shook her head.

Oh.

Errol made it safely back to his unit, regardless of the continuing tirade from the spectre of Mrs McGuffey. I left them to it, and let myself into Granny's place. Her L shaped unit was miniscule. She sat at the small dining table against the wall between the kitchenette and the lounge room. "Thank you, my darling. That man is unstoppable. The ageing process forgot to notify his libido."

I placed the bags on the floor, and gave her a hug and a kiss on her weathered cheek. "He has good taste, at least." Patting Granny's shoulder, I turned towards the fridge. "When did it happen?"

I put the groceries away, knowing she was shaken, but understanding that she wouldn't want me fussing.

Continuing with the mundane chore while she expressed her sadness was a distraction for her … and me. A reminder that life continued. We'd been through this several times now. I was terrified that she would be next. The carton of milk sloshed and banged loudly against the shelf, as it slipped from my shaking hand. I remained hidden behind the fridge door, trying to pedal back the panic as she answered my question.

"We haven't heard anything official yet, but she showed up here about three hours ago. She's been wandering around the garden, muttering about the dead flowers, and trying to get the hose to turn on. Of course, that was about as useful as cleaning up a flood with a tissue. Then she saw Errol heading this way and got mad as a hatter. Why she ever wanted to stake a claim on that man, I'll never know. He's as randy as a teenager!"

Her arms flailed with the dose of comic relief. I smiled as I watched her, dressed in her fashionable T-shirt and shorts, with the ghastly floral couch that she loved so much behind her. Despite her anachronistic taste in furnishings, she refused to be stuck in a time warp when it came to her fashion sense. Apart from her straight hair, it was like looking at me in fifty years' time. Slightly withered and weathered, but with a spark in her eye, nonetheless.

"Some women go for the bad boys. I didn't even know she was sick."

"Yeah, she went to the hospital two days ago with a bad chest infection. Darn humidity, breeds the bugs."

"I'm sorry, Granny." I leaned down and gave her a gentle hug. She was so fragile now, I was always afraid of getting over enthusiastic and snapping something when I hugged her.

"Me too, but it's a fact of life. We all have our time."

Her words cut through my heart. My biggest fear verbalized. The thought of Granny leaving me was so painful I had trouble breathing. I loved her to bits. She was my home. She had been my grandmother, my mother and my best friend. My only friend, really. The one positive thing about this curse of mine is that I'd still be able to talk to her after she'd gone. But it wouldn't be the same.

"Veronica, you really need to let me teach you about your gift, honey. Life would be so much easier for you, if you were able to control it." Granny leaned forward, encasing my hands in her grasp. The love and concern she felt for me transferred through her touch, reaffirming what I'd lose when she was gone.

I slid my hands into my lap, and cleared the lump from my throat. "We tried that, and you know how that worked out."

Ghost party. Ten o'clock. My place. Bring your nasty.

"You will never find happiness until you embrace your true self, and be the person you're meant to be."

My eyes dropped to the floor. Reigning in the need to shiver, I went back to the kitchenette to get some ingredients for dinner.

"Is an omelette okay with you?"

Granny huffed out a breath. "You're as stubborn as a mule … Fine," she waved her hand and dismissed the topic. "What about your living arrangements? I assume Felicity is having a night of drunken debauchery for her minions?"

"You assume correctly, as per usual. You can say I told you so, I know you want to."

"Oh, darling. I'm not going to do that. You have the right to make your own choices. I'm more than aware that you don't want to know anything about the future or being psychic, but they're all part of who you are. I didn't argue too much about your decision because I believed you needed to know this girl for a reason. But now's the time to pull your finger out. It's time to go, Big Brother style."

I huffed out a laugh. "You have such a way with words." My hands got busy chopping spring onions and capsicum.

"Seriously, honey. Do not let that girl play any more power games with you. You aren't helping her by staying there."

"Why the heck would I want to help her at all?"

"Because you are a decent human being under all that spit and sass."

"If I go home to find vomit or other bodily excrement anywhere near my stuff, she'll find out just how indecent I can be."

The sound of the knife embedding itself into the chopping board echoed in the tiny space.

"Prepare yourself. That's all I have to say."

Her face was a grim reflection of her warning, before a conspiratorial smile swept away the darkness. The sudden swing made my neck tingle. I had to look down at what I was doing, because I sensed that I wasn't going to like what was about to happen.

"Okay, enough about that. So, you've met him, finally?" I felt her eyes drill into my face.

The neck tingle became more of a burn. *Damn. She knows.*

My hand jerked, and I dropped the knife before I sliced off my finger. I was sure my eyes were as wide as saucers, and I had to bite my lip to stop my mouth from falling open.

"Who?" I replied, still looking at the veggies.

I knew it was pointless to play dumb with Granny and yet, stupidly, I pursued this path. I absolutely did not want to talk about *him*. Peeking out from the corner of my eye, I caught Granny's wide, satisfied grin. A groan slipped out. Both hands covered my eyes, forgetting that I'd been chopping up spicy vegetables. My hands flailed under the tap, splashing water everywhere in a desperate attempt to evict the capsaicin from my eyeballs.

"Honey, you know you can't shut everybody out forever. You don't want to end up old and alone. I don't want that for you. Imagine if I'd never fallen in love with your granddad. I wouldn't have you. I shudder at the thought."

I refrained from squirming. I knew what she said was true, but I wanted to play ostrich for a bit longer. Just the thought of letting anyone in was terrifying. Was she joking? I'd spent my entire life, up to this point, feeling like an outcast—harassed, and plagued. So, my standard defence was to keep to myself. If I absolutely had to interact with people, I was damn good at being a bitch.

My gut was telling me that I no longer had a choice. I couldn't run from an intangible force like fate. But, I'd do my damnedest to hold it off for a while. After all, I didn't know his name, or even where he worked. He knew nothing about me, apart from where I run occasionally.

My brain slowly reconnected with the here and now. I realised I'd been staring straight through my granny while she watched patiently, a small smile on her lips and a furrow in her brow. I knew she was worried. I knew she had a fair idea of what was in store for my future. I didn't like to ask her about her predictions, because I really prefer not to know. That was my inner ostrich talking, though slightly muffled due to her head being in the sand.

I shook my head, and blinked a few times. Granny lifted her hand and pointed over my shoulder. I turned my head around to look through the lace curtains, my whole body stiffening at what I saw. The little stalker. She was staring at me, hugging herself, and bouncing from one foot to the other, as if she was cold. *Shit!* Oh, but this girl knew where to find me anytime she wanted. Even with my head in the sand. *Ugh! Why me?*

Single white female, indeed.

———

Brad

God, I loved these old buildings. Even the smell of decades piling up got me high. My biker boots thumped on the old wooden decking, as I smoothed a palm over the beautifully crafted, sandstone walls of Old Government House. It amazed me when I thought of the artistry created with only the most basic tools, and the hours of labour it required. I'd be designing my own structures soon enough, when I start uni. These buildings are my inspiration. Yes, they were styled from European influence, but the use of Australian timbers and natural rock … it converged the foreign with an Aussie flavour, and stamped these buildings as our own.

I darted around the display in the foyer, while some tourists occupied the chick at reception. I hated that they'd closed off some of the house to the public. I'd have loved to get a squiz at the guts of the building.

The security guard looked me up and down as I sauntered through the rooms. I tipped my chin up in his direction. "Hey mate. How's it going?"

The guard maintained his stern face, but gave me a nod. I felt his eyes glued to my back as I walked off. I suppose I looked a bit shady with my ripped jeans and faded T-shirt, carrying a biker jacket in one hand, and my helmet in the other.

The original carpeting was long gone, replaced by a modern, Tree-of-Life patterned carpet. It was beautiful, but out of place in the grand old elegance. Just like me. I snickered to myself while I climbed the staircase.

The William Robinson Art Gallery occupied the top floor. I loved that a painting of a bloke holding two fish won the most prestigious art award in Australia. But I came here to see my favourite painting by far— 'Professor John Robinson and brother William'. It depicts the artist's brother, wearing graduation robes over a suit, standing beside William in his pyjamas and bathrobe. Classic Aussie humour. He was absolutely taking the piss when he painted it.

Striding down the hallway to my favourite room, I heard a throaty, feminine laugh. It sounded like it came from somewhere deep and genuine. It did things to me, drawing me toward it with an invisible string. I'd never get tired of looking at the painting, but when I scooted around the corner, the vision in front of the painting absolutely floored me.

It was her … again. Fate was definitely taunting me, or giving me a sign … I couldn't tell yet. I tried to breathe as I watched her having a good laugh at William Robinson's depiction of the career structure in his family. Encasing those slim thighs, a figure hugging skirt went all the way up to her ribcage. A tiny little shirt covered her slim shoulders and pert tits. Her head was tipped back, causing that tumble of curls to reach all the way to her arse.

When my eyes reached her feet, a laugh bubbled out of my throat. She was wearing runners. The conflicting style told me more about her than she probably realised. She was classy, but liked to let her hair down. She didn't mind negating fashion in favour of comfort. She was disciplined and serious, but wanted more freedom and fun in her life. She was saying, 'come hither, but if you do … I'll run'.

I'm going to catch you.

My eyes travelled up to find her staring at me in fright. *Shit.* I'd scared her with my ogling. And the way I was dressed probably wasn't helping. I took a step back and gave her my friendliest smile. "Funny painting, isn't it? It's my favourite of his collection. 'William and Josephine' comes a close second. Which one do you like the best?"

Her lips pursed and I watched her throat manoeuvre a swallow. She opened her mouth to draw in a laboured breath. She blinked, but didn't speak. I'd struck her dumb, it seemed. I took another step back and shrugged. "It's okay. It's hard to choose. Let's face it, they're all good."

"Mmm." The sound fought its way out into the air as if her throat had closed. She bent down and grabbed a handbag that I hadn't even noticed, looping it onto her shoulder. A pair of black heels poked out the top. She turned and walked away from me, again.

She was damn good at the Cinderella disappearing act. She even remembered to take her shoes with her. No worries. I didn't need a glass slipper. I'd find her again. I could feel it in my gut and my balls. I smiled up at the Robinson brothers. They had helped make my day.

Chapter
3

Ronnie

The imposing beauty of Old Government House filled my vision. I stood like a statue on the perfectly manicured lawn in front of the sandstone magnificence. My stomach tumbled, and the skin of my neck and arms prickled with fear and excitement. I loved old buildings. Old, haunted buildings. I just couldn't bring myself to go inside them. I spent a great deal of time avoiding spirits, so the idea of putting myself in their path, on purpose, went against my instincts. Ridiculous, I know. But this was all about taking back control.

I pouted my lips, and slowly breathed in and out through my nose, shaking my arms and legs in preparation for battle. Stepping into the building, I could almost feel the people who'd lived here generations before. It smelled of ingrained dust. Not the dirty kind. Just the irremovable layering of years in the pores of every surface. Rich burgundy shaded the walls, complementing the rich, dark wood of the windows and doors. This was the womb of the house, dark and crowded, but cosy.

The receptionist started her welcome speech, offering me a brochure, and pointing the way to the courtyard café where I 'might like to end my tour'. *Not likely.* I took it by my fingertips, careful not to make contact, and moved past the people watching a documentary on a small screen.

Immediately, I was drawn to the Governor's Library, and not because of the books. I could see her. The ghost of a maid wearing a black dress with layers of skirts and a white apron. She bustled around, dusting every surface. Humming quietly, quite happy in her work. A relieved breath eased from my lungs. I could do this. The smile that stretched my face felt foreign, but welcome in this public place.

I worked my way back to the winding staircase that led to the art gallery. Yet another reason I was drawn to this place. The display of William Robinson's works. He won the Archibald Prize two times. Twice! He was more of an expressionist than a realist. A misfit like me appreciated the individual interpretation of his views on life.

I wandered through the bedrooms turned into art displays, until I reached the self-portrait of the artist with his brother, clad in opposing outfits. Comfy PJ's versus knowledge and power. Both of them depicted with solemn expressions. The laugh bubbled up from my gut, escaping without my permission, just like the smile I'd been wearing before. It felt fucking awesome to let it out. Until I heard a deep laugh join the melody of mine.

My tailbone throbbed at seeing him again. He was laughing at my shoes, not the painting. *What's so funny about my sneakers?* I watched as his eyes travelled over me, the pupils growing larger despite the bright light streaming in the windows. My heart pounded, and my muscles tightened in response. I wanted to run before they reached my face, but I was too slow. He looked at me, rendering me speechless with his smile. He didn't smile like that before. Given the circumstance of our past meeting, I probably would've slapped it off his face. Now, it's an art work all on its own.

My heart galloped along, out of control. Lord knows where it wanted to go, but it definitely felt like it wanted to leave my chest and leap into someone else's. It was scaring the shit out of me. His smile faded a little and he took a step back, and said something about the artwork. I couldn't answer. My vocal chords had checked out on me, apparently on board with the travel plans taking place inside my rib cage.

His boots thumped against the floorboards as he retreated another step. He was looking at me strangely, continuing to prattle about the painting. I couldn't figure out what he was thinking, but his feet spoke for him. Two times he backed away ... Twice. I was used to it. I encouraged it. I couldn't afford to let people in. But watching him stand there looking scruffy and dangerous ... holy shit ... he was sexy. I didn't want him to back away. I wanted him to take a step closer. But those buckled, biker boots backed up, slicing a piece off my tough exterior as they went. With my vulnerable centre exposed, the second step cut even deeper. I couldn't let it happen again. So I ran.

That's what I do. I'm good at it.

———

I woke up all stiff and sweaty from sleeping on the blow-up mattress in Granny's living room. 4:15 a.m. The sun was about to enter stage left. After downing a couple of paracetamol, I threw on my running gear and headed out.

The sky held a flotilla of steel wool, locking in the heat, and denying the dawn. The oppressive atmosphere matched my mood. This was the third time this month I'd been kicked out of my home. How many fucking parties does one person need to have? I'd refuse to leave, but there was no way I wanted to be there with a crowd of people. Especially her friends. I screwed up my nose and poked out my tongue in a mock dry retch. Flick knew it, too. That was why she did this.

Wet leaves and small branches covered the footpath after the storm last night. I slowed my pace, worried I might slip on the decomposing carpet. The air felt like warm molasses. The end of something hovered close … I could sense it. The hairs on my arms transformed my skin into a pincushion. I fumbled with my phone, as if turning up the music could drown out fate. Looking around, I couldn't see any signs of life. Not even a bird. I should be celebrating. Having a moment to myself was rare for me, but this felt … fucking creepy. My skin grew taut, my muscles tensed, as my eyes darted around on high alert. I half expected the big bad wolf to jump out at me. Debating whether I should forego the torture and turn back, I decided to suck it up and keep going.

I turned a corner to run along the golf course that overlooked the river. My unsettled thoughts hurtled back to the man from Old Government House. The guy that broke my tailbone over a week ago. I admit, I haven't been able to get him out of my head since that mortifying display of ineptitude. He was connected to this sense of unease. I knew it somehow. It made me fight his pull with all my strength. I avoided the places where I'd seen him, and kept my eyes open in case I needed to run again. A neurotic attempt at maintaining my slippery control on my pathetic life.

Breaking into my morbid thoughts, I spotted a flash of yellow and blue in my peripheral vision. "FUCK!" Hurling my body sideways, I narrowly missed falling into the bush and sliding down the river bank. I made my way back onto the path, accompanied by my little stalker.

"Good morning. You look like crap," she said with an innocent smile.

I will not acknowledge you.

"My name is Letitia, by the way."

Please go the hell away, Letitia. My arms and legs fell back into a rhythm.

"You know … I can tell my brother's really going to like you. He needs someone like you to get his head out of the clouds, and you need him to neutralise your acid tongue."

Okay, that got my attention. My head twisted to glare at her. "Christ! This isn't some dating app, you know." Was she for real?

I expected her to reply with a cheeky comment, but I was met with silence. *Ah, crap.* She looked like I'd cut her favourite dolly's hair.

"So … how did you die?"

"What?! I'm not dead." The look of horror on her face sparked an attack of the guilts. Sometimes I could be horribly blunt and obnoxious. Wiping my hand across my forehead, I tried to formulate an apology. The sound of her laughter snapped my attention back to her. I swung my arm out, swiping right through the back of her head, my hand touching nothing but air. *How unsatisfying.*

"You should've seen the look on your face."

Well, at least she looked satisfied. A small smile tugged up the corners of my mouth.

"You looked like your mother just told you off for putting ice cream in the toaster."

My smile dropped. "Who the hell told you that?" The reference to my mother knocked on the Horrible Memories Vault I stored in a dark corner. I double checked the locks to fortify the door.

"Your dad."

I must've missed a lock because the door creaked, threatening to open. I wiped my hand across my brow again and kept running, ignoring my companion.

"Sorry. It's hard for me to talk about and I always make jokes when I'm uncomfortable or upset," she shrugged apologetically. "It was an accident. Car versus tree. Mother Nature wins every time!" She flashed her teeth in a wide smile. Her macabre sense of humour was back with a vengeance.

"Lee, that's my brother, blames himself for what happened to me. Before you ask, no he wasn't even in the car."

A kookaburra made its garbled wake-up call. Oh, thank God. Another living thing was out in this molasses. Maybe it was all in my head. I looked up to see if I could spot him.

"You can't keep ignoring me forever. I can play this game longer than you can. I have an eternity, and I will never give up."

I studied her face. She was serious. Determination tightened her features, narrowing and flattening them. She looked fierce, in fact. My heart sank a little. I knew I should help her. My instinct was to help despite my best efforts to shuck that part of me. I actually wanted to. I mean, I didn't have to keep my big secret from her, right? She was the secret. Or part of it. I'd become accustomed to her presence on the fringes. It had been a week since I'd last seen her, and I'd missed her.

The light broke through in a patch of misty purple on the horizon. It drained the aura of foreboding, replacing it with a beginning. I felt my body relax. Letitia was the first 'person' I had the urge to get to know in a long time. Even though she wanted something from me, just like everyone else, I felt like she was also trying to help me.

My only friends are my grandmother and a dead girl. The realisation slapped the smile off my face. *Fucking pathetic.* I had turned into a sad, cranky, lonely bitch. I was just like Flick.

Fuck!

I stumbled to a halt, breathing heavily with my fists clenched at my sides. A vision of my future flashed in my mind. I saw a crossroads. One road was empty, but for a dense, dark fog. The other was chaotic, but full of light, colour, and swirls of energy.

"Okay," I whispered while inspecting my shoes. When she didn't respond, I looked up. Her smile had widened, her green eyes lit up. She was radiating joy and relief. For a brief moment, I basked in it, feeling like I'd done something right. Then she just disappeared. Poof! Gone. What the hell? I spun in circles, looking all around for her before I realised what I must look like.

Turning to go back towards Granny's, a man caught my attention. He stood frozen on his driveway wearing his bathrobe, with a steaming mug in one hand and a newspaper in the other. His eyebrows puckered in the middle, mouth gritted in panic. The look on his face told me that he felt the psycho woman may be a problem. I put on a crazy face and shouted, "BOO!" The belly laugh tumbled free as he jumped and scurried off inside to safety. The smile on my face accompanied me all the way back, pushing away the fog. If I wasn't careful, this could become a habit.

Chapter
4

Ronnie

I covertly shook my head at all the Ned Kelly wannabes, as I walked to the eatery on campus. Since when did suspenders become fashion for men under eighty? One guy caught me looking, and hooked his thumbs under the colourful straps holding up his skinny jeans, giving them a snap. He grinned and rocked back on his heels while stroking his beard. Pfft, hipsters. My eyes rolled on their own accord. I kept walking before he garnered the courage to approach the ice queen.

Yeah, I know what you call me.

Even with modern technology, the notice board outside the bookshop was still a popular way for people to list all their crap for sale, or lost items. After my run this morning, I spent over an hour scouring the online listings for rooms to rent. My brain was slowly turning necrotic from looking at bloody ads. I'm twenty-five, have a full-time job, and I still can't afford to get my own place. My lips flattened to mimic my brow as I scanned the notice board. Three notices today. Slim pickings. One notice said, 'Call Sam if you like to party' in scribbled handwriting, with a fringe of tear-off phone numbers along the bottom. The entire thing was barely legible. It had me itching for a red pen. *Well, Sam, your threes look like eights and you can't spell apartment.*

The second notice advertised a unit for rent. An entire unit for ninety percent of my current wage per week. *Ouch!* I was still trying to pay off my uni costs, and contributing to Granny's expenses. I couldn't live on lettuce.

The third notice had an artist's impression of a typical Queenslander-style house at the top of the page, with the details neatly typed below. Attached to the bottom, an envelope contained plain white business cards with a name and number. It was a room for rent, and it was affordable. A little further out from the city than I had anticipated, but close to the train line and the river. I grabbed one of the cards, and made my way to the library where I worked as a cataloguer.

Joseph, one of the library's Peer Advisers, leaned against the Help Desk chatting up a girl who looked like she should still be in high school. He was tall, dark, and gangly, with that cute-nerd thing going on. Glancing over her head, he glued his stare to my legs. I nodded my head at him—a complete waste of my time, as his attention wasn't on my face. He'd already forgotten the girl as he hustled over to follow me up to the staff offices.

"Ronnie. Looking fine, as always," he directed the greeting to my backside.

"Watch it, Jo. I'll report you to HR so fast your head will spin."

"I am," I barely heard him mumble. Ignoring him, I continued over to my desk to put away my things.

"Whatcha doing after work?"

Aw, he looked hopeful. "Not gonna happen." *Jesus.* Hadn't he ever heard of sexual harassment laws?

His smile dropped. "Beverly wants to see you before you start." His voice turned sullen and quiet before he walked back to where he came from.

I chewed on my cheek as I watched his retreating, deflated form, feeling bad for being a bitch again. "Thanks, Jo."

He spun back with a huge grin on his face. "You're welcome," he chirped with a wink.

Ugh! Why me?

I wiped my sweaty palms on my dress and headed towards the Campus Librarian's office, knocking on my boss's open door. Beverly's blonde head popped up above her screen, sending me a smile. "You wanted to see me?"

She removed her glasses, and left them hanging by a chain around her neck. "Yes. Good morning, Ronnie. I wondered if you wouldn't mind helping the acquisitions team for the next week or so. We're two down for the next week, at least, and we have to chase some requests from the academics. I know there was a problem with a supplier for a few of the requested texts."

"Okay." I started to turn away.

"Ronnie?"

Pausing, I tilted my head in question. Her brightly coloured Missoni dress added a burst of colour to an otherwise drab room. As did the fire engine red manicure, done to perfection, just like her French roll. Her style suited her personality. Bright, vibrant, confident, and classy. She reminded me of Granny. Holding her glasses in her hand, with a welcoming smile on her face, my nerves started to ramp up at the expectation written in her gaze.

"How was your weekend? Did you do anything exciting?"

"It was fine, thanks." I kept a polite, but detached mask on my face. Her smile faded a little, and she nodded her head before resuming her work.

My heart sank as I wiped my palms again, my eyes darting to the space behind her. Beverly was like everybody's mother, and I couldn't bring myself to accept her attempts at befriending me. I felt like shit when I shut her down. It wasn't that I didn't like her; I actually want to be her, sort of. I just couldn't strike up a conversation. What would I say? I couldn't share that her mother was standing over her shoulder, begging me to tell her to get a mammogram before it was too late. How the hell would I even approach something like that?

Sighing, I headed back to find Kylie in acquisitions. She thinks I'm a bitch anyway, so it should be easy to maintain a safe little bubble of indifference and reticence. My two favourite words.

———

Brad

"Straight arms! You're gonna wear yourself out, dude."

Mikey, my belayer, yelled from the base of the cliff. My breaths were coming out thick through gritted teeth. I was only halfway up this bastard and I was buggered already. I should've tried the nursery cliffs, but I got cocky, thinking that after climbing the indoor equivalent for the last two months, I was ready to attack the crag at Kangaroo Point. What man wants to be seen attacking any challenge with the word 'nursery' attached to it?

"Dude, turn your hip into the wall. You're gonna fall right off if you don't shift your centre of gravity closer to the wall."

Dude, stop calling me dude.

The spotlights illuminated every crack and crevice, and the veins of colour that ran through the volcanic tuff. A light breeze off the river cooled my sweaty back, as I scanned the rock to find the next hold. Four other climbing pairs were on the cliffs tonight, attempting to conquer routes with obscure names like, 'Blue Veined Custard Shooter', 'Brickie's Butt Crack', and my personal favourite, 'Slippery When Wet'. The smell of the barbecues wafted up from the picnic area below, where climbers were celebrating their afternoon triumphs.

I stretched my left arm up towards a large crack halfway up the 'Surrender' route at KP. The name drew me like a magnet. It felt important to attempt this climb. Don't ask me why. Adrenaline pumped through my body, feeding my addiction. I needed it as much as I needed air. It was becoming a beast whose hunger I couldn't satiate. I'd have flashed this climb if Mikey would've let me, but I hung from a top rope, all safe and sound in my harness. With a helmet on. It was still a rush, but I didn't feel the slice of the knife's edge to divert my pain.

The muscles in my forearms felt like they were about to shear off. I wedged my fingers into the crack, and eased my weight onto my other foot so I could turn into the cliff face and hang for a second. My foot slipped, shunting my weight too quickly onto my little finger. It was wedged tightly and didn't budge, until I heard the snap. I felt the sharp pain shoot through my finger and up my wrist. My body fell away from the cliff face, swinging out towards the river; a potential disaster prevented by Mikey's quick reflexes. I kicked my feet out to keep from slamming into the rock as momentum pulled me back.

"Ah! Fuck!" Cradling my injured arm, I cursed with every word I knew, and kicked at the wall again. An icy chill wrapped around my torso. It pulled at me, slowing my movements even further, and stopped the word storm raging from my mouth. The sensation was bizarre, like a frozen hug from a safe place. It disappeared when my body stopped swinging, replaced by a fresh breakout of sweat. The painful throb in my hand drew me back to reality.

Fuck. I've broken something. My eyes and mouth slammed shut to lock in a sissy scream. I kept them shut, refusing to look at the carnage. I wiggled my thumb and first two fingers to make sure they were okay. It hurt like a motherfucker, but only because my broken pinkie moved too.

"I heard that, dude."

"Mikey? You're not helping, *dude*."

"You didn't surrender to it. You fought it. You were reckless up there. Always ends in pain, dude. I'm gonna lower you down, okay?"

I grunted in response, though the rope had already started to slide through his belay device, bringing me back to Earth. Adjusting my weight back on to my feet as I felt them touch the ground, I continued to cradle my wrist in the palm of my uninjured hand, while looking back up at my nemesis. Mikey took care of the harness for me. The clinking of the carabiners joined the noise from the revellers in the park.

"Duuuuude." My eyes dropped to Mikey, annoyance festering in my throat, ready to spew out at him. Until I saw his face. He looked like he was ready to do some spewing of his own. The spotlight turned him even more pasty, as he eyeballed my mangled hand. I still refused to look.

"Thanks, mate. I'd help you pack up, but …" I lifted my hand a little. His eyes followed the movement, as his tongue and throat pulled up in an attempted heave.

"Look away, Mikey." I slapped him on the shoulder with my good hand, bracing the bad one against my stomach as I bent to pick up my pack. I had a steep climb up the stairs back to my car, and a night in the Accident and Emergency ahead of me. Coming down from the adrenaline rush was going to be a bitch.

———

The heat shimmered off the pavement as I walked through campus. My brand-new cast was itchy as hell, and the humidity only made it worse. Humidity made everything worse. Thank fuck for air-conditioning. And painkillers.

It was O Week at the university. Time to get oriented. Classes didn't start until next week, but I figured I'd check out where they would be. Near the Student Centre, most of the clubs had set up tables, enticing students to join their ranks. After standing in line for friggin' ever to get my ID, I headed across the lawn to the library. I pulled my hat down as some clown played his guitar, giving a free karaoke show. Judging by the looks on everyone's faces he needed to put that thing away and rethink his hobby.

The library was buzzing with the enthusiasm of new students, signalling the beginning of a new year. I was sure it wouldn't feel the same in six months' time. The stairs acted as an aorta through the middle of the building, crammed with human-shaped blood vessels pumping life into the uninspired concrete box. I didn't realise so many people would be in the library during O week. But I guess everyone had the same bright idea as me.

I reached the sixth floor where I'd find the quiet area and the design books. Making my way to the shelves at the end, a waft of something delicious hit me. Between two shelves I found my Amazonian Gazelle. Her profile was angled away from me, but I could see her holding a notebook in one hand, running her finger along the books with the other. Stretching up on tippy toes, she pulled a book off the top shelf. *Holy shit.* Stretched out, long and lean, her breasts pushed against her shirt where an ID tag hung from a lanyard. She must work here. I wished she'd turn so I could see her name. Her knee length skirt moulded to every line of her bum and legs. I gulped loudly. My heart tried to beat out of my chest. I had to clench my fists to stop myself from grabbing her and dragging her somewhere private.

Sick bastard. No control.

I itched for a hit of adrenaline. She did things to me. It was an unstoppable force coming from the same place as my adrenaline beast. The scant doses received so far were nowhere near enough to whet my appetite. Loss of control was probable. I was getting high from holding myself back, and the anticipation of what could happen if she decided to give her attention to me. I wouldn't hurt her, but I think I'd scare her. That's what held me together. I didn't want her to run from me anymore.

She wasn't at South Bank this morning. I was more disappointed than I probably should have been. I mean, I didn't even really know this woman, but she had me completely entranced. Maybe, it was *because* I didn't know her. She was an enigma. Untouchable. Uncatchable. I begged for a sighting every morning. A little dose of heaven to keep me going until my next adrenaline hit. What a pathetic sack of shit. Finding out that she worked where I'll be spending a heck of a lot of time for the next five years? I was stoked, but at the same time, I expected it to be torture.

She grabbed another book, and bent to put it on the second lowest shelf. *Jesus Christ*, the view she was giving me … I couldn't help myself. I groaned, but quickly turned it into a strangled cough when she angled her head to look behind her. Snapping straight up, eyes wide, she spun away from me and marched out of my life. Once again. *Smart woman*. Yeah, that just confirmed what I already thought. The chances that she would want someone like me, a man who lets down the people who need him? Jack shit.

Turning to look out the windows, I used the view of the buildings to block out the darkness. Seeing the beauty of man's creations opened a conduit of hope that one day, maybe, I could imagine something great. Something truly worthwhile that could take form in concrete and steel.

I moved on, my mind returning to my original plan. But my feet stuck to the carpet, refusing to go any further when I saw the back of a familiar dark head.

"Ben?"

He crouched down, checking out the bottom shelf. His head turned my way, and a huge toothy smile took over his face. "Mate! How the heck are ya?"

"Shh," someone hissed from their study corner.

I motioned to the stairs, my eyebrows raised in question. Nodding his head, he stood and we shook hands, vigorously.

At six foot, Ben was a little shorter than me. He made up for it in layers of muscle. His dark hair and blue eyes were always a favourite with the opposite sex.

We found a seat on the fourth floor.

"I haven't seen you for, what … four years?" I was still amazed to see him there.

"Yeah, since I moved to Bris Vegas for uni. What are you doing here? Don't tell me you're finally getting your degree?"

"Yup, finally." I put my hands in my pockets, my shoulders kissing my earlobes.

I hadn't exactly been in a position to start my degree. Until now. I'd rather not be starting it, because this opportunity for a better future for me meant that someone I love had theirs taken away. I'd give anything to give it back. Seeing my old mate had the memories flooding every cell of my body. I crossed my arms to hold it all in, embracing the good ones and blocking out the bad.

Ben and I went to school together. We had so much in common that we became fast friends. Our only difference in opinion was which rugby code was the best. He was a rugby union fan, while I was all for rugby league. After finishing high school, we decided to get some building site experience together before starting our degrees. Both of us wanted to study architectural design. Life cleared him a free path to the try line, while I got tackled and stretchered off before I'd even begun.

"That's great mate. Congrats. It's a lot of work, but it's worth it in the end."

"You'd be up to the masters now, right?"

He nodded. "Uh huh. Hopefully, I'll be able to register as an architect by the end of this year."

"Brilliant. Maybe I can pick your brain if I need some help?"

"No worries." He shrugged his shoulders.

Ben was my best friend, but we drifted apart when my life became complicated, and he moved down to Brisbane to start his degree. I was jealous, I admit. He had it all. He was on his way to a great career, and I was supposed to be there with him. He had a great girl who thought he was everything. I had responsibilities that most twenty-one-year-olds didn't have to worry about. I honestly was happy for him. Things had changed for both of us. I wanted to go back to the way things were before life put my plans in a blender.

"How's Andrea?" I asked, after an awkward pause.

"She's fantastic. She wants ankle biters soon, but I want to wait until my studies are done and dusted …. She's still pissed at you for not coming to the wedding."

I dropped my head, and stared into the hole I'd dug for myself. "I'm sorry, mate, I had a lot of shit going on at the time."

He patted me on the shoulder. "I know. I get it. Stewart did a shitty job with the best man speech. You would have done it better, but it's all good."

I gave him half a smile, nodding my head. I could just imagine how Andrea's brother, Stewart, would've made everybody cringe at his crass remarks. The bloke was the definition of a bogan.

"How's Midget?"

The smile dropped off my face instantly. I drew in a deep shaky breath. Bowing my head again, I looked up at him through my lashes. "She's gone."

"Gone? What …? Back to Rocky?" His face scrunched in confusion.

"No. She—she died," I choked out.

His mouth fell open, shaking his head in disbelief. "What? No."

"Six months ago."

"Oh, fuck. I'm so sorry, man."

He grabbed me in a half hug, slapping my back with his other hand. I closed my eyes to will the tears away. I was relieved when he didn't ask any more questions. Grown men didn't cry, especially not in public. We didn't hug each other either, unless there was a really friggin' good reason. I guess this warranted a hug.

He stepped back and cleared his throat, effectively wiping the ugly from the list of topics to discuss. "Come over for dinner tonight. Andrea's cooking Thai. I know you love it."

I looked at him again, studying his face. I saw genuine friendship and concern. I'd been a dumb arse, letting one of the most important friendships in my life go because my stupid ego was bruised, and I didn't want to burden him with my shit. Well, I was going to fix this, too.

"Sure. Why not. I'll eat anything. Even Andrea's cooking."

He grinned. "Excellent. You looking for some design books?" He crouched down, pulling a book off the shelf.

"Yeah." My knees cracked as I joined him, listening as he described the course and some of his projects.

A spark of light crept into my darkness. I knew where the Amazonian Gazelle worked, and I'd found my long-lost best-friend. The brother I never had. I'd really missed this. It was so rare to find that in life. A genuine lifelong friendship, where you could pick up where you left off after not seeing the person for some time. It was like time had never passed, but you valued the friendship even more because of the lost years. Any dickheadedness was instantly forgiven because they understood and, I guess, loved you. No matter what.

A cold patch of air briefly covered my back, causing a shiver to run its way down my spine. It disappeared almost immediately. Looking up, I couldn't see any air vents close to us. *Weird.* The sensation seemed to follow every turn my life took.

Ben noticed he'd lost my attention and stopped his spiel. "You all right, mate?" He frowned.

"Mm. Yeah. Just a bit sore." I waved my cast before resting it back on my thigh.

"I wasn't going to ask. Thought it might've been a masturbation strain or something."

I snorted. "You're still a dick."

"No. I have a dick, and someone to look after it. You were always the more dedicated do-it-yourselfer."

All thoughts of any X-Files shit going on were wiped from my memory, as we fell back into our rhythm. Between my obsession with an elusive woman, my adrenaline binges, and the weird sensations, I was seriously worried that I was losing my shit. Seeing Ben again could not have happened at a better time.

"It's good to see you again, mate," I told him with sincerity.

"Yeah, you too. You wanna go get some grub? I can show you around if you want."

"That'd be great."

We headed back towards the stairs. I kept a look out for my favourite librarian, but I didn't see her again. Yet. It was only a matter of time.

Chapter
5

Ronnie

A series of staircases wrapped the law building, climbing like the veins on a body builder. I made my way across a raised walkway to the law academic's offices. The only person I could find was a middle-aged, balding man, who was surfing the net for fishing gear.

"Uh, hi. Beverly sent me to drop this over." My body leaned away while my arm stretched out as far as it could go, offering him the large yellow envelope.

"Who's it for?" He didn't bother looking away from his screen. Rude bugger.

Angling the envelope so I could read it, I answered, "Derek Lindstrom."

He raised his head, blinking several times, his glasses magnifying his eyes. "Who are you?" His voice was raspy, and the action of talking sent him into a coughing fit. My feet retreated three steps, even though I was nowhere near him. I waited for him to stop, watching as he reached for a tissue. He's going to find blood, but not until next week.

"I'm Ronnie. I work in the library."

"Right, right. Derek just headed over there to see someone. You probably passed him on the way over—" Another round of hacking coughs wrenched from his chest, crumbling the last word as it broke out.

"Okay." I turned quickly away, but paused with my back to him.

He had lung cancer. The knowledge seeped into my brain from some unknown and unwelcome source. In the glass doors, my face reflected the internal battle waging between my conscience and my sanity. The stupid envelope hung from my limp fingers, like a yellow card signalling that I'd just committed a foul. If I told him, he probably wouldn't believe me. He'd think I was a psycho. I'd been branded with the label since I was a child. The news was too late to help him, anyway.

My features relaxed as I straightened my spine. "You should get that checked by a doctor." I walked out, not needing confirmation that he heard me. Even if he did, he wouldn't *listen*. I just had to try to give him a warning. Some time to sort his affairs and say his goodbyes. Milton Hanford wouldn't last out the year. His wife would retire nicely on the insurance pay-out, and his mistress would be devastated. The information didn't ease my conscience one iota. I've learned to live with it.

This troublesome yellow package needed to go.

I headed back to the library. As I passed the stacks, my attention was caught between two shelves to a couple who were having a quiet, but heated conversation. The man crowded the woman, his arms on either side of her head, his face angled close to hers. She was short, mostly hidden. If it wasn't for the fact that I recognized the Chanel skirt and Prada shoes she was wearing, I probably wouldn't have stopped. The man moved his left hand to circle it around her throat, exposing the identity of his captive. My suspicions were correct. It was Flicker. She had her back to the shelves, clutching a notebook to her chest. Her breaths came out in pants, her eyelids dropped low, almost closed. The compulsion to scrub my eyes raw was potent.

I coughed and the man slowly turned, stepping away. Flicker snapped her head towards me in surprise. The glare I was so familiar with immediately converted her pretty features into a nasty mask.

"What are you doing here?" she spat at me.

I schooled my features into the look of indifference I had perfected since moving in with her. "You're scaring the other patrons, I suggest you move it somewhere more private," I smiled sweetly.

"I suggest you mind your own business, Mantis." Such a delightful nickname, likening me to a praying mantis, and not the one from Kung Fu Panda.

Her male companion's eyes roamed up and down my figure. I could feel his visual assessment as if he was molesting me. It was vile and repulsive. I held back a gag. He looked about twice our age, with light brown hair greying at the temples, and wearing an expensive tailored suit. Gold, monogrammed cufflinks pinned the French cuffs of a crisp, white shirt, flashing at his wrists. How could she be with a creeper like him? Obviously, because he had money. *How cliché, Flicker.*

"Introduce me to your friend, Felicity," he crooned as he walked towards me.

Her expression changed for a brief second, before the mask was back in place. Was it jealousy or discomfort? "Derek Lindstrom, this is Veronica Williams, my tenant."

Tenant. Nice.

"Very pleased to meet you, Veronica." The way he wrapped his tongue around my name made me feel dirty. I almost ran to the nearest soap dispenser.

I purposely did not return his sentiment. "It's Ronnie, actually." Only the people I love, a.k.a. Granny, get to call me Veronica.

He stopped directly in front of me, blocking Flicker from my view. I braced my legs, ready to kick or run, if need be. He leaned towards me and breathed deeply before speaking again. "Are you a student here, Veronica? I'm sure I would have noticed you around."

Crossing my arms over my chest to create a barrier between us, I looked at him, eyebrow raised, mouth in a flat line. "It's a bit inappropriate to be chatting up another woman in front of your girlfriend, isn't it, Mr. Lindstrom?" I slapped the giant yellow card to his chest.

Flicker gasped. I watched his eyebrows lower and his mouth tighten, before I whirled around and left them to their sordid carry-on. The sooner I got away from people, the sooner I could get on with my day.

———

Easing my foot onto the brake, I looked up to see if the lights were on in the flat before I pulled into the carpark. Disappointment washed over me. They're on. She's home. *Crap.* The car idled in neutral as my hand gripped the keys, debating whether to turn it off, or chuck it back into drive and go to Granny's. The headlights shone on the Besser block wall sprayed with graffiti, the message telling me to 'feck off'. Maybe I should listen to it.

Flick's shiny, red Audi rested in the park directly opposite mine. BMW's, Mercedes and Alfa Romeos populated the other spaces. My little, silver Yaris cowered in its spot. A 'have not' surrounded by a whole bunch of 'haves'. I didn't belong here. Never had. I didn't want to belong here. I wanted a backyard and a dog, and a parrot that would sit on the back of the couch and watch TV with me. I wanted a safe place of my own.

My fingers finally twisted the keys as I decided to woman up. The block of ice in my stomach knocked my insides around while I trudged up the flights of stairs. The events of that morning had unsettled me. I started to worry that I might see Flick's new boyfriend in the unit. Even more reason for me to leave. Something was seriously wrong with that man. His energy was as black as midnight on a new moon. *Ugh.* I sounded like my grandmother.

My hand slid off the door handle, too slick with sweat to be useful. I wiped it off on my pencil skirt and tried again. The television blared through the crack in the door, getting louder as I opened it wider. The door jammed against something at the halfway mark. I slipped through the slim opening, and peered around to see what the obstacle was. A large moving box, full of my stuff, topped by a broken lava lamp oozing its contents over everything. *Excellent, and what the fuck?*

The slam of the door rivalled the television, as I took out my anger on the nearest object. *Where is that bitch?* My eyes scanned the living area wildly, as my shoes clicked on the tiles in search of my next target. The coffee table, strewn with empty chip packets and chocolate wrappers, was the second sign that something was wrong. A ceiling fan spun at warp speed, unable to lift the packets because they were stuck to the surface by a sticky yellow substance.

I trotted into the kitchen, finding an empty bottle of tequila, half a bottle of margarita mix, and only one glass beside the dirty blender. She was on a bender, but where was she now?

I left my handbag in the kitchen and filled a glass with water, adding some ice cubes before heading to her lair. Opening the door without knocking, because she never extended me that courtesy, I found a dishevelled looking Flick in her bed, passed out. The rank smell of vomit hit me in the face, stopping me for a second. It was stifling in here. All the windows were shut, no fan, and no air-conditioning. Walking around to see her face poking out above the quilt, I noticed make-up smudges around her eyes and lips. A small pool of vomit had collected under her cheek. What a disaster zone.

I'd never seen her the morning after one of her parties, but if this was how she looked, I was glad I'd never had to bear witness until now. Only one glass. Party of one. I wondered if all the parties were fake.

Setting the water glass down, I opened the window, turned the fan on full, and ripped the covers down. She didn't budge, still wrapped up in a turtleneck jumper and tracksuit pants. I didn't realise she even owned such sloth clothing, and it felt like it was thirty degrees in her room.

I grabbed the glass of iced water and dumped it on her head. She heaved in a deep breath as she bolted upright, eyes glassy but wide. Her stomach revolted from the movement and emptied its contents all over the bed. I jumped back in time to avoid the spray.

"Fuck!" she croaked, wiping her mouth with her sleeve. Her eyelids fluttered, probably trying to focus her blurry vision.

I glared with my arms folded, waiting for her brain to catch up to the situation. She finally turned her head towards me, wincing with the movement. "What the fuck, Mantis? You fucking maniac! What are you doing here? Didn't you understand the eviction notice at the door?"

"Oh, I saw your message. I want to know why you couldn't discuss it with me like a normal adult?"

"I don't want you here anymore. What else is there to say? Get out. Leave your key on the kitchen counter." She swayed as she placed her feet on the floor, and opened her bedside drawer to reveal a virtual pharmacy of medications. Picking out a box, she removed two pills and swallowed them dry.

I couldn't believe what I was seeing. This wasn't the in-control, immaculate woman she presented to the world. This was a woman in crisis, on edge. I couldn't reconcile the two people as one. Despite the smell, I remained locked in position, feeling like she might actually need my help somehow and wanting to give it to her. *What the hell?*

Her eyes turned icy, shooting blue dagger points in my direction. Her voice and expression hard as she gripped the side of the bed with her fists. "GET THE FUCK OUT OF MY LIFE!"

My shoulders jumped and I sprang into action, heading back into the hall. The door to my room was open, revealing splintered furniture and gouges in the plaster walls. *Oh my God, she has lost her shit.* I saw some random belongings of mine spread among the debris. None of it was important or irreplaceable. I never kept my valuables here anyway. It was a miracle she'd packed any of my stuff at all.

I scuttled down the hallway to the kitchen, ripping the key off my keyring and dumping it on the bench. The door slammed behind me, this time with me on the outside. I stopped on the landing with my meagre belongings at my feet in a soggy box. I looked back at the stainless-steel number fifty-five on the door, and saw a triple six instead.

My body slumped on the top step in defeat. Taking out my phone, I rang the only person who could help me.

"Granny …?"

"I'll see you in ten minutes. Your bed is ready. Drive safely, darling." She hung up.

Silent tears ran rivers down my cheeks. I clutched my phone between my hands, elbows resting on my knees as I sent a prayer of thanks to the telco for their service, and a hallelujah for the existence of my Granny.

With a deep breath, I placed the phone back inside my bag. As I did, my fingers touched the business card for the room for rent. I stared at it dumbly. Granny would say it was a sign.

Tomorrow. I'll ring the number tomorrow. What choice do I have now?

Chapter
6

Brad

I'd put up a plaster sheet over the vertical joints on one lounge room wall to make a smooth canvas. The paintbrush behaved like an extension of my hand, as I added some shadow into the dark forest I'd created.

I was pretty sure my Gran would have loved the idea of a mural. When we first moved in, I found a box with all the drawings I'd ever given her, and two more recent paintings on the walls. She was my groupie. I still felt her … watching over me and the improvements I'd been making to her old house.

What started out as a dark tunnel of dense trees now had a focal point of light cutting through the centre. A figure started to take shape as I painted, a dream forming clearly with each brush stroke. The centre drew the eye. It was the goal. Now, I could see what it was shaping into. It was life, it was salvation and love … It was her.

I put my paintbrush and palette down and stepped back. I gently massaged around the cast on my left hand, now numb from holding the palette. I'd gone totally fucking mad. I was putting her permanently on my lounge room wall. It was barely an outline of a person, but I knew it was her. Ben would give me so much shit about this when he saw it. I debated whether I should paint over it.

Thick clouds shifted their weight, spotlighting the centre of my wall in the streams of morning sun coming through the window. My jaw slackened, eyes honing in on that figure in the centre. Those beams of light felt like they were streaming right through my heart, filling me with go-go juice or something. I could do an ironman competition right now, and make the others all look like jokers.

She was meant to be a permanent fixture in my home, and in my life. I felt it deep in my centre. The wall was staying, even if it drove me to the looney bin.

I need to get the fuck out of here.

Walking through to the kitchen, I grabbed the phone and dialled Ben's number. I didn't care if it was six in the morning.

"Yellow?"

"Is my favourite colour. Good, you're up. Get your shit together. We're going jet boating on the Goldy."

"Hang on, I've gotta check with the missus."

"Are you fucking serious right now?"

"As a heart attack."

The scratchy hissing of something moving over the mouthpiece at his end, muffled the sound of their negotiations. It seemed like ten minutes passed before I heard his voice again.

"Andrea's coming, too. She loves all that thrill seeker shit."

"Aw that's sweet. You two can't be apart."

"Shut up, dickhead. You'll be worse when you find a woman."

My eyes strayed through the archway, falling on the mural still bathed in light. I didn't doubt him for a second. *Fuck*, I needed to do something crazy to get this rush out of my system.

"Just get your arses over here." I punched the end call button, dropping the phone on the bench. My hand scrubbed the back of my head, and I growled as I saw the figure I'd created. *Correction. Ghost.* It was a ghostly outline of a recurring dream. She taunted me, just out of reach of reality.

The lounge room light flicked on, adding more light to the painted dream. As I watched from the kitchen, I felt wrapped in a frozen cocoon. The chill banded around my heaving chest before it retreated, leaving me in a cold sweat.

As I gripped the bench with my good hand, I had a feeling the woman in the painting wasn't the only one haunting me.

———

Ronnie

It was finally lunchtime and the business card for the room for rent was burning a hole in my bag. I chickened out on my attempt at dialling the number over the weekend. After the upheaval of my eviction, and my confusion over Flick's behaviour, I just needed to chill out with Granny for a couple of days. But sleeping on a blow-up mattress, well … it blows.

I pulled the card and my phone out while walking to my favourite, quiet spot in the gardens surrounding the campus. Sitting on a bench seat under a shady Morton Bay Fig, I dialled the number.

"Hello." I felt the deep rumble down my neck, sending tingles in its wake.

"Uh … hello …" I squinted at the card, tapping my heels on the pavement. "… Brad? I'm calling about the room for rent."

"Yeah? Great! I didn't know if anyone ever looked at notice boards anymore. Did the drawing catch your eye, or was it the fact that I went to the trouble of printing out business cards?"

This guy is a talker.

And he's cheery.

This probably wasn't going to work.

"O … kay."

"Shit. Sorry, I had an energy drink and they always make me hyper. I'll shut up now. So, you need a room and I have one. When do you wanna have a look?"

I couldn't help it, I actually laughed. Maybe this wouldn't be so bad after all. "Do you often resort to drugs to get through your morning?"

There was a brief pause before he deadpanned, "Only on Mondays."

I laughed again. What was wrong with me? I cleared my throat, attempting to regain my composure. "Would it be possible to have a look at the room this evening, at around five thirty?"

As I waited for his response, I could hear the crinkling of papers through the phone line. Was he actually checking his diary? I had a vision pop into my head of a man's hand shuffling through a stack of scrap paper on a kitchen bench, searching for a pen. I saw it as if I was standing right next to him.

"Five thirty should be good. What's your name and number, in case there's a problem and I can't be here?"

I stiffened at the thought of giving my number out to a complete stranger, but it was a sensible, valid request. I told him my number.

"Aannd …"

"And what?"

"Your name?"

Oh, right!

"Veronica." *Shit! What did I just say?* "I mean, Ronnie."

"Veronica. I like it. See you at five thirty, *Veronica.*" He hung up before I had time to correct him. *Idiot! What the hell was wrong with me?* I could only blame it on the fact that my life was in the crapper.

I grabbed my wrap and threw a piece at the crow circling my feet, having lost my appetite after my error in judgement. If this worked out, I'd be living with a man. A complete stranger who could be dangerous and psycho. I was used to psycho, but I'd never felt like my life was threatened, living with Flick. In all honesty, it was a plus that he was male. Two women under one roof was not always a good thing. I was really over drama queens.

I picked up my water bottle, gulped down half in one go, and then stared back towards the campus buildings. My back stiffened and my eyes popped as I saw Derek Lindstrom stroll towards the administration building, with his jacket slung over one shoulder. He stopped to talk to one of the law lecturers. Was Flick seriously getting it on with her teacher? Were her grades that bad, that she had to resort to providing sexual favours in exchange for an academic boost? Why wouldn't someone like her just get her minions to do her assignments?

Chills raked across my skin. That was never a good sign. Something bad had either just happened, or was about to. I suddenly felt exposed. I had the urge to go for a run, but with only fifteen minutes left of my break, it wasn't going to happen.

I packed up my lunch and made my way back to work, steering well clear of the administration building. This day couldn't be over fast enough.

———

At around five thirty, I parked my car at the curb in front of my potential new home, immediately spotting the first problem. It was an old house, and its previous occupant worked in the front garden. What was it with these old women who were so obsessed with their gardens that they haunted them from the afterlife? Lush palms, bold colourful flowers, and thick leaves in all sorts of colours crowded each garden bed forming a tropical oasis. Okay, she had good reason to be proud. I wanted to go exploring.

Shades of cream and burgundy coated the wooden house. Supported by posts, vertical wooden slats enclosed the downstairs area. Topping the railing of the wrap-around veranda, burgundy lattice screened out the world. Pretty tulip cut-outs carved into every fourth slat under the hand railing. The colours and carvings made it appear less imposing, but it was a wooden fortress.

I slung my bag over my shoulder, and locked the car before approaching the house. I kept my head down in the hopes of avoiding the spirit.

No such luck. As soon as I neared the house, I heard a soft voice.

"Hello."

I didn't look up or stop. No need to encourage her.

"Hello, Veronica. It's about time you got here." Her volume increased, her tone more forceful.

Well, that made me look up and stop. Who, the hell was she, and how did she know my name? I gripped my bag tighter, and braced a hand on the balustrade of the stairs, ready to run up and bang on the double lattice doors at the top.

Before I was able to ask any questions, the front door opened, sending more shock waves in my direction. At the top of the staircase holding open the lattice door, was the man who kept popping into my life unannounced and uninvited. *Oh, for fuck's sake!* Could this day just go to hell already? He stared down at me, his face a mixture of shock and elation.

Elation?

I cleared my throat, gathered my wits, and made my way up the staircase, stopping two steps below him. Reluctantly, I looked in his eyes, my jaw going slack at what I saw. Recognition hit me deep down to my soul. He was mine. The search that I never intended to begin was already over. I was so screwed.

The setting sun cast a glow over him, setting off sparks in his grey eyes and highlighting the shades of red and gold in his hair. The splattering of freckles across his cheeks and nose was more prominent in the light. My heart beat erratically, and my ears rang as my mouth went dry. It was physically painful to look at him.

My eyes roamed further down. He wore paint-splattered jeans with a rip across his right thigh and a holey, faded blue muscle shirt. His feet were bare. My eyes flicked between the rip, the holes, and his feet, greedy for any little piece of him.

"Veronica. Hi." He pulled on the hem of his shirt. "Sorry, I haven't had a shower yet. I've been painting."

My gaze rose to his eyes, watching him take in my face. Every part of it. He was drinking in the sight of me. I felt the heat of a flush reach my cheeks. Swallowing, I tried to focus on what he'd said. His freckled lips quirked up on one side. My flush grew hotter when I realised I'd been caught staring at the flashes of skin he tempted me with.

"Oh … no, it's fine. I'm still in my work clothes." I smoothed my sweaty hands down my hips.

He glanced down at my legs, chewing on his lips. "That's a nice dress. You're more presentable than I am." His voice sounded gravelly as though he was parched for a drink. Taking a step back, he cleared his throat. "Please come in, *Veronica.*"

Oh damn! Why does he have to keep repeating my name?

His back pressed into the veranda door, holding it open so I had to slip past him to enter. My shoulder brushed his chest, and I heard him suck in a breath. He felt it, too. The anticipation. The zing. It was like a drug. I was scared I'd get addicted to it. If I ever touched him deliberately and purposely, I'd suffer an overdose I'd never be able to come back from. I might very well lose myself in this man.

I stiffened and hopped away. I couldn't get close to him. He'd find out about me and I'd be 'The Freak' in his eyes. Somehow, I knew that that would devastate me like never before.

He shut the veranda, and opened the door to the house. I admired its oval, stained glass window, which featured a kookaburra perched on the branch of a gum tree. I could almost imagine the beautiful, coloured patterns of light along the walls when the sun hit it. The long hallway stretched out in front of me, as the smell of paint fumes and dust hit my nose. I took off my shoes before entering, and placed my bag on the small hallway table just inside. My feet made a soft thumping noise on the wooden floor as I passed the doors lining each side of the hall. I counted five. The hall opened out into the lounge on the left, and the dining room on the right, with the kitchen off the dining room to the very back of the house.

Brad trailed closely behind. The house seemed to shrink, closing in around me, or maybe it was those swirls of energy he seemed to surround himself in. The man was a hazard. One I needed to avoid. What was I doing here?

"I think the living areas are self-explanatory. I'll show you the bedroom later. Would you like a drink of something before we sit out on the deck? The house stinks of paint fumes. Sorry." Looking through the French doors, the huge deck had a table setting and a couple of Adirondack deck chairs. It looked like the perfect place to sit and get some air. And some space.

I turned back to him, once again struck dumb. Dangling by his side, one of his arms was secured in a plaster cast. The other arm was bent up, his right bicep bulging out on full display, as his hand held the back of his head. The bottom of his shirt rode up, showing a strip of skin. He waited for my answer with a sheepish expression, as if he'd been caught doing something naughty.

Bicep. Strip of skin. Freckled face.

I was the one who should be sheepish. I had to clear my throat to stop from squeaking out incomprehensible sounds.

"Water would be fine, thanks."

He left me and headed to the kitchen. I followed the paint smell into the lounge, curious to see what he was doing. My hand flew to my chest, pressing over my fluttering heartbeat. A magnificent mural covered the wall behind the couch, depicting a glimpse of a lake and jetty at the end of a forest path. I wondered if it was an actual place that he was fond of, or if it was a metaphor for life. Finding your way through the dark and difficult, to the light and sanctity at the end. It was truly beautiful. The detail was amazing even in its unfinished form. I almost felt the brush of leaves against my skin as I walked toward the water. A figure sketched roughly on the jetty was only beginning to take on some colour.

I heard the clink of a glass as he placed it on the coffee table. I put a pillow down on the couch where I planned to sit. My tail still hurt when I put weight on it. He noticed and grimaced, as he took a seat on the arm of the couch.

"Thanks for the drink."

"No worries. I—I'm … Shit. I'm sorry for knocking you down. You turned so suddenly, and I didn't have a chance to stop in time. I've felt like crap about it ever since." He chewed on his lips, rubbing the back of his head again.

Damn, that was distracting.

I waved away his apology, and shook my head. "It was an accident. Not your fault. I wasn't watching where I was going." Leaning forward, I grabbed my glass and gulped down a few swallows. He watched me closely, staring at my mouth and throat with such heat in his eyes I forgot to breath between swallows, choking on the water. I coughed and spluttered. He was going to think I was a lunatic without even knowing about my curse. He jumped off the couch, slapping me on the back several times.

After regrouping, I steered the conversation to safer territory. "Thanks. The, um … the painting is beautiful. You're really talented. How long have you been working on it?"

"Thanks." He bobbed his head. "I started it four months ago. I got hit with inspiration from my muse." The words were jovial, but the intensity in his gaze told me there was more to his statement. I grabbed my drink again and sipped carefully this time, making sure to look at the glass and not at him.

"Would you like me to show you the rest of the house?"

"Yes!" I practically yelled before he'd finished the final word. Heat swept my face again. *Jesus, who am I?* This whole meeting had been utterly ridiculous. I felt like I was back in high school. I didn't want to be rude and leave before seeing the room, but my feet itched to bolt.

I followed him onto the deck and down another set of stairs leading to the backyard. Much like the front, it was dense with tropical plants, separated by a series of winding pathways. In the middle of the yard, a small pond and bench seat formed an oasis.

"Are there any fish in the pond?" I asked as he led the way down.

"No fish, but I think we have a family of frogs. They're bloody noisy at night. Especially after it rains. Fair warning." I barely heard what he said. The rear view of his broad shoulders and bum was very distracting. Another rip exposed the back of his knee. He had the body of a swimmer.

Shoulders. Bum. Knee. Jesus!

He unlocked a gate to the right of the stairs, and led me under the house. The vast area, broken up by thick wooden posts, was cluttered with boxes and various outdoor equipment. A couple of bicycles and a canoe hung from the beams overhead, and a washing line zigzagged across the ceiling.

Brad opened the door of a built-in room to our left and towards the back of the space. "This is the laundry and there's also a small bathroom through there." He pointed to another door past the washing machine and sink. I peered through, not wanting to squeeze past him again. "There's a dryer you'll probably need to use in the summer. I don't know if you're from here, but it can get pretty humid and wet. It's hard to dry the washing, even hanging under here."

"Why do I smell sawdust?" I wrinkled my nose, even though I liked the smell.

He stepped back and swung an arm towards a workshop in the front corner. A homemade bench was cluttered with tools and sawdust, standing beside a motorcycle tyre that peeked out from under a cloth cover. "I like to build stuff. It's pretty grotty under here. I promise not to get your washing dirty." I nodded as he directed me back to the staircase, letting me go first.

The bench near the pond provided the old lady with a front row seat to the spectacle. Who was she? "How long have you lived here?" I turned my head to ask, and caught him with his eyes glued to my behind.

He jerked his eyes up to mine. "Oh—ah … two years," the words blurted from his mouth. "This was my Gran's house. She left it to us in her Will."

Us?

I spun my head back to the pond. *Hi Gran.* She dipped her head, sending me a smile. Brad moved into the house, opening the first door on the left of the hallway and standing aside so I could see in.

"This is the main bathroom. We'd have to share. It's too much of a pain to use the one downstairs unless you're already down there. Sorry. You can use whichever one you feel comfortable with."

It was adorable how he kept apologising. I chewed on my cheek to stop a smile.

Shutting the door, he pointed to the next one along. "Separate toilet." He beckoned me into the room across the hall. "This is my workroom. You can put a desk in here too, if you want. Or there's room in your bedroom for a desk."

My hand flew to cover my heart, again. A large, old-fashioned Draftsman's desk rested against the wall under the window, but what caught my attention were the drawings pinned to the walls. Consisting mostly of buildings, and some landscapes, there were also a couple of scenes with people. His talent astounded me.

"Do you sell your art?" The words fell through my thin breath.

He choked on a laugh, "No. I'm just an amateur." He stood crowding the doorway, without any idea how he was affecting me. Not a clue as to how he was putting me under a spell.

Swirls of energy. Oodles of talent. Humble. Clueless. Freckled face. Gah!

"You're kidding, right?" I said, incredulous. "I've been to the art gallery; your art would fit right in."

"No. It's just something I do for shits and giggles. I'm starting a degree in Architectural Design, so I guess the drawing will come in handy." He rubbed the back of his head. Modest and adorable. What a killer combo.

We headed to the front of the house where he opened the last door on the left. "This is my room."

Right. Well, I'm not going in there. I hung back, resisting the smell of him, more potent and intoxicating where he slept on the king-sized bed. Cologne mixed with his own unique scent. He had a chest of drawers against the wall at the end of the bed supporting the obligatory television. I gasped. On a table beside the bed sat a lava lamp. *You've got to be shitting me.*

My gaze kept getting dragged back to the bed. I was filled with visions of limbs entwined, sweat-slicked skin, hands grabbing and squeezing. I stumbled backwards into Brad, not realising he'd moved closer behind me. He steadied me with his hands around my waist, sucking me into that vortex. My eyes drifted shut at the divine feeling.

Hazardous Brad.

I used all my strength to spin out of his hold. I pushed past him, and grabbed my bag to search for my phone. "Ah—I just remembered, I have a thing. A—my granny. I … I have to go." Where were my bloody shoes? My head swivelled from side to side, looking up and down the hallway.

"But, you haven't seen the room yet." His legs were braced apart, arms out, as if he was face to face with a rabid dog.

"I'm sure it's great, just like the rest of the house. I'll be in touch."

Fuck the shoes. I threw my hand on the door handle and yanked it towards me. *There they are.* Shoving my feet in my shoes as quickly as possible, I barely got them on before I raced down two steps at a time.

I jumped in my car and waved out the open window at a bewildered Brad, standing at the top of the stairs in the fading light of dusk. His Gran waved from the front garden, mouthing, "See you again soon," before I sped off.

I had a sinking feeling that she might be right. I felt like I'd lost control of my life. I wasn't in charge anymore.

The swirls of energy chased me down the road. I wriggled in the seat, trying to shake them off, but they stuck like glue. My mind stayed behind in that bedroom. On that bed. I'd brought part of him with me and left part of me behind.

Hazardous Brad.

Chapter
7

Brad

Ben occupied one end of the dining table, while I sat at the other. Our laptops, textbooks and other study resources covered most of the space between us. Andrea was having a girl's day out, whatever that involved. I didn't want to ask. I was supposed to be studying different theories in design, but my mind was still trying to figure out what the hell happened yesterday with Veronica. She seemed fine until she saw my room. Maybe my lava lamp spooked her. I didn't give a fuck if they were lame, the thing provided me with hours of entertainment. That might be a deal breaker, right there. Who was I kidding? I'd smash it if she asked, just to see a smile on her face.

"You're frowning again. Is there something you don't understand?" He peered at me over his laptop, with a pencil stuck under his nose, fish lips keeping it in place.

"Yeah. Women."

He snorted, making the pencil clatter onto the keyboard. "Join the club, man. Who's got you all twisted up?"

"Veronica."

"I didn't realise you were seeing anyone. Andrea will be hounding you for an introduction."

"Oh, I'm seeing her. She's not seeing me in return. She's a pro at doing the bolt."

"Huh?"

I told him the story, including the parts where I injured, her, scared her, and made her run for the hills.

"Mate, how long since you changed your sheets? They probably fucking stink. Did you gas her out with your methane chamber, or what?"

"Fuck …" I leaned my chair back, balancing on two legs and inspected the ceiling for the answer. "Nah, I changed them the weekend before last." The thump of the chair returning to all fours was like the rap of the gavel on the bench. Case closed.

"Well, there ya go." He pointed his pencil at me in accusation.

"Whadaya mean?"

"That's over a week's worth of sweat, farts and BO. She couldn't stand your pong, you rank bastard. You're supposed to wash them *every* weekend."

"Shit!"

I shoved the chair back, heading to my room so I could rip the sheets off and throw them in the wash. Ben's laughter followed me down the hall. My ringtone chimed from the kitchen bench. "Can you get that?" I yelled from my room. Ben spoke in low tones, giving me no idea who it might've been, but I had more important things to deal with.

Arms overflowing with dirty sheets, I turned around to find Ben blocking the doorway. He held my phone out with a smug smile on his face. "What? Who is it?"

"It's her." Ben's legs were buried in an avalanche of sheets as I snatched the phone with one hand and shoved him back with my cast, slamming the door in his face.

"Veronica?"

"Yeah, um, hi. Is the room still available?"

My left arm was already doing a fist pump, albeit an awkward one, what with the heavy plaster. *Be cool.* "Yes. It is."

"Okay … Great. Would it be possible to move in tomorrow?"

"Now is good." My head nodded several times, though she couldn't see me.

"Oh, is tomorrow not good for you? Maybe I could come and get a key—"

"Nooo. Yes. Whenever you want, you're welcome whenever you want. I have a tutorial between one and three tomorrow, but other than that I'm free to help. Do you have furniture? Because the room is fully furnished. You didn't stay to check that part out." I was fishing for an explanation, a little scared she might confirm that I stank her out.

"Oh, that's great. I'm so sick of sleeping on a blow-up mattress. Well, I'll see you tomorrow morning. Thanks. Bye."

"B—" The sound of the dial tone filled the line.

She hung up. I didn't even care. I had a smokin' hot, new housemate. Collapsing backwards onto the mattress, I kicked my limbs in the air like a beetle that had its world turned upside down.

"So … I guess you don't stink."

My head jerked up, and the phone bounced against the mattress as I straightened out my limbs. "She loved my smell so much she wants more of it." My cheeks started to hurt from the grin that wouldn't leave my face.

"There must be something wrong with her, because these …" He picked up the pile of sheets and dumped it on my head, "… smell like you rolled in dog shit and then went to bed without a shower."

The last part was a bit muffled, but I heard him. I held up my middle finger in his general direction, my face still stretched in a smile hidden by the washing. I took a sniff, just to check. *Nuh. Smells like a fucking mountain spring.*

Shit. I had to clean the room and get it ready. Springing off the bed with the dirty washing in my arms, I headed out into the hall, and opened her door. My throat cramped as I took in the abandoned room. I hadn't been in there since I packed all of Tish's things into boxes, and stored them under the house. The recollection stabbed me in the chest. It still felt like a fresh wound, instead of a six-month-old memory.

Mould spores and dust lay their perfume on every surface and molecule of air. Hacking coughs hammered from my chest. *Jesus.* It was a good thing she didn't get a look at the place. I stepped into the room, glad to be hugging the dirty linen as I passed through a pocket of frozen air. The shiver was unstoppable. Darkness and chills engulfed me, momentarily dragging me back to a bad place. Somewhere I never wanted to return. The sheets provided little comfort as I hugged them closer.

My feet moved me across to the heavy curtains. I yanked them open and released a lung-clogging cloud of pollution. I was prepared for it. I held my breath until I could budge the window open. The cream carpet I remembered from my childhood visits had turned dark grey under a thick layer of dust and years of use. I probably should replace that. *Wow, I hadn't really thought this through.* She would've run away if she saw this room, for sure. I blew out a breath, glad she agreed to move in without seeing it.

When I turned around, my attention found the wrought iron bed. Sucked into a time shift, I could see a little girl jumping on the makeshift trampoline. I heard my Gran's stern voice telling her to get off. It was a bittersweet memory. Happy, simple and innocent, but marred by the sad knowledge that the girl never grew up.

I had plenty of work to do before tomorrow. Just looking at the room was sapping my energy. I felt confined by the memories, the emotions that being here brought back. My muscles tensed. I needed to get away from here.

I inspected my injured hand, annoyed by the cast acting as a tether to the mundane. Searching my mind for ideas, I chose one at random. "Hey. You wanna go ride a Segway?" I yelled down the hallway, dropping the sheets in a heap.

"Segway? You going tame in your old age?"

"Fuck off. As soon as this cast is off, we're going hang gliding off the lighthouse at Byron. It's a little hard to get a grip on anything right now."

"Why can't you use your right hand to jack off instead? Or are you worried your left one will get jealous?"

"You're such a dickhead. Do you wanna be Paul Blart with me or not?"

Ben took his time answering. "Yeah, all right. I've always wanted to try one of those things. Let's go be mall cops."

The relief I felt was massive. He didn't know my internal struggle, or how much it meant to me to have him here as I bolstered the courage to face the pain. I asked for an escape and some company, and he said yes. Simple.

Damn, it was good to have my friend back.

———

Ronnie

In five years, I had never taken a day off. I was entitled to a mental health day, with all the shit that had happened to me lately. Mother Nature was on her period this morning, having a major sob fest, drowning us all in her grief. It broke through the monotonous heat, so I was actually pretty happy about her misery.

"Don't forget that box of photos under my bed. Ooh, and the washing in the dryer." Granny reclined on the floral monstrosity, sipping a cup of tea and overseeing my last minute packing.

"You seem a bit too happy to be getting rid of me."

"I'm ecstatic!" The wrinkles around her eyes congregated to point the way to her hairline.

"Thanks, Granny. Jeez. Lotta love comin' at me, I don't know if I can stand it."

"It's because I love you so much that I'm so pleased to be rid of you."

"That makes no sense."

"It will," she sang. I hated it when she dropped cryptic little hints. Not only was it a reminder that this was a 'normal' exclusion zone, but it ramped up my anxiety levels about the future. I just wanted to be blissfully unaware. Like 'normal' people.

The ripping sound of the packing tape grated on my eardrums as I taped up the last box. I slapped my palms against my thighs, relieved to be finished. "Well, I guess I'll start loading the car." I looked from the boxes to Granny, alarmed to find her looking so pleased with herself. Like she set this all up. *Aw, shit. Don't tell me ... No, Veronica, don't be stupid.* I reminded myself that I found the ad on my own. She had nothing to do with it. *Damn it. Why does she have to mess with my head?*

The sound of Granny's giggle faded as I retreated outside with the first box. My car was parked in the visitor space about ten metres from the door. The downpour turned me to a soppy mess, instantly. My baggy grey T-shirt stuck like it was vacuum-sealed, forming wings under each arm. The moisture twisted my hair into tangled ropes. *Well, this sucks.*

After saying a big thank you to Granny, I headed to my new place, trepidation and a little excitement coming along for the short ride. When I pulled up in the driveway, Brad came running out with an umbrella. *Little late for that.* I got out of the car before he reached the bottom step, pulling the first wet box out of the back seat.

"Hi. I guess you don't need this."

"Nope. Thanks anyway." I gave him a tight smile and aimed for the stairs. It was a sweet, thoughtful gesture, but I didn't want to give him false hope that I was a nice person. My back-off signal had to be blatantly obvious.

I reached the top, surprised to find that he wasn't behind me. My traitorous heart thumped harder when I saw Brad with a box balanced on one arm, a plastic bag full of clothes dangling off his plaster. *Idiot! It was going to get wet.* He kicked the door shut with his foot, and flicked his head to the side to get the wet hair out of his eyes. My stomach clenched. *Aw, that's so far from fair it's not funny.* The rain deepened the colour of his hair and stubble, adding a touch of danger, and reminding me of how he looked in the art gallery.

Brad looked up with a huge grin on his face, undeterred by the deluge. I bent to put the box on the veranda before I dropped it. My whole body shivered, despite the warm, humid air. I chose to blame the rain rather than my reaction to him. Whatever my body has decided it wanted, it just wasn't possible. Not in the least. I wouldn't be humiliated again.

The plastic bag rustled as he put it next to the boxes. "Thanks. You didn't have to go out in the rain. I could've done it."

"No worries. I like getting wet. It's invigorating …" His eyes bored into mine before straying to my shirt for a second. "Are there any more?" he said to my forehead.

"No, that's about it." I pushed the remote locking button on my key, watching the indicators flash twice. The rain was so loud; I didn't hear the beep.

"Seriously? Wow, you travel light."

That's what happens when you don't really have a home. I turned my back on him and searched one of the boxes for a towel. Luckily, the inside was still dry, but I'd have to empty them before the water seeped through. The towel soaked quickly when I rubbed it over my head. Flipping my head upside down, I twisted the towel around my hair forming a turban. It wasn't glamorous, but who cared?

Brad's jeans added to the puddle at his feet, drip by drip. Tiny freckles, a few shades darker than his skin, covered his feet. Straightening my spine, I dared a glimpse at his face, expecting him to be laughing at my ridiculous headgear. He wasn't laughing. There wasn't a trace of amusement in his heavy lidded stare. That thumping organ in my chest grew louder from the smouldering look in his eyes. I dropped my gaze to my hands, noticing how my T-shirt stuck to my thin frame. Exposing everything. *Gah!* Pinching the fabric, I pulled it away from my body, producing a sucking sound.

"Did you want a towel? Because I only have two, and the other one is still on my car seat."

"No, thanks. I'll go and change. Leave you to it." He turned to walk inside, his shoulders and arms bunched tightly. I could feel the tension radiating from him. *What was that about?*

Slumping onto the bench seat beside the door, I let out a muffled screech when I saw that I wasn't alone.

"Hi."

"Letitia," her name came out with a hiss. "Where have you been? You asked me to help you and then you buggered off without a word."

"I've been with you the whole time. Sorry about the whole Felicity incident. That must've been rough."

That niggling worry I felt when I saw Flick so messed up came back to pinch me under the arm. Where it hurt. I mentally rubbed it to make it go away, but it lingered, wanting more attention.

"Are you going to tell me more about what you need me to do? What did you say your brother's name was? Linc?"

"Lee."

"Lee. What sort of trouble do you think he's in, and what can I do about it?"

She sat with her heels balanced on the edge of the seat, arms hugging her knees, and eyes staring through the lattice screen of the veranda. "Something bad is going to happen. I just need you to be his friend so that when the time comes, he'll choose the right path."

"Doesn't he have other friends that can help him out? Why me?"

Be his friend? I baulked at the idea. How was that going to help? Goose bumps peppered my arms as icy air drifted around her. Her energy felt suppressed, dark. I wondered if it was this place. The thought started to put me on edge. She continued to stare blankly ahead.

"Where can I find him?" My voice cracked with concern.

Maybe I was too late. I didn't like the heaviness blanketing the air around her. Why was I even worried? I didn't know this girl, and I sure as shit didn't know her brother. I hadn't even begun to figure out how to help her, or where to find him. We'd barely even spoken because she disappeared out of my life almost as soon as she wrought havoc on it. My legs jiggled as I tried to justify backing out of a promise. I hated to admit it, but I felt a connection with this spirit. She got to me, made me like her. She made me re-think my purpose. Maybe I could start to see my curse as a gift. Maybe I could be more like my granny.

Letitia unfolded herself and walked straight through the wall behind the bench, into what was now my bedroom. I squinted at the empty space left behind. *Wow, that's annoying.* I got a vague idea how crappy my aloof behaviour was for the person on the receiving end.

Pulling out some things from a box, I went inside just as Brad emerged from his room in dry clothes. "Home, sweet home." He grinned. I sucked in a breath, failing to respond. Too busy noticing the photos on the hallway wall behind his head. Photos of Brad, photos of Letitia, photos of Brad and Letitia. Photos of Brad and Letitia, and their parents, I assumed. Now that I saw them side by side in photos, I could see a family resemblance. Turning my head to the left, I saw the previous occupant of my new bedroom sitting patiently on the bed.

From the distant end of a tunnel, Brad's voice told me the furniture was his Gran's. I interrupted him with my splintered question. "Did you have a housemate before?"

"This was my sister's room. Tish died seven months ago." I gaped at him. "I mean, not here. In a car accident," he rushed to reassure me.

I looked back at the bed, and she waved at me. "Hey, roomie."

Ignoring her, I took a closer look at the photos in the hall. Brad watched me, biting his lips. "I'm sorry to hear that. Life has its head in its arse, sometimes."

He snorted. "Yeah, that's one way to put it."

"Thanks for bringing my stuff up. Do you mind if I have a shower?"

"No worries."

I smiled, closing the door as he watched through the narrowing crack, never taking his steel gaze off me.

Chapter

8

Ronnie

"I thought you said your brother's name was Lee?"

"That's what I call him. Short for Bradlee. I found it hard to call him Brad, because I associated that name with a movie star or two. Mum called him Lee as early as I could remember, so that's what I call him."

I had to sit on the bed because my legs had turned to jelly. The room suddenly felt like a padded cell. My mental health day had turned into a mental slap.

My nose registered the smell of carpet shampoo, and a dampness under my toes. I looked down, noticing the threadbare tracks between the furniture and several splotchy stains. It wasn't The Ritz. I didn't care. My head was elsewhere. Remembering my soaked-through state, I jumped up off the bare mattress, collecting my scattered thoughts until they snowballed into a mass of anger and betrayal.

Shoving my finger in Letitia's face, I started throwing snowballs.

"First, I fracture my tail bone, which still hurts by the way, thanks for asking. Then, I'm thrown out of my home …" My lip stuck out, remembering my stupid lava lamp, as if the seeping ooze which stained my belongings gave me a visual cue of the future. "I have to move in with … *him*, and then find out that I'm roomies with a dead girl, who probably orchestrated this entire situation. What's next?"

My rant started as a whisper, but my voice slowly rose in volume. *Great.* I hoped Brad—Lee wasn't outside listening. A vision of him standing at the door with his arm raised, ready to knock, popped into my head. I sincerely hoped that was just my imagination running away with my fears.

Letitia watched me, chewing on her thumbnail. Anger morphed into anxiety. What bad thing was going to happen? He seemed fine. I hoped he wasn't sick. That thought swung into thoughts of my boss, Beverly. I knew I had to do something about her situation. I wouldn't be able to live with myself if she suffered because of my cowardice. And I was a total coward. *Aargh, my God.* I was all over the place. Felicity, Letitia, Beverly, Brad—Lee.

I didn't want to do this. I didn't want to reveal my curse. I didn't want to butt into people's lives, where I knew I wasn't welcome. Did Letitia expect me to tell him I could see and hear her? I didn't want him to know. The ringing in my ears increased with a tide of taunting memories from my childhood, and I felt myself unravelling.

I focused on the closed door. There was something about him that gave me hope that maybe, just maybe, I might have found someone who would accept me fully. Curse and all. But I didn't know him well enough to chance it. I wasn't ready to take that risk. Even if it was as simple as befriending another person who wasn't currently dead, let alone becoming more than friends. If I was being honest, I wanted to be more than friends with him.

But I didn't want to want him. I felt trapped all of a sudden. The padded walls seemed to pulse around me. I closed my eyes and pursed my lips to slow down my breathing.

The sound of my ringtone interrupted the silence. I scrambled into the hall, snatching it from my bag before it stopped.

"Hello," I yelled into the receiver, returning to the room and shutting the door.

"No need to yell, Veronica, I'm not losing my hearing just yet."

"Granny." My shoulders sagged. She always knew when I needed her. She may be psychic, but she also had a mother's intuition.

"How do you like your new room, sweetie? I'm glad you finally left that other wretched situation. Poor girl, she's in a bad way. She'll get the help she needs, all in good time. How's young Bradlee? He's a looker, isn't he? I always did like freckles on a man. Makes them look more rugged."

My free hand covered my face. "Why do I feel like I have no control over my life anymore?" I sat down on the damp floor. Tish remained frozen under the weight of my anger.

"None of us have control over life, sweetie, that's up to the higher powers. You can only control your actions and reactions to what is thrown at you. You couldn't have run away from him, Veronica. You two were meant to meet, no matter what, no matter where."

I didn't even know what to say to that last statement. Flopping back to stare at the ceiling, I just sighed into the phone.

"I know you're right about the control, but I thought I was safe in my cocoon."

Her cackles reached through the phone. That was her way of saying, 'Silly girl.'

"I want to meet Bradlee, officially. Next Sunday, dinner at your place. Pick me up early so I can get home in time for my show?"

"I'll have to ask him."

"Nonsense, it's your house now, too. You're allowed to have visitors. He invited people without asking you first. You might want to remind him that he's out of coffee before your dinner guests arrive tonight. Maybe you could cook your Italian risotto. They'll love it."

"What?"

"Anyhoo. Get out of those wet clothes or you'll catch a cold. As much as Bradlee would enjoy tending to you, I don't think you're quite ready for that yet. See you here at five on Sunday. Bye now." The line went dead.

What the hell is happening? I threw my phone on the mattress, and stared up at the water-stained ceiling.

"We need you, Ronnie." Letitia's quiet voice made me jerk. I had completely zoned out.

"Can we talk about this later? I have to go and have a shower. Apparently, there are visitors coming, and we need coffee."

She giggled at me, her dark mood now gone. "There are sheets for the bed in the cupboard off the dining room. Lee forgot that you might need them."

"Right, okay. Thanks."

———

Brad

"So, how long have you worked at the library?"

The smell of garlic and mushroom pervaded the air as I stood at the stove stirring the risotto. Veronica was behind me putting the pine nuts and feta on a roasted sweet potato and spinach salad.

"Five years, but two years of that were during my masters."

What? Hang on. I turned to the side so I could watch her. "How old are you?"

She flinched. I'd have missed it if I wasn't studying her so closely. I felt like a dick. I was making her uncomfortable on her first night with my rabid curiosity and loose lips. I half expected her to run.

"Sorry, that sounded really rude." I turned my back to her again, examining the stickiness of the rice.

Stupid dickhead. Are you gonna ask for her birth certificate next? My cast clipped me on the forehead as I delivered a palm to the face.

"Don't beat yourself up. You can ask me whatever you want, and if I don't want to answer, I won't. Simple."

The tension drained from my muscles. Beautiful, smart, and no bullshit drama. My smile was uncontrollable.

"I'm twenty-four." She shrugged her stiff shoulders.

Twenty-four. She started working there when she was nineteen?

"Next obvious question. Did you do summer semesters, or did you start your schooling at the age of two?" *Fuck, there I go again.*

"I did summer semesters. I graduated a year early, and finished high school a year early, too."

Damn. She was a genius and I was a dumb schmuck.

The wooden spoon in my hand stirred itself. My attention was elsewhere. My chest expanded as I took a deep breath, in an attempt to inflate my shrinking ego.

"What made you want to be a librarian?"

"Any librarian will tell you that it's because they love books, or the search for knowledge. Something noble like that, right? I just wanted a job where I could tell people to shut up, spend my day putting things in order, and charge exorbitant fines when people did the wrong thing. Parking Inspector was my next choice."

The laugh exploded from the depths of my belly. She was sharp. I noticed her mouth quirk up at the corner, though she pretended to be engrossed in the task of clearing the bench. The sight awakened something much further north than my crotch. My heart stuttered. I thought I might have peeled back the first layer of the onion, and I felt like I'd just conquered a small country.

"Why were you looking for a new place?"

"My ex-housemate is the wicked witch of the east." She smirked.

I loved her sense of humour. She didn't have a clue how sexy she was. She didn't try to hide it, and she wasn't shy, she just … didn't see herself that way. I could guarantee that every male within a ten-metre radius, saw her that way. I wanted to growl at the thought.

"How did you end up in that situation?"

"Answered an ad." She looked at me from the corner of her eye, with a raised brow and a grin.

"Gotta be careful of these people that advertise for someone to live with. Lotta psychos out there."

"Yes. Yes, there are."

Her laugh trickled out across my skin, warming me down to the bone.

She was obviously coming out of a bad situation with the last housemate, but she didn't seem to be curious about me.

"You're not going to ask me anything?"

She shook her head, eyes dropping to the bench. Her cheek caved in, as if she was biting it. I didn't know if I should be offended.

"Wow. For all you know, I could be just as wicked as your ex-landlady."

"You're not particularly tidy. You probably ran around picking up stuff before I arrived, and hadn't dusted in months. You have oodles of artistic talent, and you're good with your hands. Handy with a few tools, I'd say.

Probably been renovating the house on your own. You work hard because you need to push yourself. You're easy-going, but loyal and protective. You love having people around you, but for some reason you've been lonely and displaced. There's also a sadness surrounding you. Your sister's death hit you hard, and you feel responsible."

Fuck. That was bang on the money. She really was a genius. *I can't even ... What do I do with that?*

I felt her tense up beside me, peeking at me nervously. She was worried she'd offended me. I thought she'd floored me before. Twice. Now, I might've been slammed through to the core of the Earth. No one had ever seen through me so completely, without really knowing me. I was absolutely certain that she was the one for me. I couldn't pick one flaw. If she told me she was a drug smuggler or a sadistic dominatrix, I would bow down and do whatever she needed me to. I would literally be pussy whipped, and I'd be freakin' happy about it ... because it was her. How the hell was I ever going to get her to want me in the same way?

———

Ronnie

Silence.

Oh crap. Me and my big mouth. I chanced a glimpse. His eyes had glazed over, fixed on the wall in front. But his hand white knuckled the spoon, continuing to stir the rice. *Way to kill the mood, Ronnie. Please, don't kick me out.*

I'd resisted the urge to hide in my room when he said his friends were coming over. This was a chance for a new start. I wanted this to feel like home. I refused to hide away any longer. Plus, I made a promise to a sad, dead girl that I intend to keep, though I didn't see how it'd change anything. Blurting out my assessment of him, complete with criticisms, was not the way to go.

It was surprising how easy it was to talk to him. His curiosity was only natural. He'd be sharing his house with me, of course he wanted to know more. What I didn't expect was the look of awe that came across his face when I exposed a little of my freakishness. He didn't screw his nose up or make some snide comment. He just … moved on. It made me relax enough to actually crack a joke. And when he laughed, the sound filtered down my neck to my chest. I was glad I wasn't facing him. *Traitorous nipples.*

I'd dressed in my skater skirt and a lace, capped-sleeve top for tonight's event. I liked nice clothes, but only for my own enjoyment. Not to impress anyone else. Watching Brad's reaction when I walked out made me want to re-think my choice.

"You look amazing," he'd breathed. Heat immediately rose to my cheeks. Bless my granny for passing on her caramel skin tone.

An unfamiliar tightening started up in my stomach. My nerves were having a rave party, and it made me feel sick. I smoothed my hands across my waist to settle the discomfort. My reactions to this man's scrutiny were foreign to me. He looked amazing himself, in jeans and a fitted T-shirt.

I'd landed in the danger zone. I wanted to put up some steel reinforcing on all my protective barriers. But Brad had found the keyhole, and he had his eye firmly glued to it, trying to see what was inside.

I knew the questions would come. Work was a safe topic. I could deal with questions about work. What I couldn't deal with was the heat shearing off Brad's body. It wrapped around mine when he sidled up beside me to put the plates together. Even the way he shaped the risotto and topped it with garnish was artistic. My eyes followed every movement of his deft fingers, taking so much care to reach his idea of perfection. Having one arm out of action didn't slow him down. I thought I loved cooking. He adored it. Watching him was mesmerizing. My mouth watered. For the food, of course. I hadn't eaten this well in … well, since I lived with Granny in her old house, and had access to a proper kitchen.

He'd just finished plating up when there was a knock at the door.

"Do you mind letting them in?" he asked me without taking his eyes off his creations.

"Sure thing." I tried to sound cool, even though the idea of spending the evening with strangers made me want to scratch my eyes out.

Drying my hands, I made my way to the front door, opening it to reveal a tall, brawny man with black hair, and striking blue eyes. He had a six-pack of beer in one hand, and his other arm around a short, curvy blonde. They both grinned at me. The blonde ducked out from under Hercules' arm, and wrapped her arms around me.

"Hi, I'm Andrea. You're Veronica. We've heard lots about you. Welcome to the family." She stretched up as far as she could go, kissing me on the cheek. *Who was this woman and what had she heard about me?* She released me and gestured to the brawn. "This is Ben."

He tipped up his chin. "Glad you finally moved in and put him out of his misery."

Um. A frown marred my brow; an external sign of my internal confusion. Hercules laughed at my discomfort. Thankfully, he made no move to hug me.

"Erm … It's Ronnie, and good to meet you both. I don't know anything about Brad's misery, but now I'm wondering what he's been saying about me."

I led them through the house, finding Brad in the kitchen rubbing the back of his head. The meals were set on the table outside.

"I guess dinner is served," I announced, and moved to sit in one of the chairs.

Moths buzzed around the fluorescent light above the table. The light breeze carried the scent of a nearby frangipani to mix with the aromas of the food. The others joined me around the table, exchanging looks as they sat. I thought our guests might be in trouble. Andrea snickered under her breath, mouthing, "busted," at Ben. Ben bared his teeth at Brad, unthreatened.

Okay, let's move on and pretend that didn't just happen. "Bon appetite." I picked up my fork and dug in.

"I like this one," Ben added, as he reached for a piece of bread.

"Ignore them." Andrea rolled her eyes, putting me at ease.

"Oh, I will, don't worry." I inspected Andrea more closely. It occurred to me that she'd given me a hug, and yet I hadn't felt infused with bad medicine.

Her expression was openly curious. I wasn't getting any bad vibes from either of them. That was unexpected and new for me.

Growing up, I had a reputation that preceded me. Being seen with me was social suicide, unless they were using me for entertainment value. Any potential friendships were quashed because the risk to the other person was too great. The reason why I'd finished school ahead of everyone else, wasn't because I was smarter. It was because I wanted to get the fuck out of there as fast as I could. I studied constantly. There was nothing special about me, academically. I learned to keep my head down and stick to myself. Whatever got me through.

This was the first dinner I'd been invited to. I guess I wasn't really invited. I dropped my eyes as the warm, fuzzy feeling I was enjoying dispersed with that revelation. Still, the ember of hope glowed brightly. I had finally been given the chance to get to know people.

When I raised my head, everyone had their eyes on the new girl. I wracked my brain for something to say, only finding tumbleweed between my ears. Brad jumped in to rescue the situation.

"Ben and I met in pre-school. He was sprouting some rubbish about rugby league being a thug's game, and rugby union being for educated gentlemen. He must have heard that from his dad. I told him the Broncos could smash the Queensland Reds any day. Typical tough-boy talk. We got into a scuffle and were sent to the principal's office. The principal made us sit down and talk about things we both liked. We had a lot in common. Favourite food, favourite colour, favourite toy, our hobbies. We became instant friends and agreed to disagree on the rugby debate."

"Sensible actions from a principal well-versed in young boys' disputes."

He smiled and bobbed his head. "Luckily, we have different tastes in women, or it would've been awkward later in life. Andrea is the younger sister of a rugby friend. We used to go over to Stewart's house after a game and swim in his pool. Andrea was the annoying little shadow …"

"Hey!" she protested while Ben captured her hand, kissing the back of it.

"… always asking questions and wanting to be a part of the action. She was only fourteen, then. Two years later, she started tutoring Adam, Ben's younger brother."

"Two years later, she'd changed a lot. I noticed. She could still talk the leg off a chair," Ben joked.

I barely said a word, but I drew it all in. They'd known each other since they were kids. What would it be like to have someone who knew you that well, and still wanted to spend time with you, despite having no shared blood?

A fresh sheen of sweat broke out on my skin when Letitia joined our group. The muscles in my neck stiffened so my head wouldn't follow her movement. Words drifted through the air as the conversation continued, the staccato of laughter breaking the flow intermittently. My gaze remained fixed on Andrea's plate across from me, but my attention was firmly on my peripheral vision. If she was aiming to throw me off, it was working. Some friend she was.

Andrea asked about the mural, as Letitia spoke up. "You're being super rude."

I scratched my temple with my middle finger, hoping she'd get the hint, before focusing my ears to catch those floating words.

"About four months ago. I was hit with inspiration." Brad gave me a strange sideways look. He lifted his beer bottle to his lips, taking a sip. They were coated with moisture when he put the bottle down, before he licked it off. I couldn't help it; I did the same.

"Well, isn't that interesting?" Ben's voice barely drifted through the fog of lust crowding my senses.

The prominent veins in Brad's forearm travelled all the way to his elbow. I watched them shift with his muscles, as he rubbed the back of his neck. What was he so uncomfortable about? I was the oddball here. His arm retreated below the table and I focused back on the guests. Who were staring at me again.

"Is it my turn to speak?" My eyes were wide in alarm. *Fuck*, I was so bad at this socializing shit. Brad laughed beside me. *That sound.*

"Lee tells us you're a librarian." Ben's white teeth flashed, obviously amused by my social ineptitude.

"Yes." *What else do they want me to say?* I scanned the seats. Letitia had gone.

"That's pretty impressive at your age," Ben added.

I shrugged. Another statement that didn't require a response. I just hoped they didn't ask me to explain why I finished so young.

"How is your sister, Andrea?" Coming to my rescue again, Brad noticed my discomfort and steered the conversation away. His head tilted towards Andrea, but he snuck a glance at me, winking. The rave party fired back up in my stomach, and I parted my lips in a shaky smile, feeling a little woozy. His eyes locked onto my mouth. Heat crept up my neck, and down to other long forgotten places. My smile slipped at the expression on his face.

Wet lips. Veins on his arms. Freckled face. Hazardous Brad.

I turned away when Andrea spoke. "Earth to Lee." Andrea waved her hand up and down in front of Brad's face. "He's not even listening to me. Bree turned eighteen and has decided to become a prostitute. We're so proud. Her favourite client is a seventy-two-year-old, retired trucker, named Bazza. Oh, and Ben and I are contemplating becoming swingers. You interested?"

Ben started coughing uncontrollably, dribbling beer down his chin. Andrea and I watched as Brad returned from his mental trip, jumping up to get some paper towels.

"What the hell, Ben? I just cleaned the table this morning."

My laughter joined Andrea's girlie giggles, and I felt like maybe I didn't suck at this as much as I thought.

"What? What'd I miss?" Brad's head swivelled like a bobble head, looking for answers.

"Never mind." Andrea's voice dripped with sarcasm.

She continued telling Brad about her little sister, Bree, and about her job as a childcare worker. She was so animated and energetic. She clearly loved children. Ben fixed his eyes on her, watching in rapt fascination. I watched them like they were under my microscope. He maintained contact at all times, whether it was a hand on her leg or fingers playing with her hair. Although she chatted almost non-stop to Brad, she frequently turned to Ben with a smile.

I had no idea about relationships. I'd never observed a couple before. Did every couple behave like that? I didn't know if I was capable of being that close with someone. After watching Andrea, feelings of inadequacy swamped me. I slid down in my chair, wanting to disappear under the table. She was very comfortable in social situations. If she were the interloper, she'd still be the life of the party. I'd rather be in my room.

"Would you like another drink, Veronica?" Brad asked me for the fifth time. Every time he said my name, I felt the magnet between us strengthen. Every time he looked at me, it sent sparks of electricity through my heart and down to my core. When we touched … I squeezed my thighs together. Craving it more than anything and not knowing how to stop it.

"No thanks." I kept my eyes on the empty plate in front of him. "I thought I might get the dessert sorted. Is everyone ready for some sweets?"

A chorus of, "yes, yeah, yep," rang out simultaneously.

"Okay then. Back in a tick."

Gathering all the dirty plates, I made a move. The thumping of my hurried steps on the deck mimicked my pulse as I escaped. I dumped the plates and stuck my head in the fridge, glad for a little breathing space, and cold air to cool my fever. Grabbing the cream and fruit salad, I backed out, bumping into something solid.

"Oomph." The deep grunt sounded behind me as a strong arm came around to steady the bowls. "Sorry. I thought I'd give you a hand," Brad growled in my ear, turning me by the waist so he could squeeze past.

"Tha—nks."

I didn't move, staring down at the bench until his hands slid away. *Holy shit!* The trail of fire he left behind was volcanic. The bowls clattered on the bench as my arms trembled. I fumbled, flapping my hands about trying to save them from tipping and rolling off onto the floor.

All the glances throughout dinner. All his attentiveness. Making sure I was comfortable and keeping the conversation on any other topic besides me. He was softening my hard shell, damn it. But, that move that he just pulled? *Shit.* I'm in so much trouble.

I heard the clink of ceramic bowls and steel spoons as he gathered and placed them on the bench next to me. I was too much of a coward to look over. Trying to remove the plastic wrap from the bowls with my hands shaking like it was twenty below, was a joke. I couldn't even find the end.

Brad placed his hand on top of mine, searing my skin. My heart kicked up a storm and my nipples stood at attention. His breath feathered over my ear as his deep voice rumbled, "Let me help you."

I slowly dragged my hands out from beneath his and sidestepped in retreat. "I—I'm just going to the bathroom for a sec."

His pupils looked huge, shaded under heavy lids. So much desire; blatant for all to see. My body wanted to meld to his. I actually started to step forward, as if ready to climb aboard. My mind was screaming, "RUN."

Spinning on my heel, I ducked into the bathroom and shut the door a little too forcefully. The petrified woman in the mirror begged me for help, with wild eyes and skin the palest I'd ever seen it. I didn't really believe what Granny told me this afternoon. Despite the certainty I felt when I first met him, that he was meant to be mine, I discounted it. Surely you had to get to know someone really freakin' well before you could decide, this was it.

Brad had been acting like he'd made his decision, and he wanted me. That scared me. I'd had people, alive and dead, harass me since I was a kid. I knew that wasn't what he was doing, but his attention was intense. I'd just moved in, for Christ's sake! We were not on a date. So why did it feel like one?

The door vibrated with Andrea's soft knock. "Ronnie, are you okay in there?"

My dry throat hindered my attempt at a reply. I cleared my throat, and tried again. "Yeah, sorry. I'll be out in a minute."

I washed my hands to make it seem like I was in there for a legitimate reason. When I came out, everyone had already finished their dessert, and the table was already cleared. *Crap. How long was I in there?*

Brad looked at me with a sad smile as I sat down beside him. My bowl of fruit looked lonely on the table. The odd one out among a table full of empty ones. The oddball. The interloper.

"Are you feeling okay?" He placed his palm on my forearm, setting me off balance again.

I collected a breath. "Yeah. I guess the day has caught up with me. I'm really tired. Do you mind if I say goodnight?"

"No. Of course, that's fine. I probably should have waited for you to settle in first before forcing my friends on you."

"It was great meeting you both. Thanks for dinner, Brad. It was delicious." Forcing a smile, I managed to raise my eyes as far as his throat before dropping them to his shirt. I couldn't handle seeing his skin.

"No. Thank you. We'll have to cook dinner together every night." I heard the smile in his voice.

"Goodnight, Ronnie." Ben and Andrea both waved.

"Um … goodnight."

I put my bowl in the fridge after covering it. Hushed conversation breached the door; the low rumble of two baritones exchanging harried words. I didn't look back. The exhaustion of the day had suddenly hit me. When I entered my room, I didn't bother to undress, apart from slipping off my shoes. I fell onto the mattress, face first, not acknowledging the presence in the corner. She wasn't the last person I wanted to speak to right now, but she was pretty high on the list.

Chapter
9

Brad

"Back off, man. You're a little too intense," Ben chastised, mock punching my shoulder.

"She looked a bit scared when she came out of the bathroom." Andrea eyed me over the rim of her wine glass, eyebrows raised.

"I know I'm about ten steps ahead of her. I can't stop myself."

"You're about fifty steps ahead of her, I think, mate."

Andrea put her glass down and slid an arm around the back of Ben's chair. Their PDA's were not helping my state of yearning and frustration.

"While that's true, our Lee wasn't the only one making googly eyes. Give her time. Let her get to know you first. Breathe, Lee. Breathe." Andrea patted me on the hand in sympathy.

I huffed, attempting to expel some pent-up energy. It didn't work. The only way I was going to cool down was if I went for a run or a ride. For a second and third option, they weren't bad choices. I'd rather expend it in a much more satisfying and entertaining way, but we all knew there was little chance of that happening. For now.

Ben and Andrea stayed for another hour, talking me down from my craving for a hit. I felt like a prick for being resentful of their good fortune, and the open displays of their obvious love for each other. In my defence, I was frustrated as fuck. Having Veronica here, under my roof, was the most exquisite torture.

Instead of going for a run, I tried out my domestic side. I didn't want Veronica waking up tomorrow morning to a dirty kitchen. Clearing off the remaining debris from dinner, I brought it inside and locked up for the night.

I tried to be quiet, but the beer bottles clinked together as I put them in the recycling bin. *Shit. I hope I didn't wake her up.* Then again, maybe I'd get a glimpse of her in her PJ's. That thought sent my imagination straight to the gutter. A quiet groan escaped, sounding like a wounded animal. I laughed at the accuracy of that comparison.

A whoosh of cold air hit the back of my head. I'd just shut the windows, but I double checked them even though the air outside was nowhere near as cold. This shit was getting so weird. I felt eyes watching me. Could've been old Mrs Hammond looking over the fence again. She liked to gawk. I shook my head with a smile. The only person I wanted checking me out was sleeping soundly down the hall.

Back off, Ben said. I huffed again. My thoughts swirled like the suds in the kitchen sink. They changed

Snippet_3142339C3.idms shape, forming a brilliant plan. Andrea seemed to think there was some hope for me. I remembered the way Veronica's hands shook when I helped her with the dessert. The way she bolted after that. I took it as a bad sign, but what if she was feeling it, too?

I needed to charm her. My Gran would say I needed to woo her. Give her romance. Ben was right, I'd been coming on too strong. Basics. I've got to get back to basics, and become her friend.

Friends do stuff like run together, right? I quickly finished up and got ready for bed. Phase one; Friendship, started at sparrow's fart, tomorrow.

———

Ronnie

Running was my bliss, but I was dead tired. I woke up in the same position that I'd collapsed in the night before. The smell of coffee invaded my nostrils, making my head throb even more. I wasn't a coffee person. Tea was more my speed. But in summer, I couldn't stomach the thought of a hot drink. Apple juice was supposed to be more effective at waking you up than caffeine, anyway.

My mouth felt like a refuge for something furry and pungent. I forgot to brush my teeth before bed. *Nice.* First priority—toilet. Second priority—toothbrush.

Brad had such a hopeful look on his face when he asked if I wanted coffee, I almost felt bad for turning him down. Almost. My resolve to keep my distance was now firmly in place. I'd be friendly, but I couldn't give anyone any more than that. If I was reading Brad right, he was attracted to me. He wouldn't be if he knew the depths of my crazy. It was purely physical, I'm sure. I needed to turn him off, let him see me at my worst. My only concession today was brushing my teeth. I drew the line at pungent, post-alcohol, morning breath.

I still wore the clothes I had on last night. My hair looked like a bad eighties rock video. Deep, crease lines gouged my face from being squashed into the pillow all night. I fully expected a look of disgust on his face, but received a polite smile as he showed me where to find all the required breakfast paraphernalia.

"Do you have any paracetamol?"

"Yeah. It's in the bathroom cabinet. I'll go get it for you." He walked off down the hall and I used the opportunity to admire his rear in his workout gear, with a scowl on my face the entire time. Why did he have to be so … Brad? The name was now synonymous with so many adjectives that all boiled down to beautiful.

He returned, handing me the packet.

"Thanks," I mumbled after swallowing a mouth full of cereal.

"So, I guess you're not up to going for a run?"

"Nuh uh."

His hand scrubbed at the back of his head. He'd go bald at this rate. I didn't really care. "Okay. My last class finishes at four. Do you want to run this arvo?" He dropped his arm when he followed my line of sight.

"I'll wait until the sun has set. It's too hot, otherwise."

"Sure. Sure." His eyes drifted down my body for a second before he caught himself, locking eyes with me. "We could go to the pool instead. You like to swim?"

"No." *You are not getting to see me in my togs, Bradlee.* My eyebrows shot up. His arm crept up again, but diverted to rub his chin instead.

I decided to add to the unease. "Oh, before I forget, my granny has invited herself here for dinner next Sunday. I hope that's okay?"

Swinging his arm down, he beamed, making me blink. "Perfect. I'd love to meet your family."

Huh. Well, she's it.

Oh boy. My resolution—thwarted by my own grandmother. If I was being totally honest with myself, a small part of me was secretly pleased with her meddling. The rest of me panicked. I downed the paracetamol, hoping to dull the pain that had suddenly escalated.

"Great. Don't let me keep you from your run, you look ready to go." Did he ever.

"Nah. I'll save the run for this arvo. It's always better with company. I might go and lift some weights. Did I show you the gym yesterday? It's kind of hidden behind the laundry."

"You've got everything set up. The perfect bachelor pad." *And I've ruined it.* My lips quirked.

"It's always better to share, Veronica. Makes life much more fun," he volleyed, with a twinkle in his eye before he retreated down the back stairs.

He was incorrigible. I clearly had a challenge ahead of me.

Chapter
10

Ronnie

The library was getting steadily busier as the semester marched on. Joseph was loving the influx of young beauties beginning their quest for knowledge. This morning he was busy hawking his wares to the latest petite blonde. Poor thing probably just wanted to know where to find the photocopiers.

My head was in such a jumble after last night's events. I had to search for the correct reference numbers rather than spouting them from memory. I thanked my lucky stars that I chose to specialise in cataloguing rather than something like research or faculty librarian. Something that required more human interaction. Keeping my distance … it was what I'd always done. What I'd had to do to protect myself. So, why did it feel so wrong?

I decided to walk it off and wound up stuck at the help desk.

"Excuse me?" My eyes lowered to a short, young woman with her red hair in plaits. She stood at the desk, tightly clutching the strap of her messenger bag across her chest. A quick scan of the area told me Joseph was nowhere to be found, and neither was a library officer.

"I—I've booked a study pod, and the guy who's in there won't leave."

My eyebrows, currently in the frown position, danced upwards in exasperation. I let out a sigh. "Which room did you book?"

"Six H."

"No problem. I'll just be a second."

I ran up the stairs across from the desk, and followed the glass dividing walls until I reached my destination. The guy sitting in the room was on his laptop, surfing the web. A blond-haired, blue-eyed, pretty boy. Dressed in jeans and a polo shirt—clearly both designer brands—he was the picture of privilege.

Taking out my phone, I opened the camera app and held it up ready to snap a photo.

"Hey," I barked out. He turned his head. *Click.* Instantly, a cocky demeanour slid into place.

"Well, hello. Did you need proof to show your friends you weren't lying about how hot the guy in the library was?"

My eyes rolled. *What a dick.* "This pod is booked. You need to leave."

"Pfft. Did Pippi Longstocking send you? There are plenty of rooms to choose from." His cocky grin remained in place. I wanted to smack it off.

"All the rooms are booked. That's the procedure if you want these work spaces." I breathed in slowly, trying to calm the rising storm within. We were attracting an audience.

His smile changed to a look of annoyance, making me feel slightly better. "I've been here all morning. I'm not moving if there are other empty spaces where she can go."

"They may be empty, but they're booked. Those people could be searching the stacks or running late. You need to get out, or I'll email your photo to the library staff with the word banned in the subject line, so they'll all know you're an inconsiderate twit. Last warning. Please move."

His face turned red as his mouth tightened. "Relax …" He stood to collect his stuff. I was pretty sure he mumbled 'bitch' at the end.

I stood to the side of the pod's entrance and watched him go. The sour expression he wore made him look like the spoiled little boy that he was.

"Thank you."

I turned around to see the timid redhead smiling. I sincerely hoped she wasn't a law student. She'd never survive the shark tank. Nodding, I walked back to the stairs. My heels clicked loudly on the wooden laminate. When I reached the second last step, I froze. With her back to me, Flick watched Lindstrom retreat through the doors. She turned, and her wide-eyed look of panic morphed instantly into a hateful sneer when she spotted me.

What is it with all the arseholes today? Lifting my chin, I stomped down the last two steps and towered over her, toe to toe. "What is your deal? Because there is no way I deserved all the vitriol you have spewed my way. And what is going on between you and Lindstrom?"

"Shh, keep your voice down," she hissed. She latched onto my arm, pulling me behind the help desk, and down the hallway. I could fight her, but I agreed that this should be done in private.

"Nothing is going on between us, don't be absurd. He is a friend and associate of my father." Her voice was indignant, but she radiated despair in the way she trembled. There were shadows under her eyes. I couldn't figure out what she was really saying. "You deserved everything I threw at you. Keep your nose out of my business. I'm warning you, don't go poking the beast."

"That's a fitting analogy. You are definitely a beast." I poked her on the shoulder and she burst into tears.

O ... kay. I was totally confused. She could give it—I mean, she named me after a stick insect—but she couldn't take it. Her shoulders jerked as each sob wrenched out. Mascara ran down her cheeks, ruining her carefully constructed mask. The breath she gasped between cries of pain seemed so hard won, I felt compelled to comfort her. *Not gonna happen.* She didn't deserve it. This woman reawakened all my worst nightmares from childhood. She treated me like I was less than the mould in her shower. My bitterness towards her told my instincts to shut up, and my feet to walk away.

Ignoring both of them, I stayed put, waiting to see if she had anything more to say. An apology would've been nice.

"You talk to yourself." She broke into my thoughts with her sobs.

"Pardon?" My insides shrivelled. *She can't know.* I carefully kept my face blank.

"I know you know things. You tried to hide it, but I figured it out when you had nightmares. You told me to take a different route to visit my dad one day. It was a really off-hand comment. I don't think you were aware you'd said it aloud. I ignored you. There was a nasty accident that day, and I got stuck in traffic for two hours. When I finally made it to the office, I—my father wasn't happy."

She jabbed her manicured finger into my shoulder. "You're a freak. I couldn't be happier that you finally got the hint and moved out. Stay. Away. From me."

Spinning on her sensible heels, she stalked away. I didn't have any time to process the gravity of the situation because Beverly appeared, looking concerned. Her pale blonde hair glowed under the lights. "Ronnie. Is everything okay back here?"

My mouth stretched into something resembling a smile—I hoped. "Just an unhappy customer. The photocopiers are playing up today."

"Oh well, must be the day for it. I've got a young fella out here telling me you called him a twit."

I seriously wanted to groan and slap my forehead repeatedly. "I believe I called him an inconsiderate twit, and he deserved it."

"Now, Ronnie. We can't go insulting the students. Unfortunately, this bloke knows people in high places."

Of course, he does. "I'll go talk to him."

"If you would." She inclined her head. "Thank you. I trust you'll deal with it professionally."

I walked to the desk with Beverly following. "You have a complaint?" I asked the inconsiderate twit watching me with cold indifference.

"Yes, I do. You insulted me, and rudely interrupted my study session." He placed his hands on the desk and leaned forward.

"Your study session was taking place in a room that had been booked by another student. Your refusal to leave was interrupting her study session."

I grabbed my phone and opened the picture. "You see this, Beverly?" She nodded, resting her hands on the desk. "Notice the location of the study pod in question?"

"Yep. That's six H."

"Would you mind checking the bookings for that room, please?"

"Sure." She tapped on the keyboard.

"This picture was taken at 11:05 this morning. Who had booked the room at that time?"

"Unless your name is Theresa, it's not you." Beverly's expression was serious, but there was a twinkle in her eye.

"I didn't say I had the room booked. I'm not complaining about being told to leave. My issue is her unprofessional conduct." Twit waved his hand in my face. Like a red flag. My eyes speared into his, making sure he didn't look away.

"Are you saying that you left willingly, without insulting a fellow student? That you didn't deliberately ignore the rules, which resulted in the obstruction of learning for said student?" After that spiel, I needed a deep breath.

The twit squirmed on the spot. "I wasn't the one doing the insulting."

"Oh really? It's a good thing I recorded it, then. Beverly, would you like to listen?" I turned to my boss with a smile before pressing play on the recording. Twit eyeballed the phone with contempt. When the recording finished, it confirmed his use of the word, 'bitch'. *Twit.*

Turning back to the student, I began my closing argument. "I apologize for saying twit. My understanding of the definition is, 'someone who is behaving in a bothersome or foolish manner.' I think it's fair to say that was an accurate assessment at the time. However, you referred to me as a female dog. Would you say that's a fair assessment, Beverly?" I tilted my head towards her, but kept my eyes on the scowling pretty-boy.

"No, I'd say that's actually pretty insulting and you could file a complaint." Her lips quivered with her effort to stop a smile. "If there's anything else you'd like to add, feel free. Otherwise, you'd better get back to work."

The student turned abruptly, moving back to his desk with his shoulders stiff and his ego in tatters.

"You missed your calling." Beverly's parted red lips showed her white teeth in stark relief. My cheeks flushed. I felt chuffed that I'd pleased her.

"Nah. You have to enjoy putting on a show to be a barrister," I joked. *Having a courtroom full of people staring at me—no, thank you.*

"That was one of the most enjoyable shows I've watched in a long time. It'll do that young man some good to be knocked down a peg or two. I don't understand the attitude of some of these young kids these days. If you want respect, you have to give it first." Her gaze was unfocused. She seemed lost in contemplation. But her lowered eyebrows and crossed arms told me that she was getting ready to get things off her chest. Thinking about Beverly's chest just reminded me of my failure to help her. But I'd said more in the last fifteen minutes than I had in the last day, and I wasn't in the mood for a get-to-know-you chat.

"Do you mind if I grab some lunch? I'm feeling a bit faint."

"Sure thing. Take an hour, you earned it."

"Thanks." I headed back down the hallway where Flick and I had our altercation. My eyes followed the striped pattern on the carpet. Applause joined the muffled sound my shoes were making.

Letitia. I was really starting to hate this spot. With her hands clasped under her chin, her face showed a bright smile. Her outfit hadn't changed the entire time I'd known her. Yellow tank top and denim cut-offs.

"That was brilliant. I could almost rest in peace now."

I snorted. "Go ahead, that's fine by me." I kept walking and collected my purse from the office.

"Ooh, nasty." She stuck her bottom lip out and batted her lashes. "No can do, anyway. I still have unfinished business."

"Like what? Your brother is fine. I don't understand what you want me to do." I raised my hands in exasperation, then dropped them against my thighs with an audible slap.

"You need to help Lee paint the house."

"You … What now? You want me …" I jab my thumb into my chest. "… to *paint*? Is this some kind of Mr. Miyagi stunt?" *She has got to be kidding.*

"Trust me on this one. Please?" She clasped her hands together in mock prayer. Those big eyes, so much like her brother's, implored me to agree.

Tilting my head up to the ceiling, I let out a groan. "Sure, why not? It's not as if I have a life."

"Aw, don't be like that. You'd have more of a life if you stopped pushing everyone away."

"I'm pretty sure you know why I have to do that."

She nodded. "Yes, but you don't have to. You just need to be selective about who you let in." Her expression suddenly became alert. "Heads up, Beverly's coming. You need to help her soon. Time is running out."

"Everything okay? I heard you talking."

"Yep. Just on the phone with my granny." I waved my phone at her, and dropped it back in my bag. "I like to check in regularly."

"Okay. Well, enjoy your lunch. I wouldn't mind some tucker, myself."

I smiled tightly on my way past.

———

Returning from lunch, I headed to Beverly's office to apologise for the earlier altercation. This was why it was safer for me to stay away from people. Her door was open, as always. When I knocked softly to get her attention, she had her smile ready. To my surprise, I returned it with ease. Her mother stood guard over her shoulder, her expression impatient. I kept my gaze on Beverly.

"Back from lunch? What did you have?"

"You need a mammogram." The words spewed unchecked from my mouth. My eyebrows shot up, as my throat snapped shut. I was sure I looked like I was choking on a fish bone. She blinked rapidly with her mouth agape. The whooshing sound of the air-conditioning vents seemed as loud as a jet engine. Or, maybe that was my heartbeat.

"Uh." *Shit.* "I mean, I need a mammogram and I was wondering if you'd come with me? I'm a bit scared." *What?*

Her shock transformed to motherly concern. "Oh, Ronnie. It's nothing to be concerned about, sweetie. They squish you flat as a pancake, this way and that, then you're out in fifteen minutes. I'd be happy to accompany you. Truth is, I'm six months overdue for mine. It's so easy to keep putting these things off. Have you been to your doctor? You might need a referral because you're so young." She waited, looking at me expectantly.

Right, what have I gotten myself into?

"Okay … I'll need to book an appointment first, then. Best to get the doc to check first. It could all be in my head." *It's most definitely in my head.* "Do you need a referral, or can you just book in? I don't want you to wait if you're overdue. Why don't you book and I'll come with you? I can wait in the waiting room. Check out what it entails, so I'm not nervous if my doctor requests one for me. Then you can come with me, if need be." *Please book your appointment, now.*

"Okay, I'll book my appointment, if you book yours. How about that?"

I breathed a sigh of relief, and my shoulders sagged. Beverly's mother performed a happy dance behind her back. I disguised my laughter as a cough, biting my lips as I took out my phone.

I flexed my calves to make sure my feet were still attached to the ground. I didn't understand how much weight had piled on my shoulders from ignoring all the requests for help, and denying my gift. Using it to help was a high I never expected. *Wow.* Maybe I could do this. Maybe it was okay to be who I was. I just had to be creative with the explanations.

Chapter
11

Ronnie

The loud honk from a taxi blended with the sounds of lunchtime in the city. The rush of people on a mission to fill their bellies, and find a patch of peace to enjoy their half hour of freedom. My mission was to face my fears, and cross another old building off my list.

"What about the Casino?"

"Nope. It's too tainted. Too many people. I'd rather face a ghost than the energy surrounding hundreds of people losing their hard-earned cash. Beautiful buildings, though. From the outside."

She narrowed her eyes, and tapped her finger on her chin in contemplation. "The Old Windmill? That place is haunted. All those convicts forced onto a treadmill for hours to grind the grain. Nasty business."

"No. That part doesn't float my boat. It's the old buildings I love. I'm not aiming to visit every ghost in Brisbane. I just want to be free to pursue a love of mine without being put off by a spirit who can't let go." I looked at her pointedly. The shame of setting my sharp tongue free hit me the moment her bottom lip popped out. Years of snapping back was a hard habit to break.

"Sorry. I'm no good at this friendship thing."

"Well, you're letting me tag along with you, so that's a good start. Friends share what they love to do with each other. You know, Lee would love to do this with you. He loves buildings, new and old."

"Humph." I put more force into each of my steps. My go-to move. Running. More like power walking right now, but I wanted to run so badly the adrenaline was already surging.

We weaved in and out of the foot traffic. I held my breath every time I passed a smoker loitering in a driveway, or near the rubbish bins. The tick, tick, tick of the 'walk' signals could be heard every couple of minutes. If I timed my pace just right, I could get all the little green men all the way to The Mansions without stopping.

"You're willing to face up to a couple of spirits so that you can pursue something you love, but you can't face my brother because you're running from someone who could love you and who you could love."

"Whom."

"What?"

"It's someone *whom* you could love. And anyway, that's ridiculous. I'm not running from love. It's … the physical... Whatever. I'm not running." I shoved my mass of hair out of my face. My semblance of control was slipping.

I can't handle your brother.

"I'm pretty sure he'd like you to handle him."

"Stop reading my thoughts!"

The man walking ahead of us turned to check out the crazy lady talking to herself. *Damn it.* This is why it was better to ignore this goddamn curse.

"Who cares what he thinks? He still sleeps with his teddy bear." Tish poked her ethereal tongue out, in a wasted but appreciated gesture. I jerked my chin back in surprise. Someone other than my grandmother, willing to stick up for me? Even if she was dead, it soothed my frayed nerves.

The man's frown turned to a look of appreciation as his eyes travelled down to my legs, exposed in my shorts. I was tempted to karate kick him in the family jewels. Snapping my fingers under his nose to get his attention on my face, I gave him a verbal kick instead. "Hey, mister. How's Big Ted? Do you still suck your thumb, too?"

Alarm flickered in his eyes before he spun away, scurrying off.

"That's how you know it's real."

"Huh?" My mind searched back through our words, attempting to pick up the lost thread.

"Lee. He gets to you. He has the ability to burrow under those reinforced layers you wrap yourself in. You know it, and that's what has you crapping your dacks."

Yep, that's exactly what I'm afraid of. "Can we not talk about your brother?"

"You promised."

"I never promised to date him, if that's what you're suggesting. You set me up!"

"I may have nudged a little, but you didn't exactly refuse to move in."

"What choice did I have?"

"There's always a choice. There's the right one, and a lot of wrong ones. I'm here to tell you that you made the right choice."

"Why doesn't that make me feel any better?"

Her appearance faded to mist, as she whipped her body around in front of me. "Stop!"

"What? Why?" The panic she emitted spun a web around us.

Her icy palm encircled my bicep, giving it a faint tug. My feet refused to budge. When I looked across the street,

I saw what had her attention. My feet moved then, but it was too late. He'd spotted me.

Lindstrom adjusted the button on his suit jacket, as he crossed the road without regard for the oncoming traffic. The leer on his face churned my gut and raised my hackles. I almost hoped he'd get hit, but that wasn't something I'd ever want to witness. An iron mask dropped over my face, my shoulders pushing back in defiance and readiness for whatever assault was coming. If Flick had been saying things about me …

"Ronnie," he sneered as he assessed my casual attire.

"Lindstrom," I replied, putting as much contempt as possible into my voice. "Not doing coffee with your girlfriend this morning?"

"To whom are you referring?" he questioned as he closed in, pinning me with his icy, blue eyes.

His response told me a lot. Flick was telling the truth about her relationship with him. He probably had a harem of girls to toy with. Toying with people was his favourite pastime.

He was attractive, I'd give him that. But the outward appearance was only a thin crust that hid what lay beneath. My curse was great for seeing the hidden, and his insides weren't pretty at all.

"Don't let him get in your head, Ronnie," Letitia warned.

"Uh, I'm late so … yeah."

"Oh, Ronnie?" he called out behind me as I hot footed it down George Street.

"What?" I snapped, without turning back.

"I'll be seeing a lot more of you. Soon." The tone of voice he used was so threatening that I jerked my eyes back. He appeared to be smiling and friendly, but the eyes … the eyes told me it was a warning, and a promise, all in one.

I shuddered as fear snaked up my spine. The sense of foreboding was suffocating. This time, I felt like evil was coming for me.

"What's that supposed to mean? What is your game?" I spat back, switching to attack mode. The veneer started to slip and his evil leaked out slowly for all to see, turning his eyes almost black. Letitia shoved me from behind, making me stumble forward. Okay, so she could move things.

"Go now!" she yelled at me. I ran down the side street and found a cafe, silently willing Letitia to follow me into the toilets. I needed privacy for this conversation. Checking all the stalls to make sure they were empty, I leaned back against the sinks with my arms crossed, and pinned my stare on Letitia.

"Normally, 'I don't want to know', is my motto. Normally, I'm a stick-my-head-in-the-sand-and-go-the-fuck-away kind of girl. You asked me for help, and I thought, *okay*, because I liked you and I felt like you wanted to help me, too. I know being an ostrich is not healthy, but it has been my defence mechanism, and my protection from insanity. Now, I feel like a can of worms—no—a can of eastern brown snakes, has been opened in my bed while I was sleeping. What. The fuck. Was that?" I flung my trembling arm towards the door, as the breath sawed in and out of my lungs.

"You just need to stay away from him. Never, ever, let him get you alone. Do you understand me?" The last bit came out as a whisper. Letitia looked haunted. I felt dread in my soul, just looking at her.

"What has he done?"

Letitia looked down at her hands, twisting her fingers around and around. "You need to know that he is more dark than light. He seeks to dull the light, and you are one of the brightest."

"Brightest? I consider myself fairly intelligent, but that's not the kind of bright you're referring to. I'm not sunshine and roses. What's he doing with Flick if he wants light? I'd say she's pretty dark." Letitia stared, her poker face in place, waiting for me to clue in.

Oh. I remembered the single glass on the bench. The sticky margarita mix. The drawer full of pills. So many things about Flick made sense, now. It was so true what they said about bullies. How they're most likely being bullied themselves. I had grossly misjudged her.

You are one of the brightest. She was referring to my 'gift'. If I ever needed proof that it was a curse, this was it. My 'light' had attracted the worst kind of attention.

"Does Flicker have extra senses, too?"

"She's an unfortunate pawn in a sick power game."

"What do you mean?"

"It's not something you need to get involved with at the moment."

Normally, I couldn't agree with her more. "Is it something that will involve me in the future?"

"It's undecided." She shrugged her shoulders like it was no big deal, but her face told me another story.

Our eyes were locked. My palms were sweating. My heart was vibrating rather than beating. For the first time in my life, I felt like I was going to faint. White spots danced in front of my eyes and joined together to block out my vision. The ringing in my ears smothered her words. I forgot how to breathe.

I sank to the floor, only vaguely registering that I was in a public bathroom. Water sprayed from the sink above my head. Its heavenly, cool relief, kept me from becoming lost. I couldn't be more grateful.

My hearing returned first. I heard Letitia calling my name. Realising I had closed my eyes, I opened them to see her concerned face. She was so young and innocent. Life was so unfair.

Had I been unfair to Flick? I didn't even know the woman I'd been living with. I thought she was a pretentious, coffee-loving, shopaholic, control freak.

Maybe she'd endured harassment by Lindstrom, or worse. I was so glad I'd gotten out of there, but what had I left behind?

I had to get out. I felt like the walls were closing in on me. My reflection in the mirror showed a petrified, soggy mess. I just wanted to run home. Towards Brad, and the way he made me feel. There are much scarier and more sinister things than love. Things that could damage you in irreparable ways.

Returning to the main street, I looked across to where I'd seen Lindstrom emerge. It was a federation style building, no number marked its address. Tilting my head up to the top floor, the blood drained from my face, and my legs threatened to collapse again. The lady in the floral dress stared at me from a window. *What was she doing here?* The feeling of her icy fingers as they tugged at my toes gripped my mind in its hold. *Oh, fuck.* I think I'm in deep shit.

Chapter
12

Brad

She was avoiding me. She'd moved in over a week ago, and I hadn't seen her since the morning after our dinner with Ben and Andrea. Every morning, she was up before the sun and didn't come home until I'd gone to bed. The only evidence that she had been here at all was some washing hanging under the house. She hadn't eaten anything from here, either. Damn, that pissed me off. Not sleeping, not eating, it was going to stop, right now.

Her Granny was coming to dinner tonight, unless the plans had changed. My gut clenched at the thought. I wanted to meet the woman who had shaped Veronica into the amazing woman that she was today, and who had gained her love and respect. I needed more insight into my new 'friend'.

From the back deck, I could see the very edges of the sun's halo of light chasing away the night. A colony of bats winged their way home as I sat and waited, wondering what I could cook for our special guest. The cool breeze stirred the smell of frangipanis and moisture from last night's rain. I could taste it in the air. When the sun's warmth hit the damp earth, Brisbane would turn into a sauna.

Dressed in my running gear, I was ready to catch my Gazelle before she escaped me again. The pocket of cold to my left kept me company, as it did almost constantly, whether I was outside or in. There was no explanation that I could think of without feeling like a fruit loop. The truth was, I was comforted by it. Bloody handy to have built-in air-conditioning. Wouldn't be so great in winter, but whatever.

The noise of the toilet flushing put me back on alert. She was up. I leaned back a bit so I had a view down the hallway. The bathroom door opened revealing Veronica in a purple tank top and … were those shorts or knickers? Her mass of dark curls moved free and wild. She rubbed her eyes as she walked towards me, heading for the kitchen. Those legs, that hair. *Those legs.* I was amazed this woman was for real, to be honest.

She dropped her hands as she reached the counter, and squealed when she spotted me watching her.

"Morning, Veronica." The look on her face was priceless. I let a chuckle escape.

"What the fuck do you think you're doing?" Arms akimbo, stormy eyes, she set my heart on fire.

The flame dimmed at the sight of the dark circles under her eyes.

I grinned at her outrage, and moved inside, wanting to get closer and take away whatever troubled her. "Enjoying the morning show."

She rolled her eyes and opened the fridge to grab the apple juice. I made a mental note to keep the apple juice stocked.

"Hurry up and get your running gear on, we're leaving in five."

She paused mid gulp with her cheeks puffed out. The glass clinked on the counter as she set it down, swallowing loudly. "I beg your pardon?"

She was putting on her stern-librarian voice. I bet that worked on most people. She liked to keep everyone at a distance. Not gonna happen with me because it was making me hard. Made me want to rough her up, and show her who was in charge.

"Four minutes."

Her dark chocolate eyes grew wide as her delectable lips parted. I noted the pulse on her neck as it jumped. She liked it when I took charge. Interesting. A smile tugged at my mouth. "Three minutes. If you don't change out of those pyjamas, the neighbourhood is going to know what you sleep in."

She made a strangled sound. "Okay, Bossy Boots. Sheesh."

She had to brush past me as she navigated the kitchen counter. I breathed in deeply. Her scent wrapped around my chest, and drew my balls up tight. She made me want. She made me need. She made me forget.

In less than two minutes, she was standing in front of me ready to go, wearing black Skins and a fluorescent yellow, razor-back singlet. Her baseball cap dangled from one hand, and sunglasses from the other. I reached out to take them from her.

"You won't be needing those. We'll be back before the sun breaks."

She held her hands up in dismay. Her phone was strapped to her arm. I ripped off the Velcro, taking that, too.

She put her hand over mine. "No. I need to have music when I run."

I slowly shook my head. "You need to let your mind wander. Listen to the hum of the morning. Let yourself relax and mull things over. I do my best thinking when I run. Pictures of designs start flicking through my head. It's liberating. Better than therapy."

"Everything's better than therapy." She bit her lip as she let that slip.

I might've found a kindred soul. Her eyes told me she knew pain. The kind that I did. I almost felt like a prick for taking away her safety blanket. Almost.

I placed her things on the kitchen bench. Before I could stop myself, my thumb pressed on her chin to free her lip. "Please stop that, it's very distracting."

I heard her soft gasp. Her huge eyes seemed too innocent. It was such a contradiction to the independent, sassy girl I'd come to know.

I let my hand drop and turned towards the door. "Let's go." Without waiting for her response, I headed out the front, hoping she'd follow.

She caught up to me under a streetlight. "What did you do to your hand?"

"Rock climbing fail." I held up the offending appendage. It didn't hurt, but it was annoying. The cast would be off soon enough. I think that was the first question she'd asked me since asking about Tish. An encouraging sign. The questions I had for her were piling up behind my ribcage. I needed to let them out before I had a fit, or something. "Is your schedule that crazy, or do you have a boyfriend? I haven't seen you since the morning after you moved in."

"This is why I need music. I don't talk and run."

My head turned towards her. We were doing an easy jog. I knew she normally went a lot faster. "We're not running, we're jogging. Don't tell me you're not fit enough. I didn't peg you for a liar."

"I just don't like talking."

"Ever …? Really?"

She nodded, emphasizing her point.

"How does that go down at work?"

"I talk when I have to, obviously." She raised her eyes to the sky like I was a dumb arse.

"Do you talk to your boyfriend, or do you just play some weird game of charades?"

"Ha, ha. Okay, I'll take the bait. No boyfriend." My chest inflated. "I don't do relationships." And deflated, as she dug the knife in with her final statement. I had to take a moment to mull that over.

"Why? Have you been burned before?"

"Not the way you're thinking."

What other way is there? My thoughts whirled with possibilities. Some of them were too dark for my mind to comprehend, making my good hand clench, ready to punch someone. If anybody was to lay a forceful hand on Veronica, I'd rip their guts out through their arsehole.

"I'm imagining all sorts of bad shit, right now. You've gotta put me out of my misery."

"Let's just say I've seen a really bad example of what love …" She curled her fingers in air quotes around that word. "… can do, and I don't want any part of it."

The sound of our feet pounding the footpath filled the sudden pause. Curiosity burned in my throat. I wanted to release it … ask all the questions. But I didn't want to scare Veronica off.

"Do you have any family here, other than your granny?"

"Nope. She raised me. She lives in a retirement community now."

"No siblings?" She shook her head, her mouth in a tight line.

"May I ask what happened to your parents?"

She glanced my way with narrowed eyes, biting her lips, clearly wondering if I could be trusted with this information. Several minutes passed. There was an awareness deep down that I needed to shut up and give her this time. The pain swirling in her eyes was something I recognised too well. I wanted her to trust me with her secrets. I needed her to let me in, like I'd never needed anything before.

Keeping my eyes forward, I concentrated on running. We'd reached the Brisbane River. I led the way across the road to the path curving its way along the brown, murky, rush of water. A dog's bark followed our trail from its front yard.

"My mother left my father when I was three, because she couldn't handle who he was. I don't remember much happiness as a young girl, apart from visiting my granny. My father used to play with me, but when my mother left him, he became a shell of a man. He moved back into his mother's house—Granny's. When it was his turn to have me, I spent the time with Granny while he sat out in the back garden, staring off into space. His head was obviously a very dark place. He lost his shit and committed suicide a year later. A little while later, Mum left me because … I reminded her of him."

Holy fuck! Her story was sadder than I was prepared for. Nobody should have to suffer through an experience like that. Especially at such a young age. Now, I was even more eager to meet her grandmother. She had raised an incredible woman. After suffering so much heartache, they've come through together.

Veronica drew in a deep breath and pushed it out in a rush. "I'm never going to be like my father. I'll never put myself in that position. I think it's unrealistic to expect that you'll find a person who will accept you for all that you are, including the ugly parts, and love you anyway."

My eyebrows rose. "That's a really bleak outlook on love. I know for a fact it's possible to find that one person who will love you, warts and all. My parents were a prime example."

"Were?" She turned her body, skipping sideways.

"Yeah, were. They died in a light aircraft accident when I was nineteen. Tish was only fourteen at the time. They were our world. They cherished us, but they lived for each other. I think that's the way it should be, because they're the reason we're here. In a way, it's a good thing that they were together when they died. At least that's what I keep telling myself."

"Shit. I'm sorry, that's awful. My parents chose to leave me, but yours were ripped away suddenly. Life's unfair and cruel."

"Six months ago, I would have said the same thing. Now, I think it's not all bad." Looking at her, I had a feeling that things might turn out okay. If only she could learn to trust me. Open up to the possibility that someone could love her for all she was … and that someone was me.

We headed down another street that would take us back to the house.

Barking dogs verbalized their alarm like a Mexican wave following us as we passed. The daylight encroached on the horizon, flicking the streetlights off for the day.

"You realise you've been talking?" She grunted at me, making me laugh. "So, what does your granny like to eat?"

"She's on a vegan, gluten-free, diabetic diet."

My feet faltered. "Wha?"

Her smile was huge, sweeping away all the sad reminders with a lift of her beautiful lips. "You should see your face."

"Please tell me you were joking."

"Absolutely," she sang.

I shoved her on the arm, making her stumble to the side. Her foot caught in a divot, her leg crumbling beneath her. I grabbed her arm in time before she hit the grass. Her groan of pain was an effective punishment.

"Shit! Sorry. Are you okay?"

"Nope. Not even a little bit." She flopped herself down and clutched her ankle.

"Ah, damn. You twisted your ankle."

I looked around, gauging where we were; nearly at the corner. It was only about three hundred metres to home. My eyes dropped to the top of her head. Her gorgeous curls were caught in a ponytail at the nape of her neck. She had suffered so much. I just wanted to care for her. Show her that her mother's choices weren't because she wasn't worthy of love. Her mother was the problem.

I made the decision to carry her.

————

Ronnie

I shrieked as he bent down and scooped me up, one hand behind my back and one under my thighs, the cast sticking out beyond my legs. Secured in his arms, I forgot the sleepless night of tossing and turning. I forgot the danger that lurked on the periphery. I forgot my reluctance to introduce Brad to Granny tonight, and that I was trying to distance myself from him. I wanted to burrow in deeper.

"Wrap your arms around my neck." His grey eyes burned with familiar intensity.

I followed his command. Thankful that I had the permission and the excuse to do so. "You know, this is the second time you've injured me while we've been running." His sheepish smile was adorable. "I don't think it's safe to go running with you again."

"Bull dust," he baulked.

I gave him a single nod. "All the evidence is against you."

"Have I not picked you up and offered assistance every time?"

"Mm. There is that."

"Am I not strong enough and chivalrous enough to see to your needs?"

"I s'pose." I chewed on my cheek at the mention of his strength, and him seeing to my needs. I was six-foot-tall. I could feel the muscles in his shoulders straining, but he wasn't out of breath. We turned the corner into our street.

"Do you not feel safe in my arms?" His voice dropped to a sexy rumble.

The black of his pupils almost eclipsed the slate of his irises, and his nostrils flared. My gaze travelled back up to his. I was reluctant to admit that I felt incredibly safe with him at that moment. But the words slipped from my mouth on a breath. "I do."

His mouth parted and his minty breath rushed across my face at his sharp exhale. I felt the thunder of his pulse through the side of my ribcage, pressed to his heart. The rhythm of my own, a match for his. I refrained from squirming, but the energy pulsing through us made it hard to stay still.

Dragging my eyes away, I looked up at a cockatoo squawking its good mornings at a deafening pitch. I drew in a breath, and Brad's clean scent. "Granny likes creamy French dishes with wine."

He waited a few seconds before replying. "Sounds delicious. I'll enjoy the challenge."

"We should have all the stuff we need. I did some shopping last night." *While I was avoiding you.*

"Thank you for thinking ahead. There'll be no shopping for you today, anyway. We need to get some ice on that ankle."

I kicked my leg out to inspect my puffy ankle with its angry, red hue. "I don't think it's that bad." I'd forgotten about it, actually. *Huh.*

I felt Brad change direction, and noticed that we were back home. I started to remove my hands from around his neck, not wanting him to tackle the stairs with my extra weight. His arms tightened around me, his eyes flashing a warning.

"Put me down, I'm too heavy."

He scoffed. "No, you're not."

He began ascending the stairs. I was relieved to hear his breath pick up. It meant he was human, at least. Putting me down on the bench seat beside the door, he got out his keys. My hands gripped the seat as I leaned forward, preparing to follow him in.

"Uh uh." He scowled and folded me in his arms, drawing a huff of annoyance from my chest. "Would you just let me take care of you?"

"I can look after myself. I've been doing it for a while now."

"I know that, but I want to look after you. It's my fault that you're hurt."

I purred like a cat on the inside, feeling giddy and tingly where we touched. All sorts of alarms went off in my brain as it struggled to regain dominance. I didn't like it. *I'm a fucking liar.* I ached to hand over control of my body to this man. *Stop it, stop it, stop it!* He was a nice, genuine, caring guy. He'd do this for anybody.

I suddenly found myself on the couch, with my calf cradled in his warm palm, as he placed a couple of cushions underneath my ankle. His hand slid slowly off my leg, the feel of his calloused skin sending tingles shooting straight to my centre. I wriggled my bottom in embarrassment, certain that my cheeks were blazing. I hoped he couldn't see it.

He put two more cushions under my back, and pushed my shoulders down, staring into my eyes. When his eyes fell to my mouth, my pulse fluttered in my neck. The tingles intensified and spread to my breasts. My thin thread of control threatened to snap, as I refrained from squirming and letting out a mortifying moan. The pain in my ankle only added to the cataclysm. I was so close to unravelling.

Warm palm. Arms around my body. Eyes on my mouth. Freckled face. Hazardous Brad.

I watched his back retreat, as he presumably went to get some ice. When he disappeared, I threw my head back into the softness of the cushion and let out a loud sigh.

His face reappeared around the corner. "Did you say something?"

My neck cracked as I yanked my head up, eyes wide. The tension ratcheted up with his piercing eyes aimed at me. "Nope, no. Nothing." *How many times do you want to say it?*

"Hmm. Okay, back in a tick." His head disappeared again.

I lay back gazing at the ceiling, trying to calm my lascivious thoughts and my raging hormones. It sucked to be human. To be at the mercy of visceral reactions and processes. I wished I could transcend the flesh. I knew this man was going to lead me into trouble, and I knew I'd happily follow because I was a stupid, weak woman. *Damn it.* I wanted to punch myself. I was so angry for allowing him to get so close to me. How much longer would I be able to hold him off?

He came back with an ice pack wrapped in a tea towel. I snatched it from him before he could put his hands on me again. "Thanks," I muttered, avoiding his eyes.

"No worries. I'm really sorry. The last thing I want to do is hurt you in any way." His smile didn't quite work.

My heart plunged into my pounding ankle. *I think you might be the only person who could fracture me into tiny pieces and leave me alive.* My lips curved up, copying his sad attempt. "It's okay. It was an accident."

"Yeah," he nodded. "Do you want the TV on? The ice should be left on for twenty minutes and then off for twenty. What about painkillers? You want some?" *There goes his hand.*

Bulging bicep. Adorable Brad.

"There's probably nothing worth watching on a Sunday morning, unless you're a kid."

"Cartoons are good at any age." He switched on the kid's channel, and we ended up laughing at the juvenile antics of Wile E. Coyote and the gang for an hour. Without fail, every twenty minutes he attended to the ice pack. He must have been watching the clock rather than the cartoons. I simultaneously revelled and cringed at the attention I received. My mind and emotions were a tangled mess.

"Do you think you can put weight on your ankle?"

I gently swivelled the joint, testing its mobility. It ached, but not as bad as before. "Maybe. Why?"

"I'd like to take you out for breakfast. I'm starving. You must be, too." He pointed the remote at the TV, not really expecting an answer.

Wrapping his warm palms around my calves, he swung them around to carefully place my feet on the floor. My ankle didn't twinge. Not yet anyway. Shivers danced up and down my body as he devoted all his attention to me. Holding my hands in his, he pulled me slowly to stand. Our chests bumped together, eyes and mouths almost aligned, hands still clasped together. I couldn't feel my legs, let alone my ankle.

"Okay?" His breath feathered across my face in a delicious tease. I had to bite my lips and swallow the squeak, nodding my head in affirmation instead.

He hooked my arm over his shoulders, and led me down to his car, grabbing his keys and our sunnies on the way. When I felt his hands wrap around my waist to hoist me into his ute, I squeaked in protest. I slapped his hands away when he tried to help me with my seatbelt. The deep laugh that tumbled out of him washed through me, bringing things to life that had no business being revived.

We drove to a little café in Oxley, just off the main road, and part of a newly refurbished group of shops. Their Sunday breakfast was popular. I didn't realise so many people went out for their first meal. Brad guided me to a table in the alfresco area, while he went in to grab a carafe of water, and a couple of glasses. I examined the menu, diligently ignoring the young girl perched on a bench, holding her dog's leash just a few feet away. I didn't see her stare, but I felt the vibrant tendrils of it flutter over my face.

The border collie's nose worked overtime, sniffing out all the scents embedded in his little piece of the footpath. He yanked the girl off her seat when he found something particularly juicy in my direction, wedging his nose under my chair. The black and white fur ball whipped his head up, licking his lips after finding his prize, and shoved his nose into my knee. His wet snort sprayed saliva and fragments of food, leaving a glistening trail on my black Skins. *Aw, gross.* I recoiled at the wetness, but gave the dog a scratch behind the ears. He was beautiful. The pang of yearning for something to call my own, something that would love me unconditionally, hit me square in the chest.

"Sorry, Miss." Her blue eyes held her apology in their depths. She looked about twelve. Almost a teenager. As I watched her, a niggling feeling grazed the back of my neck. I reached under my hair to rub it away.

"It's okay. He's a dog, that's what dogs do. What's his name?"

"*Her* name is Casper." The girl's brown curls bounced as she tried to regain control of the excited pup.

"Casper. Cute. I like it." A dog named after a ghost. *Huh.* No wonder she liked me.

"What's your name?"

"Uh …" I hesitated for only a second. The instinct to snap back in defence wasn't there. "… Veronica."

"Marissa? Marissa?" A panicked voice trailed out of the pharmacy a few doors down.

"Over here, Mum."

No.

Any air I had in my lungs stayed trapped, as I stiffened. The girl's mother hurried out of the pharmacy, with an older version of Marissa by her side. The woman did a double take when she saw me, recoiling in disgust. She seized Marissa by the arm, dragging her away with the dog skidding behind.

"Muumm. What're you doing?" Both girls looked over their shoulders, searching for the horror they were running from. I wondered if they saw that it was me. If they could see the pieces of my self-worth flaking off with every step they took in the opposite direction.

"Get away from that woman, she's no good. She's sick."

The dog bounced around Marissa's legs, making growly, yipping noises as they struggled to keep up with her mother's harried pace. Moments later, they disappeared around a corner. My gaze remained locked in their direction well after they'd gone.

A heavy weight jerked my shoulder back and forth. The chair legs scraped at the footpath, and I thrashed in protest, crossing my arms over my face.

"Hey. Hey, it's okay. It's only me. I won't hurt you." The voice echoed through the time tunnel surrounding me, pulling me down into a void where I was nothing. I saw the woman. Her disgust and contempt. It coated my eyes and tongue, plugging my senses and severing me from the world.

"Veronica!"

Desperation sharpened the edge of the voice, cutting through the haze of pain. The warm slide of a hand stroking my cheek reached in, pulling me back to awareness. Brad's stricken face filled my vision. I felt his other hand tugging my wrists away from my face, and I made a conscious effort to loosen my muscles and let my arms fall. As I relaxed, my body started shaking uncontrollably. My eyes held Brad's. He kept stroking my face, my hair, my shoulders … his touch brought me back to life and calmed me. The shakes slowly disappeared like storm clouds clearing.

"Are you back with me?"

Dipping my chin in answer, we both let out a sharp breath of relief.

"What happened? Who were they?"

Biting on my cheek, I closed my eyes in denial. But I couldn't escape his probing gaze. I sucked in a breath so I could mutter the words I thought would never form on my tongue.

"That was my mother. And … my sisters."

Chapter
13

Ronnie

"Are you sure you're okay to drive? We could've done this another time." Granny's hand squeezed my elbow in a soothing gesture.

"I'm fine."

Keeping my eyes on the road, I flexed and relaxed my fingers on the steering wheel in a refusal to let that woman get to me. It was the shock of finding out that I had sisters that made me feel like I'd been through a spin cycle. I'd never get to know those girls. I thought my mother no longer had the power to hurt me … I was wrong. They knew what it was like to have a father and a mother who loved them. I bet they were close with my mother's parents, too. Their father was acceptable, where my father never was.

"I honestly didn't see that one coming. It has always been difficult to tune in to your mother. I hope she's treating those girls better than she treated you."

"I guess we'll never know. I'd really appreciate it if you'd change the subject."

She put her hand back in her lap. "Okay, sweetie. I'm looking forward to meeting your new beau."

Oh, good Lord!

"He's not my beau. He's my housemate. Please don't embarrass me. I do have to live with this man." For now, anyway. I shifted down a gear and tapped on the indicator to enter Moggill Road. Granny vibrated with excitement, all dolled up in a flowing kaftan.

"Why would I embarrass you? Always be yourself when you first meet someone. That way, you sift out the people who don't click with you. Will save you a lot of pain later, believe me. Why would you waste your time and energy on someone who wants you to be something you're not?"

A timely stop at a red light gave her words a chance to penetrate. If only my father had taken that advice. Then, I wouldn't exist today. I wouldn't be struggling with his legacy. The 'gift' that was the catalyst in his demise.

"Stop it. I know what you're thinking. Your father made his choice. When the heart latches on to someone, it can become an addiction. If he had taken his time and stood back a little, he would have realised that your mother wasn't in love with him like he was with her. He would've had a chance to save his heart for someone who'd truly cherish it. But, you were absolutely meant to exist, Veronica. You're going to do great things."

We drove over the Walter Taylor Bridge, and I tried to focus on the road, though I was unnerved by what she said. I wanted to pretend I didn't hear her, but Granny's expression was a mix of determination and compassion as she scanned my face.

"I don't want to do great things. I just want to keep my head down and get through each day."

"That's a really good strategy for getting through tough times, but it's not a good plan for life. That's a one-way street to depression. Life is for finding your purpose and fulfilling it. Take a risk, live loud, be you. Like-minded people will come along, and you will get to help each other on the journey." Again, she reached over to squeeze my elbow, my skin absorbing the infusion of calm.

The closer we got to the meet and greet, the more terrified I became of Brad finding out my little secret. My hands ached from gripping the steering wheel. I turned into the driveway and parked next to his ute. Granny waited for me to come around to help her out, her movements stiff, impaired by a metal hip and aged, brittle bones. After a bit of shuffling, she made it to the edge of the seat and I scooped her out, holding her by the elbows until she was steady enough to take the walking stick. I didn't think of the stairs when I moved in here. We'd have to take it slow.

She hooked her hand through the crook of my arm. When I moved towards the stairs, she tugged me towards the side of the house instead. I used my free hand to open the gate, and push the palm leaves out of our way. My shoulders bunched and my throat emitted a grunt when I saw who Granny was heading for. Brad's Gran was waiting on the bench seat in the back garden.

"Hello, Martha," Granny offered in greeting.

"You two know each other?"

"Of course. We used to play Mahjong." She eased herself into the space beside her departed friend.

Oh, here we go. This was exactly what I was worried about. I positioned myself to the side in an attempt to transform my body into a screen. I hoped he'd heard my car and gone to unlock the front door. If he was standing at the kitchen window, it might look like I was showing Granny the garden, and she'd needed a rest. I crossed my fingers.

"Keep your voice down."

"Relax. He's out front, wandering around. He can't hear us." She flapped her hand at me.

"You look well, Amelia."

"Thank you, my dear. I assume you're staying to make sure young Bradlee is taken care of?"

Martha smiled, dipping her head at Granny before looking at me. "I'm very pleased to see you again." Her pronunciation was like polished silver. This was a classy lady.

"I didn't have much choice, at the time."

"Psh. We always have a choice. This was the best one. Meant to be." Granny's self-assured smile did nothing to appease me, before she dropped a bombshell. "Didn't I tell you all those years ago, Amelia?"

"Wait, what?" I set my hands on my hips, frowning.

"There you are!" Brad came around the side of the house.

I was too confused to acknowledge him as he stopped beside me. Ignoring my rudeness, he stretched his hand to introduce himself. "Hi. I'm Bradlee, and you're the famous Granny. Very pleased to meet you." He bent to kiss the back of Granny's papery hand, adding a roguish grin and a wink. He was laying it on thick.

Granny giggled like a school girl. "You've grown into a fine young man. I was just telling Veronica that we've met before. You played together when you were toddlers. I used to bring Veronica with me to visit your Gran. You were here for the Christmas holidays one year. The two of you ran around in the sprinklers in your underwear."

My hands covered my face in denial. *Oh, my God. Kill me now.*

"Really?" He drew the word out, wicked amusement lending a musical quality to the word.

"Actually, you used to chase Veronica around, trying to kiss her, and pull on her pigtails." I peeked at her through my fingers, willing her to shut up. "It was so cute. You were a year older, and much bigger than her, but she was quicker." The wrinkles on her face were as deep as her delight at the memories. *Traitor.*

The slide of Brad's arm across my shoulders increased the heat of my embarrassment to fever pitch. With his other hand, he removed mine from my face. "Not much has changed, then."

I raised my eyes, watching him peer back with adoration, and silver flecks of mischief lighting his irises. He tightened his hold, shocking me by planting a quick peck on my temple. The touch of his lips spurred a rush of blood to my face and a thundering behind my ribcage, readying me for … what? Him? I swallowed against a parched throat.

"Who's hungry?" I squeaked, clapping my hands together as I ducked out from beneath his arm. My body screamed at me to get back under there.

"I'm starving," Brad's voice rasped. "How about you, Granny?"

Granny reached out her hand to Brad with a wide smile. "Help me up, and lead the way." He patted Granny's hand where it grasped his elbow, and guided her carefully up the back stairs.

They chatted as if they were long lost friends. It was disconcerting the way seeing them together warmed my heart. This beating, bloody organ in my chest wanted to let that man infiltrate it, and spread the ensuing warmth throughout my body. A big part of me didn't want to be his friend. I didn't want to endure the torment of it. I wanted more. I wanted to be a part of his family. Seeing him with Granny, I knew we belonged together. The realisation stunned me. I had to clench my fingers on the railing halfway up the stairs to let it sink in. How could I survive letting him in, only to lose him in the end? I wasn't going to end up like my father.

Take a risk. Granny's words came back to me. What she said about my mother not being as invested … it was true. I saw that now. If she had loved him, she would have talked about him all the time. I would have had a picture of him in my room. She never would have left him just because he saw things, knew things. If she loved me, she never would have left me. That thought was better left in the vault.

I couldn't deny myself or him any longer. I wanted to feel like I belonged to a family, not just my Granny. It was him, I knew it was him. He was the one. I just had to figure out if he felt the same. If he could be strong enough to take on my demons with me, and come out the other side, still holding my hand.

"You coming?"

My eyes shot to Brad's as I refocused. "Mmm."

He blocked the top of the stairs, and held his hand out for mine. I looked in his eyes before I took it. I needed to see an indication that he felt what I did. His slate eyes penetrated the depths of mine as I asked my silent question. Something shifted inside me, a piece of my soul latching onto his. I reached out, accepting his hand. He received it with a smile. The symbolism wasn't lost on me. I felt like I'd let go, just by holding on. I jumped a barrier that I couldn't retreat behind, ever again. Actually, I think I just kicked it down.

Only several more barriers to go.

————

It was raining bacon. The smell was divine, soaking into my nose, down into my oesophagus, prompting an answering grumble from my tummy. From the deck, I watched the fried flesh strips fall and bounce on the grass ... splashing in the flood of maple syrup that oozed from all the maple trees ... Wait ... There aren't any maple trees in the backyard.

"Wake up, Gazelle."

Huh? That's Brad's voice.

With great effort, I opened my eyes until they were narrow slits. Brad had his hand on my shin, and a wicked smirk on his face. What was he grinning at? I closed my eyes again, letting my mind drift back to the deliciousness. His hand was so warm. I could feel him making small circles with his thumb, causing hot sparks to shoot around my body. Waking up my core, well before my good sense. I focused on the smell of the bacon, maple syrup, and pancakes, evidently in existence in the house somewhere. Even more delectable, I smelled freshly showered man. Slowly, my level of consciousness rose, so I was able to register that it was morning, and Brad was in my room—stroking my bare leg.

My leg was bare.

I bolted upright in the bed, startling him enough that he snapped his hand back. The sheet was on the floor and I was only wearing a thin singlet, and my knickers. I could feel the girls at full attention thanks to his ministrations, and a restless night's sleep spent dreaming of a certain freckled wonder.

Freckled face. Warm palm. Adorable, kissable Brad.

"Morning," I grunted, pulling my knees up and covering my face with both hands. Attempting to wake myself up, I rubbed vigorously. "What time is it?"

"It's 6:30 a.m.," he laughed. "Wow, avoiding me must have been exhausting. Caught up with you now, though, hasn't it?" I fanned my fingers over my face so I could blink at him through the gaps. He laughed louder. *Cheeky bugger.* "Come on, Gazelle. The sun's up, and we've got lots of painting to do."

I recalled agreeing to help paint the house. Last night. No thanks to Granny.

"You've done a fine job of fixing up the place. Still need a lick of paint in places, though. You could use some help with that, couldn't you, Bradlee?"

Granny had turned 'the look' on me. That look that mothers have perfected through the ages. The one that said, 'you better be reading me loud and clear'. There was no way I could say no to that look. And, I guess I trusted her guidance. I didn't listen to her when she told me not to move in with Flick. That was something I'd always regret.

"What did you call me?"

"Gazelle. I think it's how you run. Fast, long, lean, and graceful."

Huh.

I swung my legs over the side and stood up, completely forgetting that I was wearing next to nothing. Brad held his ground, unabashedly staring. I resisted the urge to shield myself with my arms. "Um. A little privacy please?"

His eyes wandered back up to my face, tracing each of my features in the way he often did. His gaze was like a feather tracing over my skin, stroking me … pulling me towards him.

"Sure," he said lazily, turning to leave. The connection between us stretched uncomfortably, urging me to follow. I had to push all the air from my lungs, and shake my arms to release some of the tension before I exploded. I had a feeling when we lit this thing up, we were going to do just that. I had danger coming at me from all sides, but if I had to choose between fear or love … love won every time.

Whoa. Is that what this is?

After I had a quick wash and got dressed, I sought out the delicious smell coming from the back deck. The spread of food looked incredible. My nose was correct. Bacon and pancakes, with maple syrup and strawberries. On a Monday morning. Lucky I had the day off.

He'd pushed the table into the corner to make way for a drop sheet covering the wooden deck. Three different paint tins and various painting paraphernalia made a home on the sheet. How long had he been awake? Tish wiggled her fingers at me in greeting.

Brad watched my reaction carefully. "We'll need some sustenance today if we're going to get the job done. It can be pretty exhausting." His gaze dropped to my shorts and faded ACDC T-shirt. "You didn't have to change on my account, but this outfit works just as well."

The tension snapped back full force. I chewed on the inside of my cheek, and loaded up a plate. "Looks good. Smells yum."

"Mm hmm," he almost groaned. I could feel him looking at me again, but wasn't brave enough to return the favour.

"What are we painting today?"

"The hallway and the dining room. We'll do the bedrooms another day. And then we'll be finished."

"Oh, okay. That's not so bad."

"You see? I wasn't asking for a kidney," Tish piped in.

"Yeah, I know," I conceded, nodding.

"Hmm? What do you know?" About to devour a pancake, Brad waited for my explanation.

Oh shit. I said that out loud. He'd made me relax and forget.

"Um … That it's exhausting. Renovating a house." I stuffed a pancake in my mouth, and chewed like my life depended on it.

"You've renovated a house before?"

Tish slapped a hand across her mouth to hold in a giggle. Not that he'd hear her. I made a show of chewing some more and swallowing before answering. "I've helped at my granny's old house. Before she sold it." *Sort of.* Okay, no. That was a lie. I ordered new carpet for her, and I finger painted the wall once when I was a kid, but that was it.

I hated having to lie, and make up stories all the time. It was a big part of why I didn't let anyone in. It was too draining. Lying to Brad made me want to regurgitate pancakes and strawberries over the side of the railing. Reminding me that I couldn't let my guard down all the way with him, no matter how I wanted to. I grabbed another strawberry, and ripped off its leaves.

In such a short space of time, he had become so important to me. I didn't want to let that feeling go. It was too hard to find. I was willing to take a chance with him because I'd rather have him for a little while, than not at all. I'd just have to keep that part of me locked down tightly.

The tug of war inside me agitated my gut. Pushing my plate away, I leaned back, holding my stomach.

"You okay?"

"Yeah, just full."

"You've had one pancake and one strawberry." His eyebrows went up.

He's counting my food intake?

Tish moved to his side, putting her hand on his shoulder as she leaned down to nab a strawberry. *What is she doing?* The strawberry tumbled off the top of the pile to the edge of the plate. Brad picked up the stray red fruit, and shivered in reaction to her touch, frowning.

He felt that?

"Don't tell me you're cold." I joked as a distraction, pulling the plate back towards me to take a piece of bacon. My hunger had returned.

"No, I just felt a cold patch. It's weird. I've been feeling them everywhere I go. Maybe I should go see a doctor." He bit the strawberry, juice dripping onto his lips and chin. I stared transfixed, as he licked it up with his tongue.

"I think you're in fine health." The truth slipped out uncensored, making Brad and his sister smirk at me in unison.

They were a beautiful pair. Watching them together, her presence unable to be fully appreciated by her brother who clearly loved her, leaked a sadness into the moment. She should be the one here with him, not me. I almost wished I could share my gift with him. Let him know she was still looking out for him.

I cleared my throat, shaking off the regret. "Hurry up. We've got a lot of work to do."

"Says the woman who would've kept sleeping if I hadn't woken her up."

"I was quite happy to keep sleeping."

"I could tell." A flush raged up my neck and face, leaving tingles in its path. Brad's look held me in its powerful grasp. His lips hinted at a smile. The full force of his desire hit me between my thighs. My body would have readily spent the day doing other things besides painting. I was aware that was where we were heading. Probably sooner than I was ready for. I'd never be able to let him in completely, but he was the only man who'd come close to making me want it all.

He stood and circled towards where I sat, mesmerized. Holding out his hand, he silently asked me to stand. I didn't think my legs would support my weight. They were shaking that badly. He clasped me by the wrist where my pulse hammered and pulled me to my feet. I couldn't stop trembling. The tips of his fingers, poking from the cast, brushed my hair away from my face, and came to rest on my collarbone. *Fuck.* The fire had spread throughout my whole body. I relinquished control over to him. He inched towards me until our bodies were pushed up against each other. There was no hiding my physical reaction to him, nor his reaction to me. It turned me on, knowing I did that to him.

His lips found mine, brushing softly, hesitantly, as if he was afraid I was going to bolt like the gazelle he called me. *Silly man.* I couldn't run if I wanted to, and I didn't want to at all. My lips parted on a sigh. This was what I'd been waiting for. I've denied myself for far too long. I pressed more forcefully into him, and wrapped my arms around his neck. I wanted to seal our connection forever. Brad grunted and sank into my mouth, tilting his head to get closer. I tasted maple syrup, and all the treats we'd shared before.

Tantalising Brad.

Brad fisted my hair in his good hand, pulling me closer. If that was even possible. His stubble grazed my jaw and my cheeks in a rough tease. I was running out of air. I had to break the kiss and pull away to regain my sanity.

We both let go, gasping. I took a step back, doubling over to grip my knees. *Whoa.*

"Holy fuck! I knew it. I fucking knew it!" he said, breathless. "You're not getting away from me again, Gazelle … You've just been caught."

I continued looking at the wooden decking in my bent position. I agreed with him, and I was pretty bloody excited about the possibilities.

When I straightened up, I saw Tish through the window in the dining room, one brow cocked. "Thought I'd give you some privacy."

Well, most of the possibilities. If he found out I could see and talk to his dead sister, it was possible he'd never want to speak to me again. My bubble of desire deflated, dropping my shoulders with it. My curse would always come between us. I'd never be able to give all of myself to him. I wanted to cry in protest. It wasn't Letitia's fault. It wasn't anybody's fault but my own. I was the one that hadn't learned to deal with my reality. My eyes swung back to Brad, still watching me from under heavy lids, and struggling to compose himself. I needed to find a way, and fast.

"Let's paint." Marching past Brad into the house, I didn't look back when my statement was met with a long silence.

"You're welcome!" he finally yelled out, before I heard the pop of a paint tin opening.

It was going to be an interesting day.

Chapter

14

Brad

Pouring the paint into a small tub seemed so simple, but it was bloody difficult while my muscles were strung so tightly I could barely move. That kiss. I still felt the imprint of her body all over me. I could barely stop myself from going inside, and ravishing her mouth again. She felt it, too, I knew she did. She was vibrating in my arms, devouring my mouth with as much hunger as I had for her. Then I watched as the shadows crowded in, snuffing out the blazing fire we'd ignited.

I was starting to understand the depth of her scars and pain. Watching her in the aftermath of yesterday's shock scared the shit out of me. She was obviously in some personal hell zone, trapped in her memories of a fucked up past at the hands of that woman. I wanted to hunt her mother down, and make her come back to witness the pain she'd inflicted. I wanted to wring her neck. What the fuck was wrong with her? How could she not love Veronica, but be a mother to those girls? Why them and not Veronica? I didn't get it. It just made me want to protect her, and never let anyone hurt her again.

With that thought, the bitter reality of my past bubbled up, burning the back of my throat. I wasn't able to protect Tish. Logic told me it was just an accident, but I should've been there to drive her home. Seems I wasn't good at protecting anyone …

But I have to try. The need to protect Veronica was even fiercer than it was with my sister. Especially because she'd been hurt so badly. She was mine, and I just wanted to be hers already. She was still keeping a part of herself hidden from me … I could sense it. I felt like there were a thousand doors I needed to open before I could reach her heart. But I opened the first one yesterday when she told me her story, and I opened the second as we poured our feelings into each other's kiss. It was a good start … and I would keep picking all the locks on her doors until she was mine.

I picked up the tubs and a couple of paintbrushes, taking them to the hallway where Veronica waited.

"We'll do the cutting in first. These VJ's are a bit of a pain to paint. We'll brush over the edges and joints, and then roller over the top. I only have one ladder. Do you want to work down low or up high?"

"I'll take the ladder."

Gripping the metal, she climbed up, leaning down as I passed up one of the tubs and a brush. "Here you go." My face was level with her firm bum. Holding in a groan at the view she presented, I focused on her eyes, watching her dark pupils dilate.

Before I stepped back, I gave in to the urge to look at those legs. Goosebumps dotted her skin. I blew out a long breath, making the fine hairs stand up further. The temptation to run my palm along her leg was almost too much to resist. Forcing myself to step back, I picked up the tub, and got to work on painting around the edge of the skirting. We worked with only the sound of paintbrushes slicking on the wet colour for about an hour.

"Do you mind if we put some music on?" Veronica broke the silence.

"Sure thing. Do you want to use your phone, or do you trust me to pick the tunes?"

"My phone. Definitely."

"I'm offended. What if your taste in music is crap?"

"It's not." She climbed down and grabbed her phone from her room, plugging it into the speakers in the lounge. Hard rock and the screaming vocals of Brian Johnson pumped into the air. She sauntered down the hallway, hips swaying to the beat as she smiled widely at me.

"ACDC. Goes with the T-shirt. Nice." *I'm in love.* A woman who appreciated classic, Aussie rock. "Have you got Chisel on there, too?"

"Yup. I have all sorts of things on there, but none of that sugar pop shit."

"Oh, thank God." The roller made a hissing rattle as it moved in wide strokes to the beat of the song.

"Tell me more about Tish. What's the age difference between you?"

"Five and a half years. She was fourteen when Mum and Dad died."

I heard the roller pause and turned to find her watching me with sympathy. "You were only nineteen, and suddenly responsible for a teenage girl. Wow, that must've been hard."

Turning around to block out her concern, I continued the therapeutic to and fro with the roller.

"Neither of us took their deaths well, but Tish was a total wreck. She closed herself off from everyone, and became consumed by school work. She'd break down if she didn't get one hundred percent on an assignment. I guess she decided to be the perfect daughter, to honour them. It freaked me out."

"But, you guys looked so happy in the photos."

"Yeah. No." I laughed bitterly. "We had our moments, I s'pose. Things were strained. She'd just started becoming a woman, and her mother was killed. I didn't know anything about all that stuff. My girlfriend at the time was pissed with me because I didn't spend enough time with her. I was working as an apprentice chippie. Tish had to get herself to school and back. By the time I'd done the dinner and whatever else needed to be done, I was knackered. Ben and Andrea left for Brisbane to start a new life together, and then I found out my girlfriend had been cheating on me, and my sister had been stealing feminine hygiene products, because I was an idiot and didn't think to buy them. She was too embarrassed to ask. I made so many mistakes with her …" I trailed off, as my throat closed.

My icy companion covered the left side of my ribcage. Shivers formed a layer between it and me, but broke away with the addition of a tentative hand on my opposite shoulder. I dropped my head taking in the twin sensations. Warmth versus chill. Strangely, both of them made me feel surrounded by love.

"She seemed to be getting back on track when we moved here for her to start her degree. She was going to be an engineer, just like Dad. She started seeing this guy. She seemed happy, and then she had the accident."

The weight of Veronica's arm landed across my shoulders as she pressed into my side. The roller fell to the drop sheet, forgotten, as I gave in. I folded my body around hers. I absorbed her compassion and warmth, letting it fill me up with hope for a better future. One where I got to keep someone I loved, forever.

She understood about loss. We'd both lost too much. Maybe I was stupid to put so much faith in her, in us. The girl with all the walls, and the guy with all the baggage. What a pair we made. She was afraid I'd get too close to her, but she wanted to know me. She was asking me to let her in, and I was powerless not to, no matter how much it hurt to relive my failures and pain.

A faint sniffle brushed my ear, and I pulled back to find her crying. "I'm sorry. I didn't mean to be such a downer."

She swatted an invisible fly in front of her face. "No, it's not that. I wanted to know your story. I just … I think your sister and I would have been best friends. Two studious nerds with mummy issues," she said with a rueful smile.

"You would have hated her taste in music."

"Oh, really? What're we talking about? One Direction? Justin Bieber?"

"Techno pop."

"Oi, Jesus!" We both shuddered, having a laugh before picking up where we left off.

It wasn't until much later, as we sat watching the box, that I realised I hadn't felt the need to run off and do something crazy for an adrenaline fix, or reach for a bottle. Whether that meant she was helping me heal, or that she was becoming the fix that I needed, I wasn't sure yet. I didn't want to analyse it right now.

Reaching across to link my fingers with hers, I pulled the back of her hand to my lips for a kiss. She didn't stiffen up, or stop me. She smiled. That was all the confirmation I needed. Whatever role she fulfilled for me, I was doing the same for her. And that was something to be damn happy and proud about.

————

Ronnie

Before my lunch break, I searched for Beverly, hoping she'd seen the doctor by now. It had been a week since the mammogram. My concern for her overwhelmed any qualms I had about getting close to another person. Beverly was all about caring for others. It was about time I returned the favour. She was one of the most open-minded people I knew. Very new-age. She'd probably be okay if I suggested she look into a crystal ball. Not that I was into that sort of crap.

"Hi, Beverly!" Where I'd pulled the cheer from, I didn't know. That ought to make anyone suspicious. *Ronnie's all cheery. Call the cops 'cause some crazy shit must be going down.* Her blonde hair bobbed as she raised her head, giving me a view of the dark circles and bags under her eyes. The smile fell off my face.

"Ronn—" She choked on my name as a sob wrenched free.

Shit! I rushed around the desk, encircling her in my arms. Her tears soaked the sleeve of my shirt. The grief pouring out of her was so raw and unbound it burrowed into my soul, unleashing my own pent-up anger, frustration and sorrow. I felt like I did this to her. Like it was me mutating her cells and sentencing her to months of misery, if not death. All my complaining about being an outcast seemed juvenile in the face of her battle for life.

"How bad is it?" I asked her when the deluge became a trickle, standing back to give her some space.

"Locally advanced breast cancer. It's in the lymph nodes. They want to pump me full of poison, and possibly nuke me with radiation to shrink it first. Then, they'll take my breast. They think I have a pretty good chance, if I survive all that."

"You will. You have to fight, but you will." I knew it. I could see her old and grey with a grandchild on her lap. "When does all this start?"

"First treatment is on Friday. John is taking the day off. We haven't told the kids yet … and I really don't want to."

"Maybe, let John do that. Can I do anything for you?"

She shook her head and ripped another tissue from the box. "No. Thank you. I honestly can't say that enough. If it wasn't for you, I'd have waited too long and had no chance at all." She squeezed my forearm.

I didn't know what possessed me to say, "Actually, I'm just the messenger. Your mother badgered me to tell you. I should've said something sooner. I never know how to deal with these things, so I usually just ignore it. But I knew I couldn't ignore this. I'm so sorry you're suffering." I clasped my hands together and dropped the bomb. "Your mum, she's watching over you. She's a determined lady."

Her puzzled expression was unexpected. "You've seen my mum?"

I bobbed my head, bracing myself for the criticism.

"Is she the one who's been hiding my bras?"

Was not expecting that question. "Ah ..." A movement to my right caught my eye. Beverly's mother shook with laughter. "... I'm guessing yes, but she's unable to speak at the moment."

"She was an imp, my mother. Her nickname was Tinkerbell." Beverly sighed. "I'll have to apologise to John. I thought he'd developed some weird fetish."

The snort ripped out, unfettered. "Do you feel up to having some lunch?" I asked.

"Absolutely. I've got to gorge myself while I can, before my extreme cleansing starts."

"What a way to diet." I rubbed the sudden pain in my stomach as we headed out to the closest cafe.

———

I sat alone at a table outside under an umbrella, while Beverly contemplated her dessert choices at the counter. Her finger pointed to several different delicacies that she discussed with the manager. *This could take a while.*

People from all walks of life ambled by. Across the green, Twit was with a group of his mates, making rude gestures behind a young woman's back. *What a dickhead.* That would have been my preferred term for his behaviour several weeks back. The young woman threw them an annoyed look, but skittered away, a scared little lamb among the wolves. The rumbles of laughter from the pack carried across the open gardens.

Flick rounded the pathway behind the group, strutting in her sensible heels with her head held high. I admired her self-possessed attitude. She swept past them before suddenly coming to a halt. Twit was eyeing her with a creepy grin. She turned to him, raised her right hand and wiggled her little finger before flipping him the bird, and marching off. His face was priceless. A caricature of shock and anger. His mates all looked away, hiding their snickers behind their palms.

"What's so funny?" My head snapped towards the voice.

"Andrea?" *I probably shouldn't greet her with a frown.*

Luckily, she laughed at my question. "You don't get out much do you? You're supposed to say, "Hi Andrea, it's great to see you again. How are you?" and then, I'll reply and ask you what you were laughing at, again." She took a seat beside me, plonking one elbow on the table and resting her chin in her hand.

"Uh. Hi Andrea. How are you?" She twirled her finger in the air, urging me to continue. "Um … It's great to see you again," I added, twisting my mouth to stop a smirk.

She nodded in approval. "I'm great, thanks for asking. Hello backatcha. I just finished lunch with my other half when I saw you cackling to yourself. So, what's so funny?"

I tossed my head towards Twit and company. "Big man on campus just got knocked off the podium."

"Tall. Blond. Polo wearer?"

"Mm hmm." I swigged some water from my bottle.

"That guy. He's a law student. His name's Matt. He tried to make a pass at me at a club last weekend. Ben was at the bar getting us drinks. Matt pawed me from behind while I was dancing. I elbowed him in the gut, then stilettoed him on the foot." She jumped up to demonstrate the motions, as I sat in horror. *Sit the fuck down!* "Had it sorted out before Ben got back," she finished in a bored tone before sitting down again, much to my relief. "Ben gave him the look." She glared at me.

"The look?"

"Yeah, you know?" She aimed her finger at the example she was showing on her face. "Get-the-hell-away-from-my-woman-or-I'll-break-your-face.   That look." She scoffed.

"Right." I tugged my chin down, wanting this conversation over already, and for Andrea to stay seated.

"Lee would do the same thing if that happened to you. He's not as intense as Ben, but he's still a guy."

"No, he wouldn't. I'm not his girlfriend."

She burst out laughing. "Ah, yeah … you are. You want each other something bad."

I could feel the heat rising up my chest all the way to my forehead. I distracted myself by checking to see if Beverly had finished ordering. No such luck. I silently begged her to hurry so we could run away.

Andrea tapped my shoulder. "What's your deal? I don't mean to be rude, but Bradlee means a lot to Ben and me. He's been through hell. If you don't like him that way, tell him now. Don't play games. He doesn't deserve it."

My eyelids fluttered. "I do like him that way." I whispered the words, too scared to speak and bring them into reality, and too annoyed that I was admitting it to Andrea and not Brad. "I'm not playing games. I don't know—" I pulled in a breath and bit my cheek, using the pain to aid my truth. "He confuses me. I was happy ignoring everyone, and now … I've been thrust into living, and participating in friendships, and I don't even know what to call what Brad and I have. He told me about Tish and his parents. I understand what he had to go through more than you'd imagine. I don't want to cause either one of us any more pain. That's why I'm reluctant to progress things any further than … whatever. Part of me still thinks it'd be better to back off. I'm just … confused as fuck, to be honest."

"You better figure things out. I like you. You make him happy. Please don't hurt him." She gave me a tight smile, and tapped the table before she trotted off.

I sighed with relief, feeling wrung out and slightly nauseous from the interrogation. Andrea was right. I was fooling myself if I thought I could get close to him without exposing myself completely. I watched her wave at someone as she walked, an eternal spring in her step. I couldn't imagine her ever hiding anything from anyone. She was as clear as glass. I was envious of her freedom to be herself. She might be quirky and perky, but no one would ever accuse her of being a fruit cake.

"What's the frown for?" A plate with a slab of cheesecake landed on the table with a thunk, before Beverly sat down. She was either not aware that she'd been gone for ten minutes, or she didn't care.

"Never mind … Two forks?"

She picked one of the utensils and carved a chunk of creamy delight, holding it up for inspection. "You like cheesecake, don't you? Dig in." She demonstrated by shovelling the cake into her mouth. I shrugged my shoulders and followed her lead, already feeling better, or maybe I just needed the sugar fix.

Watching my boss as she scooped another piece onto her fork, I realised that she was my friend. Although she didn't really know me, I'd known her for five years. She knew my secret now, and I knew hers, but I didn't feel vulnerable. I was even relieved and thankful to be given the chance to make a positive difference to someone's life. Someone I deeply respect. A welcome smile slipped into place. What if it were this easy with Brad? What if I cut all my wounds open and bled before him, and he was able to stitch me back up and love me anyway? The spark of hope was tentative … but it was there. If anyone could fan it into flame, it would be Brad.

Prickles stabbed into the back of my neck, warning of a looming danger. My second piece of cake stuck in my cheek, and I nearly bit my tongue. I jerked my eyes around, looking for the source, nearly spitting my food everywhere when I found it. Several metres away, just off the footpath, Derek Lindstrom held his mobile to his ear. His sickening stare bored into me, and one side of his mouth lifted in a sneer, pleased that he had my attention. I struggled against the sensations he evoked, but I'd be damned if I let him see the effect he had on me.

"I've never liked that man." *Thank you, Beverly. Perfect timing.* She looked me over with concern. "Are you all right? You look like you're going to be sick."

Using my tongue to manoeuvre the food, I pushed it down my throat and paused to make sure it stayed down. "I'll be fine. Too much sugar. Are you ready to go?"

"Absolutely."

He was planning something, and my senses told me to stay as far away from him as possible. Men like him had to be in control, and I'd slapped him down a couple of times now. One thing was certain. I needed to find out what he was up to. I needed to know what was in that building in town, and why he was there.

I need to find the ghost from the window.

Chapter
15

Brad

A piercing scream jolted me out of my sleep. I flicked on my lamp and hit the ground running, smacking my shoulder into the doorway as I tried to coordinate lethargic limbs. Veronica's body contorted and twisted in the sweat drenched agony of a nightmare, as I watched through her door. My hand frantically rubbed the back of my head, searching for a plan as I stood at the foot of the bed. I couldn't touch her. That'd make her more terrified. Her room was fucking freezing, but she was drenched in sweat.

"Veronica." I spoke low and calm, hoping to break through her horror. Her body curled up in a ball, and she gasped furiously for a breath she couldn't seem to catch.

"Veronica, it's me. Brad. It's okay. You're safe."

She whimpered, stuck in the foetal position, her hair a wild tangle on the pillow. *Fuck.* I felt so helpless. This was as bad as when she lost it after seeing her mother. She was in some headspace that I couldn't reach. No amount of physical force or determination would get me where I needed to be to help her. My fist tightened around a clump of my hair, and I pulled in frustration.

"Veronica!" Desperation forced the words into her ears. "It's a dream. It's not real. Come back to me. Wake up."

Tears ran from her eyes, and down her temple to wet the sheets. The keening sound she made pierced me. I had to touch her. Placing my hand lightly on her shoulder, I smoothed it down her arm, talking to her the entire time. Letting her know it was me. She slowly relaxed, stretched her legs out and rolled onto her back. I watched as her eyelids fluttered open, and her dark, tear-soaked gaze finally focused on me. Her eyes widened, then those lids dropped closed, and her hands covered her face.

"Hey." I gently held her wrists and tugged down, so I could see her and make sure she was okay.

"Sorry 'bout that," she croaked at the ceiling.

"Look at me." After a moment's hesitation, she turned her eyes in my direction. "Are you okay?"

"Yeah. I get nightmares. A lot. Although I haven't had one since I moved here. Guess the holiday is over. Sorry that I woke you."

"Don't worry about me. Do you want a drink of something?"

"Yes, please. Cold water would be great."

I padded down the hallway, feeling the temperature change as soon as I left her room. The nights were getting cooler, but it was nowhere near winter, and the air-conditioner wasn't on. I scrubbed my hands up and down my face, unable to comprehend how bizarre that was at two in the morning. I flexed my left hand. It felt weird without the cast, like it weighed nothing.

After filling a glass, I handed it to her, watching her drink. If she told me to leave, I would have. But I had a strong compulsion to stand guard over her all night.

She put the empty glass on her side table, and scanned my face through wet lashes. "Would you mind if I slept in your bed tonight? Sorry, I know I'm being a wuss. You can say no. I'm a bit freaked out—"

Even better.

I was a little stunned that she'd suggest it, so it took me a few seconds to respond while she kept apologising. "Yes." I threaded my fingers through hers and pulled her behind me to my room. She climbed up on the bed, curling away from me. I knew she was shaken and might need some space, but I was wired up, and needed to hold her to know she was okay. Flicking off the lamp, I wrapped an arm around her waist and pulled her back into my front. "Is this okay? I need to hold you."

She didn't make a move or a sound for the longest time. I wondered if she was asleep already.

"Yeah. It's good. Thanks." Her hand covered mine, and I felt my panic ease.

I spent hours listening to her breathing, and watched the lava lamp as I worried myself sick. She said the nightmares were nothing new. There were things that plagued her, and they were out of my reach. The shadows behind her eyes slayed me. They were buried deep, and I couldn't reach in and clear them away. And that pissed me right off. I fucking hated feeling useless. I felt that way when Mum and Dad died, when I found out Tish had been stealing, and when she wouldn't do anything but study. I'd felt like a complete waste of space when she'd died.

If all I could do to help Veronica was hold her, then this was where she needed to be every night. Right here in my arms.

Ronnie

I didn't have to find her after all. She found me, infiltrating my subconscious with her movie reel of horrors. Her name was Candace. I heard it on the lips of her killer, as he thrust into her body, encircling her throat with strong hands. Her choked sobs eventually stopped as she died. Even more sickening, there had been witnesses, and one of them caught the murder on video. I couldn't see their faces as they stood back in the shadows, but I could see the little red light blinking. Recording the sickening act in digital clarity just confirmed how fucked in the head her abusers were.

She didn't show me more than the few moments before and after her death, but I got the impression that they'd been torturing her for a while. Bound and gagged, her dress was torn and bunched up, barely covering anything.

I bit my cheek, forcing myself to get a grip. Brad surrounded me in the cocoon of his overheated body, providing the grounding that I so desperately needed. As rattled as I was, I found comfort in his touch. I covered his hand with mine to let him know I was thankful, and that it was okay, more than okay, for him to hold me. I shuddered at the thought of him not being there to bring me out of the nightmare.

Tish appeared at the side of the bed, crouching down to my level. I curled back into Brad, not sure if I could handle another visit from the beyond.

"I'm sorry. I tried to keep her away. She wanted to answer your questions."

I wanted to ask about the building and the woman, but obviously there was no chance of doing that, for now. I think Tish knew exactly what had been going on, but she's been trying to protect me. Come to think of it, the ghostly visitations had lessened since she appeared in my life. My own little guardian angel. I gave her a shaky smile and closed my eyes. Brad moved my hair on the pillow so he could burrow his face closer. His sigh brushed over my ear and across my neck. Timing my breaths with his, I slowly descended into peace.

Chapter
16

Ronnie

"This is your favourite?"

"Yeah."

"Gotham Tower?" Craning my neck back to take in the towering mass of glass and steel, I shook my head in amusement.

"I call it the Batman Building, but Gotham Tower works just as well. It's the State Law Building, actually. I always get a kick out of the fact that a building dedicated to justice looks like something straight out of a Justice League comic book."

"It's true what they say, then?"

"What do they say?"

"That all men are just little boys at heart. You never really grow up."

"Hey. I'm all man. And Batman is a legend. Why wouldn't I be ecstatic that we have a real life Gotham Tower here in Brissie?"

"It's pretty ugly."

Brad scoffed. "Beauty is subjective."

"That's true," I agreed, amused at how passionate he was about a building. Like me.

"The gothic styling was added in '93 as a way to conceal the new plant facilities. The designer must have been a Batman fan. I mean, come on. It's too obvious. Genius, if you ask me." He clapped his hands together and turned his face back to mine. "Okay, your turn. Where are we going next?"

"Can we head down towards The Mansions?" *I never did get to see them the other day.*

"Lead the way." He gestured with his arm. Taking a step forward, I reached for his hand and pulled his arm down, twining my fingers into his. I'd rather walk beside him than lead him anywhere. I'd been alone for so long, it felt nice to finally have someone to share things with. Tish was right. I thought she'd be tagging along, but she was nowhere to be seen. That didn't mean she wasn't watching, though.

My stomach tightened with urgency as we got closer to our destination. It was one thing to have my safe place infiltrated by nightmares, but to actually pursue my demons was … fucking insane. *What was I doing?* I had to call on my deepest reserves to hunt down and face my darkest fears. Somehow, holding Brad's hand, his unfaltering steps in sync with mine, I found what I was looking for. I wanted to see inside that building, and get it over with.

"Before we get to The Mansions, there's a place I've been wanting to see. It's just down there."

We walked a little further, weaving in and out of the crowd. I did my best to avoid touching anyone as I breezed past. Not an easy task on a Saturday morning.

I came to an abrupt halt when we reached the large, brown house. It was beautiful. A turn-of-the-century, decorative facade covering a sinister deceit.

Brad surveyed the place from the footpath. "Federation Filigree. Just like my place. See the iron fringe and balustrade? I don't have a parapet, though. I mean, this is a mansion, and my place is just a regular Queenslander. Looks like they rendered it when they restored it. Shame. I hope it's not sandstone under there."

"I tried to find out what this place was on the internet, but there's no mention of its current purpose. It was sold to a private buyer back in 2010. They built it for a banker and his wife in 1897. They had eleven children and plenty of money, so I'm guessing there are quite a few rooms. He sold it when he went broke. I think it was used by the military during the first world war."

The ornate wood and stained glass front door suddenly opened, and I grabbed a fistful of Brad's shirt, dragging him behind a tree. It earned us the attention that I was trying to avoid, but only from passersby, curious about what we were hiding from.

"Uh, what're you doing?" Brad looked pointedly down at his shirt still gripped in my fist.

I let go of him, smoothing out his shirt, while peeking around the tree to see who'd exited the building. Air hissed between my teeth when I caught a glimpse of Lindstrom and his associates. He was in a huddle with four other suits, looking like they'd just convened a meeting. On a Saturday. Not out of the question, I suppose. The four men left the grounds as Lindstrom waited. The door opened again, revealing a pudgy, red-faced man. He descended the stairs on dodgy legs to join the professor.

I felt Brad collect my hand in his, and realised I'd been smoothing his shirt the entire time. One more person emerged before the door finally closed. At that moment, I was so grateful that Brad was with me. Flick wiped her face as she joined Lindstrom in the yard. But before the door closed, I saw Candace and two other women. Dead women. Standing at the entrance, pointing their wispy fingers straight at me. My legs began to give way, but Brad's strong arms propped me up. I buried my face in his chest not wanting to believe my eyes. My pulse raged, the taste of coppery blood lined my tongue as I started chewing on my cheek.

I focused on Brad's clean, soapy smell, and the feel of his arms around me, as I tried to calm myself. I hoped like fuck they didn't need to come this way. *Please let them be parked on the side street, or even behind the residence.* I didn't think it was a residence. But whatever it was used for, bad things had happened there. *That wasn't a business meeting.* What the fuck was Flick doing with Lindstrom and his cronies? Had she set up an internship with Lindstrom's firm? She sure as hell didn't look happy about it. And why were dead women haunting a law office?

Because that's where they were killed.

"Veronica!" I lifted my head, as Brad gave me a gentle shake. "Jesus. You scare the shit out of me when you fade out like that. Where did you go?"

I kept my palms firmly attached to his chest, as I spun my head around to check that they were gone. "Um …" *Shit.* "Sorry, I don't know what happened." My head was fuzzy, stuffed with images and questions. Scattered pieces of a puzzle that I had yet to put together.

Frozen hands rested on my shoulders, plunging my body temperature and trapping the breath in my chest. It wasn't Tish. I sensed it. I'd felt those icy hands tugging on my feet before. The shiver was uncontrollable, transferring from my body to Brad's. I blinked up at him, unable to say anything. His face changed when he read the panic that must be so blatant it was screaming through my eyes.

"Come on. We can come back another day."

Brad's arm curled around my shoulders, shoving the frozen touch away, replacing it with his blissful heat. As we turned to walk back, I took one last look at the building. There she was again, in the corner window on the second floor. It was only a blurry outline through the sheer curtain, but I knew it was her. A delicate hand protruded through the curtain, through the glass, beckoning me to come. I felt the force of the gesture, as if she'd just reached into my ribcage and scooped out the contents. I heaved in some air to reassure myself that I still had lungs, and hurried away.

Fuck. I felt like the future was an endless black hole threatening to engulf me. I desperately clung to Brad's gravity in the hopes that its force was powerful enough to change my path. To fill me with light and drag me away from the darkness. An unwelcome thought seeped in. What if I dragged him in with me, and we were both lost forever?

———

"Your juice is on the table for you. Do you want scrambled eggs this morning?"

"No, thanks. I'll just have cereal."

Brad has been so sweet even after seeing some of my craziness. First, my nightmares, and then the incident in the city. Not to mention my breakdown when I saw my mother and sisters. Instead of running the other way, or looking at me like I was a weirdo, he'd been more attentive. More doting.

And I noticed that the woman taking shape on the lounge room wall looked more and more like me.

He was peeling back my layers, getting to the damaged core. I was still afraid he wouldn't like what he saw when he reached deep enough. But he was still here after all he'd seen.

I was utterly in love with him.

I had been for a while. When I thought I'd put him in danger by stupidly dragging him into my mess, I panicked. Mentally, I beat myself black and blue.

What if Lindstrom had seen him? I didn't know if he did because I was too busy doing my ostrich act to watch them as they left. Lindstrom hadn't even done anything to me yet. It could all be in my head. Letitia shook her head, mouthing, *no, it's not*. Her truth joined the instincts in my gut, reminding me to listen.

I felt the danger crowding me. The Monday after seeing Lindstrom and Flick in the city, I found him watching me from across the courtyard as I got to work. He was making note of my habits. Calculating his next move. Waiting for his opportunity. I had no proof, and yet I knew exactly what he was doing. I sensed it as if I could read his thoughts. I didn't have to see him to know he was near. His twisted energy cloaked me in its filth. A cloying, oppressive heaviness on my being. Only someone who was really fucking psychopathic had that kind of energy.

"Hey." Brad smoothed a hand down my messy hair, and kissed me on the forehead. My eyelids fluttered closed, blocking everything else out so I could savour the moment. "You okay?"

"Yeah. Sorry, I was just thinking."

"About what?"

You don't want to know. "Work."

"What's going on at work?"

I pursed my lips and blew out a breath, as I started making some breakfast. "I think I need a change of pace. I'm getting bored of cataloguing." First time I'd really thought of it, but yeah, it was true. I was bored. I guess I wasn't happy being holed up anymore.

"What are you thinking of doing?"

"Maybe assisting with research. You know, compiling resources for literature reviews, stuff like that." *Where was this shit coming from?*

"Well …" He looked me in the eye. "… I think you could do anything you put your mind to."

I fucking love this man. So hard.

I was ruining things with Brad because I was letting a vague threat mess with my head. I smacked the cereal packet back onto the pantry shelf, and slapped the door shut. I needed to shed the scared mouse act, and attack this thing head on. That was how I'd always dealt with bullies of the living kind. Now that I had a safe place to catch my breath, something more to fight for, and someone who would fight for me, I needed to toughen up and block the bad shit out. This was what bullies did. They made you insecure until your self-esteem was so shrivelled that you didn't want to leave the house, and couldn't interact with anyone in a healthy way. I knew that. I'd lived that. I didn't want to succumb to anyone else's bullying tactics anymore.

Granny helped get me through the dramas growing up. Now, I had this solid, generous, incredible man, and a ghost on my side. I should have the strength to conquer anything.

Chapter
17

Brad

I loved the smell of paint. A coat of paint made everything better. At least that's what I was banking on. For the last two weeks, something had been missing. Ever since we checked out that house in the city, the light in Veronica's eyes had dimmed. Something happened to her while we were there, right in front of my eyes, and I couldn't see inside her to know what it was. I felt like I was reliving the dramas with Tish after our parents' deaths, and it was stirring up an ugly gnawing inside my gut.

I'd been hovering over her like a bad smell. Insisting that we run together, cook together, watch TV. She snuggled with me on the couch, but when it was time to sleep, she said goodnight with a chaste kiss on the lips, and retreated to her room. I even coerced her into coming rock climbing with me, now that I was all healed. On the surface she seemed fine. She smiled and laughed, but there was trouble brewing in her eyes, snuffing out the spark. Her snappy mouth had gone quiet. She was curled up like a pill bug hiding in its armour. I needed to coax her out.

After breakfast this morning, Veronica helped me clear out my bedroom furniture. My mattress was on the floor in the lounge room where I'd be spending the night … maybe two nights. I might like the smell of paint, but I'd rather not choke on the fumes all night, and it was too cold to sleep with the windows open.

"Are you seriously sure about this colour?"

I crouched over the open tin, inspecting the deep, blue-grey shade Veronica had chosen for my room. It was nice, but it was a big change from the off-white walls that had served a few generations, and bolder than anything I would've chosen.

"Positive."

The word was said with such conviction I had to tilt my head back to see her face. Her gaze penetrated mine, sending a silent message, but my brain cells switched off at the sight of her watching me. She was so fucking gorgeous. All those wild curls were tamed in a braid that hung low at her back. Old, ripped jeans hugged those legs all the way to her slender ankles, and the ACDC T-shirt had reappeared.

Whatever was bothering her, it hadn't dampened the desire that ignited the air between us. It wasn't just a physical pull, although my cock made its wishes known whenever she was near. My heart wanted in on the action just as badly. Everything I felt, I saw echoed in her soulful brown eyes. Her craving coated the air, mingling with mine to paint the air in lustful colours. I wanted to say, "fuck the painting," but I needed to know that when this happened, it was because she really wanted it. Not because she was escaping from something.

"It's going to look so serene when it's done. You'll find it hard to get out of bed."

Her cheek caved as she bit it, and her gaze slipped to the paint can between my knees. I looked down, waiting for it to boil from the heat of her gaze. *Damn, it wasn't safe for me to stand up.*

"I believe you ..." I muttered. *How the hell do I distract her?* "... uh, I think I forgot that angled paint brush. Could you please check the deck?"

"It's right behind you. You're going to get a cramp if you stay like that for much longer."

I have a huge cramp ... in my dick, thanks to you. She raised an eyebrow, waiting for me to move. Well, she'd asked for it. If she skittered away when she saw my body's reaction to her, then I knew she wasn't ready for this. For us.

"Great. Thanks." My thighs tightened and stretched, as I unfolded my body to its full height. Her eyebrows arched up as she followed my movement. Her pupils dilated when she caught a glimpse of my arousal.

She stepped closer, watching me. The tiny smile teasing the corner of her lips widened to a cheeky grin, ramping up the ticking of my heart. She crouched down in the same position I was just in, and diligently filled a container with a splash of colour. She was totally calm, enjoying my discomfort. I was a tower of raging hormones and frustration.

With a growl, I grabbed her around the waist and lifted her to her feet. "You think this is funny?" I smiled down at her surprised face when I pulled her body closer to mine. A whimper escaped her, the sound shooting to my balls, which tightened painfully when she burrowed closer. "This is your fault. You did this to me."

"I know."

My eyebrows shot up at her cockiness. "Do you, now?"

"Mm hmm," she hummed, nodding.

I wrapped a hand around her braid, gently tilting her head so that our lips lined up. The puff of her breath against my mouth sent shock waves shooting south. She had all the power. I might be the one holding her, but I was rendered helpless under her spell. I knew she didn't understand, but that was my fault. I hadn't told her with words. I'd shown it every time I made her breakfast. When I held her hand in mine, or played with her hair when we had quiet time. But never in words.

Stroking her mouth with mine, I wanted to show her how I felt in every way possible. But I also needed to tell her. The words lined up in my throat, ready to be set free. There was no stopping them anymore. The way her body vibrated under my touch, the way her tongue came out to stroke mine, told me that she was ready to hear them. She was practically drawing them out of me.

"I'm in love with you." Sliding my thumbs over her collar bones, I felt her shiver.

Heavy lids shaded dark eyes, holding me as her soul poured into mine. They told me so much without a sound. I felt what she wasn't saying, but she opened her mouth to speak, anyway.

"Yeah, I know." Her words stayed suspended. I wasn't sure if I should take them on board or let them drop.

Her arms wrapped around my neck, pulling me back down for a deeper kiss. I bent at the knees slightly so our bodies were aligned, chest to chest, hip to hip, soft to hard. She tasted like apple juice, so sweet I couldn't get enough. Our hands roamed, and I grasped those words and swallowed them down. I no longer cared if they weren't the words I was expecting. It wasn't what she said … it was how she said it. The message behind her words was worth everything.

"Do you feel this? Tell me you feel this." I rested her palm over my thundering heart, making certain that she did. She needed to know that I was done for. I was all hers. I had been ever since she'd bolted past me like a swarm of bees were chasing her.

"I feel it," she panted between kisses.

"Thank fuck for that."

I dove into her mouth with more fervour, needing it all and taking what I could. My palms latched on to the backs of her thighs, lifting her, and wrapping her long luscious limbs around my waist. I sidestepped, somehow remembering the paint, and strode down the hallway towards the mattress on the floor.

Sinking to my knees, I kept her right where she was so I could rub my aching cock against her sweet spot. She moaned into my mouth, letting me know my aim was spot on. She rocked her hips to help me out. Hell, she was helping herself out, too. I loved that she was taking control of her pleasure. She was welcome to use me as much as she wanted, however she wanted.

I felt her fingers tugging up my shirt at the back, and I was all on board with that plan. Reaching behind my head, I ripped the shirt off, and flung it at the TV. She plastered her mouth on mine, and I pulled her shirt up as I leaned forward, laying her flat on the mattress underneath me. Where I'd had her in my dreams countless times. The reality was so much better than my feeble imagination.

Her arms stretched above her head as the T-Shirt rose. I kissed every inch of her golden-brown skin as it was exposed, taking extra care to go slow over her chin, her mouth, cheeks and her eyelids. Leaving the T-shirt bunched around her wrists, I slid my hands down each arm and over her breasts, covered in purple satin. Feeling the hard nubs of her nipples, I couldn't resist. I wanted to suck on them.

"Can I take this off?"

"Yessss," she hissed, letting me know that she was right there with me. I was so fucking happy about it that a chuckle escaped. My tongue licked at the skin covering her breast bone as I unhooked her bra.

"What's funny?" she panted as she writhed under my tongue.

"Not funny. I'm just happy. Fucking delirious, actually."

"Oh." Her eyes rolled back before closing, as I sucked one dark nipple.

The taste of her. *God.* My eyes rolled and slammed shut, too. I could suck on her tits forever. Unable to resist, I sank my teeth in and pulled. Her back bowed up off the mattress, hands digging into my shoulders. I gripped her waist to pull her closer. Lavishing the other nipple with the same attention, I was rewarded when she started grinding her pelvis on my erection. The friction was pleasure and pain at the same time.

"You're mine. You know that, right?" Pushing her back on the mattress, I tugged at her jeans, needing to see all of her. Her stomach hollowed with each gasp. She unravelled before my eyes. Handing control to me. Needing the pleasure I was ready to give. I wanted to dip my head between those legs and taste her.

"Nobody else would make you feel this good, Gazelle. You. Are. Mine."

"Nobody … never had this before." She reached for my zipper, her fingers fluttering along my stomach as she fumbled to get it open. It felt like she was striking a match along my skin, burning me with want.

I was so turned on it took a few seconds for her words to sink in. I stopped her hands as she pushed my jeans down to my knees.

"What? Never had this? What do you mean?" I didn't mean to growl, but could barely think. She had me on edge, and it was about to get worse if she meant what I thought she meant.

"Never mind. I'm all yours."

She surged up, pushing her tongue into my mouth, and her fingers into my undies, springing my erection free. *Ah, fuck. The relief.* I reached down and squeezed my cock, pumping a couple of times until her hand covered mine and took over. My back hit the mattress. Everything went taut as her hands stroked my cock. She held me nice and tight. Just the way I liked it. Then, I felt her hair tickle my chest, and her hot tongue licking over my nipple. I nearly shot my load.

"Ah, Gazelle. Fuck. You're …" She bit me, and it jolted me like a kick of some drug. I couldn't take it anymore. "Come here."

My hands dove into her panties, dipping into the slick heat I was dying to taste. She cried out in the sweetest sound I'd ever heard. I needed to hear that sound again. Her head rested on my shoulder, as I circled one hand into the back of her knickers, clenching a handful of that arse while the other hand worked her from the front. She still had one hand pumping me, while the other fluttered over the sheet beside my head, trying to find an anchor.

Those sounds, they were hot on my chest, urging my heart to beat faster and harder just for her. Her hips rolled in a stilted rhythm, as she neared her climax. The tightening muscles of her pussy grabbed at my fingers as they slipped in and out easily. Her hand went loose, sliding up to my chest, and she pushed both arms straight, arching her body, pushing her tits in my face. My mouth salivated as it latched on. My fingers rubbed more frantically, and I smoothed my middle finger down the crack of her bum, adding pressure behind. She cried out. Her face was a mask of agonized ecstasy … so beautiful. I wanted to remember her like this. I needed to see her like this … again and again.

I eased off the pressure and let her come slowly back to Earth, fluttering down to a soft landing on the bed below. Grabbing a condom from the drawers, I dragged her satin knickers down those long, lithe legs. The room smelled like sex. It was heady … and the scent drove me wild. I was rock hard, it fucking hurt, but I had to dip my tongue in for a taste of her heat. She cried out again, yanking clumps of my hair. Pushing me away, pulling me closer. She wanted more, but she was so sensitive now. I licked a few more times just because I was a greedy bastard.

Kissing a path over the smooth skin of her thighs and belly, I looked up through my lashes over her heaving chest as she watched me.

"Are you ready for me?"

She whimpered, but nodded, licking her lips. I grasped her ankles, bending her knees, opening her up for me. Holding the base of my cock, I rubbed the tip along her entrance.

"You sure?" I asked.

"Yesss!" she hissed it again, breaking off to a gasp as I slid in, slowly.

Fuck, she was so tight. I pushed on the backs of her thighs, opening her wider and changing my angle. I could barely move, her pussy gripped me like a vice. Her boobs bounced from the force of her breaths, her eyes squeezed shut.

"Relax for me, Gazelle. Are you okay?" I gritted out.

"Yes, just move, please?" she pleaded.

I stroked her clit with my thumb, and her hips started to undulate, pulling me in deeper until finally, I was as deep as I could go. She released a long breath through pursed lips, a smile unfurling as if she'd finally found her home, just like I'd finally found mine. Leaning down, I pushed my tongue into her mouth in the same way I was surging into her body. We kissed and we fucked, building the ecstasy until we'd somehow left the Earth and found ourselves tangled in each other … somewhere no one could find us. My hips bucked in jerky movements, filling her with my orgasm as her muscles clenched around me, riding her own to completion.

We lay in each other's arms for what seemed like hours, stroking our hands over each other's bodies, drawing out the connection before we had to return to reality.

She gave me one last kiss, and turned glowing eyes on me. I loved that I could put that look in her eyes.

"We should probably paint your room now."

My arms tightened, and I glided a hand down to her butt cheek, giving it a squeeze. "Mm. Maybe later. Wanna go another round?"

She leaned up on her elbow, giving me a view of her bare tits, urging my hand to slide up and cover one. "Maybe later. Let's paint. It's probably got a film on top by now."

"Bah, we'll just peel it off. It'll be fine." I tweaked her nipple, making it pucker. I didn't want to let her go just yet.

Veronica slipped out of my grasp, and stood naked beside the mattress. I greedily drank my fill, starting from her hair, coming free from its braid, to her beautiful face watching me with undisguised amusement and affection. All that smooth caramel skin, breasts peaked with dark nipples, showing signs of stubble rash where I'd feasted on her. The contours of her firm stomach, and the dip of her navel in the middle, leading down to the thin line of curls that led to heaven—yum.

"I'm going to clean up. You're welcome to stay here and let Mrs Palmer entertain you with her five sisters." She wiggled her fingers at me, before spinning on her heel and sauntering away.

"Cheeky minx. You'll pay for that later." Her laughter bounced off the tile walls of the bathroom; the best kind of music.

I dressed quickly and met her in our room, feeling more enthusiastic about getting this job done. If she thought she would be sleeping across the hall after that experience, she was dead wrong. This was our room now. She picked the colour, putting her stamp on it. She could decorate it however she wanted. I didn't care, as long as she was in it. With me.

———

Ronnie

We spent the next several hours transforming his bedroom into a tranquil oasis. I was right. The stormy grey, the same colour as his eyes, worked well with the white trim and ceiling, and his wooden furniture.

I was exhausted, but I'd never been happier. The soreness in my muscles lingered as a reminder of what we shared through work and play. The way his talented hands knew exactly how to draw out my pleasure. My mind wandered to the way his tongue had tasted me that morning, every time I stroked the paintbrush. He stopped what he was doing every now and then to cross the room and plant a kiss on my lips. My jeans had paint hand prints on the bum from his tight grip.

As we fell onto his mattress again after a productive day, I lay on top of his body, our skin still damp from our shower. We never bothered to get dressed afterwards, opting to fall into bed to continue what we started under the spray of water.

He gripped my face and I gripped his as we sat chest to chest, our bodies intimately connected. Limbs tangling, hips rocking, our harsh breaths scored our faces as we looked into each other's eyes. I didn't want to lose this. I'd opened up something powerful, something that meant more than I could've imagined. There was no way it could be contained again.

I felt vulnerable, like my body had been flipped inside out, with my heart and organs exposed. Everything that was going on inside of me, there for him to see. Nervous panic and liberation battled for the same space in my soul. But Brad drained my fears with long drugging kisses, and the words, "I love you," whispered into my neck.

Pulsing electricity spread from my centre. I could happily drown in this tsunami of erotic sensations. Brad groaned and encircled his arms around me tighter, absorbing the pounding waves, taking back everything he gave me. He lay my limp, satiated body back on the mattress, placing the covers over me to keep away the cold while he left me to take care of the condom. Slipping under the warm cocoon with me, he pulled me close and picked up a few of my dark curls.

"I love your hair."

"I love your hands in my hair."

"Really? Thank God, 'cause I wanna touch it all the time. By the way, did you leave the light on in your room?"

I hadn't been in there since I woke up. "Uh, no."

"Hm. Weird. Must be a faulty switch."

No, it's your sister.

"Probably be best if you move into my room. Just to be safe."

"Oh, really?"

"Definitely. It's the best room, and I'm a good sharer."

Placing my hand on his chest to feel the steady beat of his heart, I had to ask, "Are you sure that's a good idea? We've only known each other for four months. Yeah, we live together, but that's *moving in*, moving in. You wouldn't have any space of your own in case you got sick of me."

"I've known you for a lot longer than that."

I tilted my head up. The steady beat under my palm thumped harder. "Huh? What are you talking about?"

"Erm, well … I saw you last winter. I wasn't in a good place after Tish died. I was doing reckless shit and binge drinking every weekend. Nearly lost my job. Let's just say I'd had a bad night with no sleep and a run-in with the cops. I decided to sit at South Bank to watch the sunrise and cool off. You raced passed me. I noticed you. I've been watching out for you ever since."

I let his words sink in. Not really knowing how to react.

"Don't freak out," he continued. "I never followed you home. Without really knowing you, you inspired me to do better, be better. So I got into a routine, and if you happened to be there then my day got a little brighter. I never expected to actually meet you. Definitely didn't expect to shirt-front you. Sorry 'bout that. Again."

Surprisingly, the frantic drumming in his chest helped to soothe me. I inspired him? Me, the freak who thought I had control over my life? I understood now that I really didn't, and still didn't. Would it be so bad to lean on him? To put all my trust in him and let him be my foundation?

"Wow. Um. What do I say to that?"

"Say that I haven't scared the shit out of you, and that you'll *move in*, move in with me."

"I'm not scared … I'm flattered. I don't think I deserve the ego stroking, but I'm enjoying it anyway."

"Can I stroke something else?"

I snorted. "You're incorrigible."

"My ego could use a little stroking." Twisting his hips, he nudged his semi-hard cock into my thigh.

"Could it, now?"

"Mmm." He hummed into my neck, quietly breathing me in for several beats. "Are we going to be roommates?"

What else could I say to that but, "Yes."

Chapter
18

Brad

Ben tapped the end of a chisel with a mallet, wood chips flying in all directions as he crafted a new bookcase. His garage was chock full of his tools and projects. There was no room for the cars, which were relegated to the driveway. It was a handyman's dream in here.

My head was in a dream of its own. The mural was finally finished. I'd woken up this morning, hit by my muse and went with it. Veronica left extra early so she could have breakfast with her Granny before work. I gave her a kiss on the lips, a smack on the arse, and sent her on her way because I was bursting out of my skin to finish solidifying her form on my wall.

My chest was swollen with pride as I took in the finished work. It was a scene from the late 1800's. She was poised at the end of a jetty wearing a long, white, cotton dress with lace trimmings, and a wide brim hat with ribbon tails flowing over her loose hair. It was my life on the wall. Coming out of the darkness to find her. I could've said the same about my second chance at a friendship with Ben.

The smell of wood as it transformed into something beautiful and with purpose … it warmed my blood. I loved it. Have done so since I was a kid watching my dad work in his shed, and I'd carried that love through my apprenticeship with my best mate by my side. I had so many good memories locked inside me. I felt stupid that I'd forgotten them for a while. That I let all the bad shit accumulate and eclipse all the good. I lost sight of the fact that life continued on and morphed into something else. Sometimes worse, sometimes better, but the point was, it was fluid. I felt so stuck in hell that I escaped by putting myself in danger. That kind of hell would've been permanent.

"So, you and Veronica are getting along well."

"Yeah." There was no hiding the perma-grin taking up residence on my face. I'd found cloud nine, and her name was Veronica.

"I like her, man. She's tough."

Relief rolled through me. If my best friend didn't like her, I'd be disappointed. I might even be pissed, but it wouldn't make me doubt my feelings for her. They were rendered onto the surface of my heart. If anything was to change them, it would crack open and drain of life in a big, bloody mess.

"Yeah. Her brain is so sexy."

Shoving my hands into the back pockets of my jeans, my eyes blurred as a memory montage played across my vision. From the moment I first saw her, to the nights we'd spent together. She was the ultimate woman. There wasn't a thing I'd change about her. I wished she didn't have to endure the agony of losing her parents, especially the way she did. But she'd built herself up to be an educated, disciplined, capable woman. I had so much respect for that. It made me proud of her. She'd be pissed if she thought I was putting her on a pedestal. I knew she wasn't perfect. Nobody was. But fuck if I could see anything not to like. She was smokin' hot, but she didn't play it up or down. She was comfortable in her own skin, and that was what made her even more attractive.

Switching my attention back to Ben, I realised I'd been standing there with my mouth open. Like a love-struck wanker. Snapping my mouth shut, I cleared my throat. "That's a huge bookcase, are you sure that's going to fit?" Ben was a perfectionist, there was no way it wasn't going to fit. I just loved pulling his leg.

He rolled his eyes. "Hand me that sand paper?" Smoothing off the rough edges, he narrowed his eyes. "It'll fit, dickhead." A couple of stray woodchips fell from his hair as he shook his head at me. "Something about her, it's … I dunno. She's been hurt. Just take it slow. I know you have a tendency to go balls all in, but Andrea's getting a bad vibe. Protect yourself."

"Oh, yeah? Like you did, huh?"

"No, tosser. Don't fuck it up like I did." He paused his sanding and frowned at the wood as if he saw something unpleasant. "Andrea reckons Veronica might act tough, but she needs someone to look out for her."

"What's that supposed to mean?"

He turned his gaze to me. "Who knows? This is Andrea we're talking about. She doesn't know what it means until after shit happens, and then it all makes sense."

I knew she needed someone to care for her. She'd been through so much. I still couldn't get over her mother treating her like a disease. What the fuck was that? Maybe that was what Andrea was referring to. What's been dragging her down, lately. Discovering that she has sisters, and then five seconds later watching their backs retreat as their mother ushered them away from her … horrifying. I didn't think I'd ever get over watching her lose it.

The old house. Something happened there, too. I didn't know if she knew those people, but she felt like she had to hide from them. What was she hiding?

"Hi, Lee!" The tiny, blonde, bundle of energy rocketed her body at me like she hadn't seen me in forever, snapping me out of my daze.

"Andy, my love." I gave her a squeeze.

"She's not your love, she's mine," Ben growled.

"He knows that." Andrea released me and kissed her husband. The envy I used to feel was long gone, no longer required. "Stop beating your chest, he has his own woman. How are you, Lee?"

"Talented and hung like a horse. I keep telling you, you picked the wrong man."

She beamed while Ben scowled. "Nope. I picked the right one. He gets the job done and his swimmers are strong little buggers."

"Gross, Andy. Why are we talking about his swimmers?"

"First one to the egg makes Baby Ben," she sang, her eyes twinkling.

"Wha? Are you … Really?"

"Yup. Four months. You're going to be an uncle, Lee."

"No wonder you need more storage. Congrats, guys." I kicked up some sawdust as I crossed the garage to give Ben a handshake and a slap on the back. "You're naming him after me, right?"

"Fat chance of that. When you have a little ranga of your own, you can name him after you, and let him share your stash of sunscreen."

"You bastard. You're just jealous because you can't play dot to dot when you're bored."

"Boys!" Andrea edged towards the door. "Are you staying for lunch, Lee? I just bought some bread rolls and a cooked chook."

"Sounds great. I'll help you."

"Aw, thanks. You're so sweet to look after the pregnant lady." She blew me a kiss and disappeared again.

"Make sure you aim the chisel away from your dick. Sounds like Andrea might need it after all. You know what they say about pregnant chicks." I gave Ben one last slap on the back as he told me to fuck off, and headed inside after Andrea.

I did want to help her, but I also wanted to pick her brain. She already had all the food spread over the counter, and was busy chopping tomatoes. I couldn't see any sign of pregnancy yet, but she was wearing a loose top over her shorts. I bet Benny had noticed.

"Have you been feeling sick? You look as healthy as ever."

"I'm totally fine. I didn't find out until a few weeks ago. My appetite is huge, though. That's what finally tipped me off. I've been so busy with unpacking and working at the day care, that I haven't been paying attention. Oh, and my boobs are sore."

"Do you want me to rub them better?"

"You wish, gutter brain. Don't you have another set of boobs to fondle?"

I probably had a dumb look on my face as the memory of sucking on Veronica's nipples seized my mind. "Mmm."

"Okay, keep it clean. How is Ronnie?"

"She's … beautiful. I'm in love with her and I'm pretty sure she feels the same way."

Andrea handed me the rolls to butter, while she tore up some lettuce. "Pretty sure? Not certain?"

"Well, she hasn't said it, but I feel it … I think." Now, I wasn't so sure. I cursed when the knife gouged into the bread a little too far.

"Hey, I didn't mean to make you doubt yourself. If it's any help, I think she's in love with you, too. She looks at you the way you look at her … but there's something off."

Andrea opened the bag of chicken, and ripped off chunks of flesh with the tongs like it was never a living thing. Like it never had blood pumping through its veins. Like she just did with my heart.

"It's a sinking feeling in my gut, when I see her. I don't know if it involves you or what, but … there's something wrong. Sorry, I can't be more specific."

"She's had a rough time of it. Worse than what I've had to deal with, and she only has her Granny to lean on. She keeps things close to her chest. I don't know how much she shares with her grandmother."

"Does she share things with you?"

I think back to when she told me about her parents. How it all came out a little like she was reciting a shopping list. I didn't expect her to spill her guts for me. Some things were too painful to rehash. But what about the old house in the city? She wouldn't talk about it. At all. "Not everything."

"I think you have your work cut out for you. She's worth it, though. Right?"

"Yeah. Yeah, she is."

"Is there anything else you can do to help her, to show her what she means to you? That you're not going to run away?"

I watched Andrea's hands as they packed the fillings into the rolls, and thought of all the times Veronica and I had cooked together. She'd been helping me paint, helping me study, doing all the activities I suggested. It's all been for me. Here I was thinking that asking her to put her stamp on our place was my way of saying that I wanted to include her in my life. I hadn't once done something that was just for her benefit. *Jesus, I'd been a blind idiot.*

"Here. Eat your chicken roll. You'll feel better with a full stomach."

"Thanks, Andy. You're good at this mum gig."

Ben joined us in the kitchen after he brushed off about a kilo of sawdust and washed up. It was the quietest meal I'd ever shared with them. My head was elsewhere, planning how to put a smile back on Veronica's face, and let her know that she had me now, and always. Ben and

Andrea were having a grinning contest with their full mouths. They had something big to look forward to. Maybe that was what Veronica needed.

I had an idea. I had no clue how I was going to make it happen, but it was going to happen. She needed this. And she needed me, whether she knew it or not. Whether she wanted to or not.

––––––

Ronnie

"Beverly ..."

My normally vibrant and vivacious boss sat behind her desk, hair in a haphazard pony tail, dark circles under her eyes, and hollows in her cheeks.

"... you don't look so good. Should you be here?"

In answer, she leaned over, grabbed the bin and dry heaved into it. I sprinted to the small staff kitchen, ripping out a few paper towels, wetting a tea towel, and filling a disposable cup with cold water. Seconds later, I was back in the room, making sure to close the door behind me. She hunched over in the chair, gasping into the bin that caught nothing but the tears dripping from her cheeks.

"I'm just going to put a cool cloth on your neck, is that okay?"

Her head bounced once, eyes not moving from the bottom of the bin as I moved around to place the towel. There was no mess to clean up as far as I could see, so I put the paper towels and the cup on the desk. "Are you due for your nausea meds?"

"Useless," she gasped, still trying to catch her breath.

"Have they got you on the basic motion sickness one or the serious, kick-cancer's-arse one?"

"Arse."

"Damn." My heart sank when I brushed her hair out of the way, and some of it came away in my hand. Her skin burned hot. "I think I might have to call John to come and get you. You feel feverish."

"'Kay."

She pushed her phone towards me, unlocking it so I could search the contacts. John answered immediately, and I heard his keys jingle as I relayed the situation. She had good support at home. That eased my worry a little.

"Can you sip a little water? It might help."

Her hands tightened on the bin, as if she was scared I was going to take it from her.

"Nuh," she grunted.

I grimaced as she dry heaved again. It must be an effort just to breathe, let alone speak, and here I was asking her twenty questions.

A brusque knock at the door gave no warning before the door started to swing open. My temper spiked at light speed. Anyone who knew Beverly was aware that if her door was shut, it must be for a bloody good reason. I bolted around the desk, pushing my weight behind the door before the person behind it could see her. A low grunt sounded from the hallway. I slipped out, prepared to unleash my anger on the unsuspecting visitor.

The anger spat and fizzled on my tongue, turning into fear at the sight of Lindstrom. I was somewhat appeased when I caught him rubbing his nose. At least until his eyes pinned me to the wall, turning dark with hatred.

I knew I should apologise. I ordered my voice box to cough up the words, but it refused to do so.

"Ronnie. How lovely to see you … again." His practiced smile said, 'Gotcha'. I bet he used it in the courtroom all the time.

"Lindstrom. Sorry about the door, but Beverly is unable to take visitors at the moment. You should've waited for the okay before barging in."

His nostrils flared, eyes narrowing to deepen the creases at his temples. I just poked the devil. Me and my stupid sharp tongue.

"I saw you. With your boyfriend, in the city. Were you spying on me, Veronica?" His harsh tone was a drill, poking holes in my feeble attempt at bravery. "Did you enjoy the show?" His finger traced a slimy path from my temple to my chin, hovering just above the skin. My head smacked the wall as I jerked to get away from him. "If you want to come and visit me, all you have to do is ask. But, I don't take kindly to unwanted guests barging into my space." His fingers dropped to run along the air above my collarbone. Where Brad's touch made me tremble, Lindstrom's phantom touch made me shrivel inside from fear. "Next time you want to see me, let me know. I'll be sure to let you in." He let his teeth clash together near my ear as his hand slid down near my breasts, still not touching, before he released me.

I sagged against the wall when he turned his back.

"Oh, and Ronnie?" He continued walking, not bothering to look back as he spoke. "Keep your nose out of my business. I wouldn't want anyone to get hurt. Those old buildings can be hazardous. Tell Beverly I need to speak with her, please?"

Holy shit. Did he just threaten me? My instincts were right. Why haven't I learned to listen? I shivered in the wake of Lindstrom's words, and the way he made me feel violated without actually touching me. I couldn't even report any abuse. What did he actually do? He invited me to visit him, and told me to be careful around old buildings. *Shit.* He was slick. This was a game. He was a veteran player, and I was just the uncoordinated newbie.

I set the thoughts aside and gathered myself together to care for my friend. She needed me. What she was battling was far more aggressive and threatening than Derek Lindstrom. I had to help her any way that I could, because her needs were more important than mine at the moment.

Quietly shutting the door behind me, I looked her over. White, pasty skin drawn tight over her despondent face changed the woman I knew into an exhausted shadow of her true self. But she was the same amazing woman at her core, and I knew she was a fighter.

"How are you feeling?"

Leaning her back against the chair, she attempted a smile.

"It's eased off a little. I feel hot now. Really hot. Hot flushes, hot. I've done menopause—amen, that's over. I never want another hot flush in my lifetime … Who was at the door?"

"Nobody you need to worry about. Do you need me to do anything for you?"

"Could you cancel my meetings? I've left my calendar open on the desktop. You should be able to notify the attendees. I'll deal with the consequences later. Oh, Brian, the Director of Libraries, is coming here at three. The notes for discussion are printed out there." She pointed a shaky finger at her in-tray. "You know enough about what's going on around here to deal with it. If you can't answer any of his questions, just call Brenda, she might be able to help. Um, what else?" She rubbed a hand over her eyes and flopped it back to her lap, as if the effort in that small movement was too much. "Derek Lindstrom has been having some trouble with the work of one of our research librarians. She refused to deal with him personally, so there are some revised papers in a big, yellow envelope under the discussion notes. That man is the bane of my existence." She huffed, tipping her head back before fixing her eyes on me again. "Thanks, Ronnie."

"Knock, knock." Her husband, John, poked his head through the door, and I watched her mask of composure slip from her face. Her pale bottom lip quivered, as moisture coated her anguished eyes. I backed up into the corner to give them space, feeling like an intruder in their bubble of pain and love.

"John. I'm a bit sick, love," she choked out.

"I'm here to look after you, sweetheart. Come on, chook." He reverently clasped his wife's hand and helped her to her feet, slipping a supportive arm around her back. "Thank you," he murmured, as he guided his wife out the door.

The room screamed 'vacant'. My back slid down the wall as my legs folded underneath me. The shakes rattled my bones, once again. Swinging from one emotion to the other had wrung me out. Folding my arms around my knees, I tucked my head down. Maybe if I held onto myself tightly enough, my body would get the memo that the crisis, no … crises, were over.

The way John and Beverly were with each other—It was truly beautiful. That was love in motion. To be so devoted to someone that you'd weather the greatest challenge standing by their side, unwavering.

Knowing there were people like Derek Lindstrom who made it their mission in life to snuff out that kind of beauty—gutted me. He thrived on perpetuating pain and suffering, and somehow, I was going to have a taste of it.

How did I know this?

I just did.

What do I do about him?

Fuck knows.

Chapter
19

Brad

Heavy panting filled the car with the excitement consuming my passenger. She was fogging up the window with her smelly breath. The odd hair flew through the car with the force of the air blowing from the vents. It was a freakishly warm day for May. I stopped at a set of lights, and reached over to scratch her behind the ears. Leaning into my touch, she lifted a hind leg to help.

Just like me, she was a redhead. Well, we're both more 'dirty rust' rather than 'carrot'. I'd walked along all the cages at the RSPCA, feeling god awful that I couldn't take more than one home. When I spotted her with her rusty, mottled coat, and boundless energy, I knew she was the one. We were going to have to do something about her breath, though. The back of the ute was stocked with everything she might need. If Veronica spotted me before I had a chance to get out of the car, my surprise would be spoiled.

Pulling into the driveway, I quickly looked up at our bedroom window to make sure she wasn't looking. The windows were angled open. For a brief second, I thought I saw someone. But maybe it was just the heat and my nervous energy getting the better of me.

We headed up the stairs, leaving all the gear in the car except for the leash. I could let myself in, but I knocked because I wanted her to open the door. Ruby's claws clicked on the decking, as she shuffled at hearing the door unlock. The dog seemed to know what was about to happen.

Veronica's puzzled face peered through a crack in the door before she opened it wide.

"Did you lose your k—"

Ruby barked her hellos, doing little hops on her front legs, itching to jump all over her new friend. I knew just how she felt. Veronica's shoulders stiffened at the sharp noise, her eyes disbelieving as they honed in on our new housemate. My stomach clenched at her reaction. For a horrible second, I thought I'd fucked up, until she dropped to her knees and smothered the dog in affection. Releasing a long breath, I let the leash fall, and joined them on the deck.

"What's her ..." She looked between the dog's back legs. "... yeah, her name?"

"Ruby. Her owner died a month ago. The neighbour brought her into the shelter. She's fully house trained. Only three years old, though. Full of energy, so she'll love to run. Cattle, Kelpie cross. She's all yours if you want her."

Ruby sat with her tail sweeping the deck in a wide arc, making grunting, happy noises. Veronica's beatific face turned to mine, her smile stretched wide.

"Really?" The word came out as more of a squeak.

When I nodded, the smile faded, and her eyes filled with tears.

I relaxed back on my heels, watching the scene unfold. My heart grew to twice the size, and lodged in my throat. I'd made her so happy … she cried. I hadn't known her for all that long, but I was pretty sure Veronica didn't let tears fall from her eyes. Not as often as she should, or at all.

"I'm sorry you lost your owners," she whispered in Ruby's ear with all the compassion of someone who'd been there.

God, she pulled at my heart. I swallowed the lump in my throat, wishing Tish could be a part of this, too. Now *my* eyes clouded over.

"Can she come inside?"

"She's fully house trained, supposedly. Yes, she can. I don't think I like the idea of shutting her outside."

Veronica took the leash and showed Ruby through the house. The dog headed straight for the kitchen, sniffing around the bin, and then scooted into the lounge before jumping on the couch.

"Ruby, no," Veronica scolded.

The dog put her head down, and sat on the floor at her new master's feet. Okay, house trained, but overexcited.

They travelled back up the hall to the bedrooms, inspecting the grey one first. Ruby let out a big sneeze. The paint smell still lingered. I guess it was too strong for her sensitive nose. She pulled out of Veronica's grasp and barged across the hall to the other bedroom. She launched into a barking rant at the bed, and dipped her back legs to pee on the floor.

"Ruby!" The dog had the gall to look over her shoulder and raise her eyebrow, not bothering to stop her destruction of the carpet.

Veronica tugged on the leash. Casually, the dog trotted out of the room, through the house and out the back door, with Veronica in tow. I was left dumbfounded. I thought it was only boy dogs who marked their territory. Guess I'd better find an old towel that Ruby could claim as her own. I was sure as hell not using it after it had been soaked in dog pee.

Welcome to the family, Ruby.

———

Ronnie

Oh, my God. The smell of pee-soaked carpet was repulsive.

We shut the door yesterday after trying to clean the spot as best as we could. But the carpet was so badly stained, there was no saving it. Vile odours just about knocked me out when I opened the door this morning. Instead of going for our run, we shifted all the furniture out into the lounge and dining room before Brad had to leave for uni. I didn't have to start work until later, so I thought I'd ditch the carpet down the front steps.

With all the furniture gone, the carpet looked even worse. It was torn in one corner where the chest of drawers had been. That was going to make the job easier than I thought. Gripping the loose edge, I yanked hard to free the tiny nails that kept it in place. Fine fibres sprayed out, adding a dusty smell to the putrid animal stink. I folded down the carpet, rolling it towards me. Large patches of mould blackened the underside. I would've been breathing that in for months. *Gross.* The turbulence in my stomach intensified.

Five minutes. That was all it took because the backing fibres were so perished they tore as they were released from the sharp nails. Folding the roll in half, I tossed it out the door into the front yard, and went back for the foam underlay. The amount of dirt and dust that had collected on the wood flooring underneath was astounding. I didn't want to replace the carpet. Not if that was what happened over the years.

I dragged in gulps of air trying to cleanse my tarnished lungs as I searched the house for the broom, finally finding it tucked beside the fridge. It'd be quicker to sweep, than to drag out the ancient vacuum that didn't work well anyway. I got the job done quickly, and stuck my head out the window to breathe in some fresh air. There, outside the window, I looked down on Letitia's long chestnut hair as she rested on the bench by the front door.

"What're you doing?"

She didn't move an inch. "Waiting." The flat tone in her voice set off alarm bells.

"For what?" I asked with caution.

"You'll see." Her unmoving form appeared to fade as I gazed at the crown of her head, before she turned to wisps of smoke that blew away to nothingness.

I whirled around, scanning the room from ceiling to floor. What was she talking about? I saw nothing but the pile of dirt I'd just swept into the corner. *I'm missing something.* I could feel the anxiety scratching at my lungs, making my breathlessness worse as I sought out the dustpan and brush.

I ran back to the room. I needed to know what she meant, but I had to leave for work soon. After scooping the dirt into the pan, I noticed that the floor boards had been cut, leaving a small, rectangular section loose. Someone had drilled a hole near one side, and threaded a thin piece of rope through, with a knot poking out as a handle.

I felt my heart pound as I put the brush and pan aside and reached for the knot. My arm flexed and my hand clenched tight with the effort required to budge the piece of wood. Gritty sand crunched as it fell into the join. The door gave way with a pop, revealing a small compartment under the floor.

Oh no. This was where Tish hid her secrets. I was sure of it.

Inside, I found her bright, yellow, daisy-covered diary. Why else would you hide your diary if it didn't contain your secrets?

Taking the treasure out, I returned the door in place and stashed the book in the back of my sock drawer, for now. I wasn't opening that book. I had to talk to her first. But I suddenly felt like I wanted to be violently ill. My weary bones sank into the couch, and I let my head drop between my knees for a minute.

My hands gripped my phone hard as I shot off a quick email to work, to let them know I'd be a bit late.

"Letitia," I hissed as I typed.

"Yeah," her small voice was alarmingly close and I dove in the opposite direction, rolling off the couch onto my old mattress on the floor.

Growling as I crawled back on the couch, I pinned her with a hard stare. "You set me up, didn't you?" Her doleful eyes refused to look at me. "What's in that diary that you didn't want anyone to read?"

"I want you to read it."

"No. Tell me what's in it."

Her hair swayed as she shook her head. "The truth. Read it, and then give it to Lee. Don't leave him. Stay with him. He needs you."

Her form evaporated as my distress escalated. "Gah."

She'd put me in this position where I had to be the bearer of shitty news, and probably crush the heart of the man I love, all over again. My legs jiggled up and down in distress. My clenched fists bounced on my knees as I tried to cool the swirl of angered panic I was feeling.

Ruby trotted in and curled her body next to me. She was intuitive, this dog. She knew when I needed her, already so in tune with me it was like she was made for me. I unclenched my fists so I could stroke her coarse fur. I couldn't even be mad that she was on the couch because if she wasn't, I'd be balled up on the floor crying at the unfairness and injustice of it all. I finally found someone who loved me and whom I adored, and I had to destroy him and make him hate me.

Yay for me.

Chapter
20

Ronnie

"You're playing a very fucking dangerous game?" Flick ground the words into my ear, as she drilled a finger into my shoulder blade. Her sharp nail actually hurt.

My quick temper surged. After a really shitty start to the day, I escaped my desk to have a break, and some privacy under my favourite Morton Bay Fig.

"Get your finger off me, and hello to you, too—" Shock seized my tongue when I turned to catch a glimpse of the woman formally known as Felicity Stevens. "What has happened to you?"

She looked gaunt; the weight had fallen off. There wasn't a speck of make up on her face, and her hair was in a ponytail. I'd never seen her hair tied back like that. She always said the style was too domestic. And, she was wearing a T-shirt. I didn't know she even owned one.

She scowled, ignoring my question. "Why were you there?"

Shit! She saw me, too.

"I was checking out the sights of Brisbane. There's no law against looking at private buildings from the footpath is there?"

"Oh, my God! If you think the law has anything to do with this, then you're more naive than I thought. Haven't you done your research? Some librarian you are. Derek is not a man you'd want to mess with. He's the lawyer that gets the bad guys off because he knows people. He knows how to manipulate the system. He's untouchable. If you go after him, you'll pay. Your friends will pay. Your family will pay." She dragged in a jagged breath, blinking rapidly to clear suddenly glassy eyes. "I warned you to stay away. Don't you ever fucking listen?" Her voice cracked on the last word as she slumped her body on the bench beside me, eyes fixed morosely on the garden.

"I kicked you out so he couldn't find you. Now he's seen you with that guy. He'll be looking for him, too."

No. No, no, no, no. "What the hell does he want with me?"

"He wants what he always wants. To control. To manipulate. To taint the light." My sandwich threatened to come back up as her warning sank in.

"If he's such a threat, why aren't the police involved?"

Her face said, *are you stupid?* "He's untouchable. He knows people," she repeated it slowly like I was a dumb arse. "It's probably too late now. Unless you leave the country. You're going to have to get to him before he gets you, and I don't see how that's going to happen. If there was a way, I'd have done it … I'm sorry. You were in the wrong place at the wrong time. Me? I was dragged into this mess."

"What mess are you talking about?"

I watched her fingers as she opened and closed her palms, alternately hiding and exposing their twisted forms. The wait for her answer stretched uncomfortably, making me squirm on the bench.

A pocket of cold encapsulated the seat, spreading goose bumps over my skin. Twisting my neck to the left, my gaze found the source. She was here. The ghost from the house, eavesdropping on our conversation, and boring holes into my face.

"You're next," she whispered.

The statement was so blunt, and yet it stabbed me like a scalpel. Her eyes swung from me to Flick, agony contained in their misty depths as she stared at Felicity. I wasn't sure if she meant me, or Flick, or both of us. Looking at her bruised neck and torn dress, recalling my nightmare and how she died, my breath hitched in my chest. I was under siege from both sides, not knowing where to centre my attention.

"The house is the office of Lindstrom and Associates ..." Flick's voice broke the moment, and the woman drifted back into the ether. "... but it's also the base for an exclusive, secret club. There's a hidden door in the back of the butler's pantry that takes you down a staircase, and another entrance from the building next door through an underground tunnel. They're not aware that I knew about that one, but I followed my father one day. I think he owns that building."

"Your father?"

Her throat moved as she swallowed, closing her eyes. "Yeah. He was there that day you saw me."

"Does he have trouble with his legs?"

"Yes. You remember." Her hands continued their action loop. "I see you there. In the basement."

What did she mean, she *sees* me there?

"I've struggled to tell you about this, because I couldn't be sure if having this information is what sends you there. But, I decided that you had to know ... so you can be prepared, if ever ... But, Ronnie ..." She dragged her eyes away from her hands and fixed them on mine. "... stay away. He will torture and kill you." She rose to her feet and merged with the crowd, out of sight.

The warning echoed in the chasm of my brain. Everything else emptied, but for those few words. *He will torture and kill you.* Everybody seemed to speed up, buzzing about their day while I remained frozen in horror. Images flicked through my mind, Lindstrom's face, Felicity's, Brad's, Tish's, Ruby's, and my granny's—so much like my own. Each image deteriorated as it passed, until their flesh looked like it dripped from their skulls. But not Lindstrom's. His expression morphed from a smile to a sneer, before it turned red and twisted with malevolence.

"Veronica." A warm hand broke through the ice to rest on my knee, shaking gently. As my vision returned, I saw Brad's frightened face, his eyes wide, mouth turned down at the corners. "Hey, you've gotta stop tripping off on me. I don't like it when you go somewhere I can't follow."

Oh, Jesus. Like his sister did? And his parents, and now possibly me too. *Fuck.* I was so worried about him hurting me, but he was the one who was going to be hurt. Again. Because of me. I didn't know what to do anymore.

For the second time in as many days, I let the tears pour out. All of my grief, my despair, my utter shock and panic—it all forced its way out of my tear ducts, and I let it. Everything seemed inevitable. For once, I didn't want to run. I wanted to burrow into him.

The bench bounced when Brad dove onto the seat beside me. He scooped me onto his lap and enveloped me in his strong frame. His smell engulfed me as I turned my face into his shoulder, where I continued to pour out my dismay for who knew how long. This man, as strong and steady as the buildings he'll design, cared for me. He calmed the storms that raged inside me, patiently waiting until they subsided.

He patted my knee. "Can I take you home? You shouldn't be here. I don't really give a shit if anyone will miss you. I'm not leaving you here like this."

Oh, God. I was so relieved that he was here, taking control.

Rising to his feet, he kept one arm around my middle, as he helped me stand on shaky legs. My thoughts were distracted throughout the trip home. Finally, I was safe in bed, tucked up, with Ruby lying on the floor watching over me. Brad hadn't even asked why I flipped out. Had I done it so many times he had accepted it as part of who I was? *Bloody hell.* I was a mess. How could he love me? And he didn't even know the worst of it.

My eyelids drooped from exhaustion. I emptied my mind and focused on the soothing rhythm of Ruby's breathing. Somehow, it helped block out the demonic face in my future. I tumbled into sleep.

Chapter
21

Brad

"Shit."

Hissing the four-letter word at the drop sheet as it caught the foot of the ladder didn't make me feel any better. I'd rather throw the ladder out the window, but that wouldn't help anyone, least of all my sleeping Gazelle across the hall. I didn't know what to do for her, but she looked wrung out. So, I figured the bed was the only way to go. I paced the house, unable to work on my design project, unable to eat. Definitely too twitchy to lie quietly beside her. Ruby was the obvious choice for that job. I may have saved the dog's life, but she was saving ours, right back.

I vented my frustration and worry on the walls, trying to paint as quietly as I could so as not to wake my Gazelle.

My hand ached, the muscles in my forearms strained as I controlled each stroke. If I lost my restraint, I'd be likely to snap the damn roller.

Veronica picked a lemon-yellow colour for this room. It amazed me how she was so instinctive. Yellow was a favourite colour I shared with her. She'd badgered me to paint this room yellow. All too late, the job was getting done. I heard a crack as disgust tightened my grip on the cheap plastic handle.

Recalling the look on Veronica's face when I found her under the tree, I started worrying again. I was losing her. I understood nothing, but that. I was losing her, and I'd only had her for a split second.

Deliberately slowing my movements, I placed the roller back in the tray before I broke the handle. Stretching up onto my toes, I lifted my arms above my head and spread my fingers wide, every muscle going taut. The rubber band just before it snapped.

"Hey."

Her voice came out of nowhere, and my hands slapped down on my thighs as I relaxed. I whipped my head to the doorway. She was framed in the entrance. The light from the room threw shadows against her cheekbones and eyebrows, the darkened hallway at her back. Cuddled in a knitted jumper with her hair loose and slippers on her feet, she took away my need for oxygen and replaced it with *her*.

I felt the tension leave my muscles and fill the room, as she tried on a smile and failed.

"How are you feeling?"

"Better. Thank you for finding me and bringing me home."

Her eyes were huge in her face, her cheek caved on one side where she was probably digging her teeth in. She looked so fragile, I was afraid if I asked one question she'd crumble to pieces. But, I needed answers. I needed to know what was wrong so I could fix it. That was what I did, I fixed things. I was a carpenter for fuck's sake. I'd been using tools my whole life, and it killed me that I didn't have the right tools for this … whatever was wrong.

I kept my voice low and my body relaxed so I didn't frighten her away.

"I've got to be honest and tell you that I'm worried, Gazelle. Are you going to tell me anything? I want to help you, so badly, but I'm in the dark here."

Her eyes sank to the floor, and she pulled the jumper tighter around herself.

"Have you spoken to anyone about what's got you so … freaked out? Your granny?"

She shook her head no. With a heavy sigh, I brought my hands up to scrub my face, probably smearing paint, but who gave a fuck. My pleading eyes found hers again.

"Please … let me in."

———

Ronnie

Before I could respond, my ringtone sounded. Ruby scrambled to her feet and followed me to my handbag. Pulling my phone out, I frowned when I didn't recognise the number.

"Hello?" The word drew slowly from my mouth.

"Is this Veronica Williams?" The authoritarian voice commanded my attention.

"Uh, yes. Who's th—"

"My name is Sister Faulkner. I run the Accident and Emergency at the Princess Alexandra Hospital. Your grandmother was brought in over an hour ago after suffering a myocardial infarction, sorry, a heart attack. We've stabilised her for now. The doctor will be able to give you more details when you get here. Are you able to come straight away?"

Without answering her, I handed the phone to Brad.

"Granny's had a heart attack." I didn't know how I squeezed the words through my narrowed throat.

Over an hour ago. Why didn't the home call me sooner?

Stormy grey eyes roamed my face in concern. "We're on our way," he told her before hanging up. "Which hospital?" His arms banded tightly around me.

"The P.A." It came out as a whisper, my voice had deserted me completely.

He nodded and whisked me out to the car.

I felt like I was floating behind him, like all my cells had separated, leaving gaping holes filled with polluted air. This was too much. Too much, toooomuuuuch. The need to scream overpowered me. I screamed it into my elbow, the pillowy wool absorbing little of the shriek of pain.

Brad laid a firm hand on my leg. "We'll be there soon. Just hang on."

His foot hit the accelerator, revving the engine as we sped down Fairfield Road. The car was too slow. I needed light speed. I needed to be with her over an hour ago.

I didn't wait for him to turn off the engine before I leaped out and ran to the Emergency entrance.

"Amelia Williams? Sister Faulkner called," I barked at the triage nurse.

She looked unimpressed under her furrowed brow, but I didn't care. She dealt with this all the time. The life and death of others must be so normal and tedious for her. My behaviour wasn't pretty, but I was prepared to get ugly if she didn't get me to my grandmother, now.

"Through those doors. Wait for the buzzer. You'll find Sister Faulkner at the nurse's station."

"Thanks," I yelled behind me before feeling a large hand rest on my lower back.

My rock. He was still with me smoothing the edge off my mania.

Entering the A and E was like entering a beehive. Bodies in scrubs raced here and there, saving lives. Commotion played out behind flimsy curtains. I heard raised voices throwing out instructions in one corner.

Someone yelled, "CLEAR!" before the zap of a defibrillator charged the air.

"Sister Faulkner?"

I swept my eyes over the three possible candidates hovering around the desk. A tiny woman with short, spiky, rose-red hair peered at me over frameless glasses.

"Miss Williams?"

"Yes. My gran—"

She nodded, and held up a hand to silence me. "Sister Faulkner is with your granny now. They're doing all they can—"

"Where is she?" I was in no mood for placation. My eyes narrowed dangerously, fists clenching at my sides. Her gaze flitted to the corner with all the ruckus. *No.*

"It's probably best if you wait ..." I darted for the curtain in the corner. "... in the waiting room. Miss Williams!"

Strong arms banded around my middle as Brad hauled me back against his body. My hands held on tight to his arms as I fought the reality playing in front of me. Words like ECG, epinephrine and cardiac enzymes were flung into the air like arrows aimed straight for my heart. I watched the bottom of the curtain as feet gathered around the trolley, shuffling positions, doing their best to save the woman who'd raised me. The only mother who'd loved me. The incessant high pitched alarm announced to the room that all that effort was in vain. There was a finality to that sound.

Behind the curtain, all went quiet. The noise of the battle waging in the room ceased. The only sound left was the silence of my grandmother's life. She was gone.

No.

A single plea. A hopeless prayer. The last thing I thought of before my legs gave way and I surrendered to the pain.

Chapter
22

Ronnie

Five days.

I'd been staring at these yellow walls for five. Whole. Days. Hating them for their cheery disposition when all I wanted to see was black.

The door rattled in its frame as Ruby's body moved against it. I heard her snuffles under the door, catching my scent. I knew she'd been watching me, waiting for me to give her some love. Brad had finally left me alone, but only because he couldn't skip out on his exams. He's been hovering over me, trying to prod me awake with food, and plying me with his affections … hoping for something in return. I wished I could, but I had nothing to give. I was empty. My grief sapped everything I had left. The molecules in my body crumbled under its weight. I may fade away and no one would even know where to find me.

Ronnie.

Was that someone calling me? "Mm." The automated response vibrated my throat.

Ronnieeeee.

My face and body felt slack, vacant of energy, but for the vibration in my voice box.

"Mm hmm."

"Veronica."

Zap! My grandmother's command fired through my system, shocking me back to life. A violent jerk tossed me onto the floor.

Ruby's frantic bark shot under the door, her claws scratching at the wood.

"I'm okay, Ruby."

"Oh, Thank goodness. You had me worried." Stretching my neck back from my position on the floor, I got an upside down view of Granny and Tish eyeing me with concern.

I scrambled up, full of excitement, ready to grip Granny in a big hug, and deflated again with the understanding that it'd never be possible.

Tish turned to Granny. "She's been catatonic. Lee's a mess. The dog is the most human thing left in this house."

Granny's eyebrows jumped. "Haven't I taught you anything? You have people who love you and need you. And there are forces in motion that you need to prepare for. That's why I've come to you now. You don't have time to mope around mourning an old lady. It was my time. I'm fine."

No nonsense. Straight to the point. I missed her so much. I was so grateful then for my ability to see the dead. It was a small consolation, but it was a comfort that those who didn't have my curse would never know. It was like a painkiller injected straight into my heart.

"Do you remember finding the diary?" Letitia's intense gaze targeted me.

My eyes bugged out. *I totally forgot!* "Yes."

Granny's shoulders shook as she tittered at my sudden animation, cutting into the serious moment before urgency descended again.

"Read it, child. Take it to him. He needs to know what happened to her. You need to fix this. Don't let that diary fall into the wrong hands."

Granny's wise, dark eyes looked younger. She appeared more vibrant, free of the physical bindings of an ageing body. I relaxed a little. She really was okay. Her soul was free.

"Yes, I'm fine. Now focus on the diary. There isn't any time."

Where did I put it?

Tish pointed to the chest of drawers in the corner, and I dashed for it, banging my knuckles as I grappled for the handle.

"Shit." I pulled out the drawer with one hand, while shaking the pain from the other. A corner of bright yellow poked out from under my clothes.

"Terrible, potty mouth," Granny tutted in disgust.

"Sorry, Granny."

Ruby's scratching and high pitched whines frantically worked at the barrier between us, and I cringed at how mean I'd been by shutting her out. Tish opened the door.

"Ruby!" Launching herself at me, the diary clattered to the floor as I caught the fur ball in my arms. "I'm so sorry, baby. I'm so sorry. I'm back, now." I put her on the bed with me—needing her close, and not caring if the sheets got dirty—and leaned down to pick up the book. The bright daisy pattern, a ruse for unsuspecting readers.

A few photos fell out, fanning across the floor. One in particular drew my attention as I flipped through them. It was a selfie of Letitia with Twit behind her, looking away. He didn't seem aware that the photo was being taken, but she had a big smile on her face. *What the fuck? What did Andrea say his name was? Max. No, Matt.*

Ready to shoot questions at Tish, I looked up to find that they'd both disappeared. Ruby cocked her head at me as I grumbled. I scratched her behind the ears and looked at the next one.

The law building provided a backdrop to a meeting between Twit and Lindstrom, mid stroll with their heads angled towards each other. Even though it had been taken at a distance, it was clear who they were. Twit was a law student, so I wasn't surprised to find him talking to a law professor. I tossed the picture aside, and grabbed the next one. Twit and Lindstrom again, exiting a shabby, red brick building through a nondescript door. It looked like they were in an alley, judging by the industrial bin behind them. I didn't recognise it.

The last photo made my jaw go slack. It was Letitia … and Flick. With their arms around each other, smiling. That little manipulator. She knew Flick all along. They were friends. The muscles in my jaw strained from clenching. Dropping the photo into a pile, I rubbed my palm down my face and picked up the diary.

First day of uni. Engineering. Was I insane when I chose this degree? The facilities here are incredible. I'm a little intimidated by the male to female ratio in my lectures. Where are all the women?

I did meet Felicity Stevens, though. I wanted to write her name down before I forgot it, so there it is. She let me follow her to Student Services and we grabbed a coffee after getting our IDs. She's cool. Anyway. I'm gonna crash. Too tired.

All right, so that was how they met. I flicked through her entries, until I found an entry about Twit.

Holy Moses! I met a man. He's a blond. It's my weakness, what can I say? Matt Lindstrom, lawyer in the making. Could it be true love? Watch this space …

Lindstrom?

Matt's acting moody. He snapped at me for hugging him in public and apologised later with flowers. He told me he loved me, but something didn't feel right. He's probably just stressed with his workload. Felicity keeps telling me I should dump him and run. But I love him.

Bad vibes turned my stomach to stone. I wanted to skip to the end, but I needed to find out how she got there.

Matt introduced me to his father, Derek. He's a lecturer at the uni. The guy is a creep. He works with Felicity's dad in this amazing, old house. Felicity was there, too. She showed me around while Matt talked to his dad about something. She didn't seem happy to see me and actually pushed me towards the door. What is her deal?

My hand trembled as I turned to the next page.

I want to peel off my skin and scrub out my insides. Matt took me to the basement where his father and a group of men were waiting for me.

I couldn't stand this. I had to skip ahead. Several weeks of blank space screamed at me before the black scribble reappeared.

I'm so sorry, Lee Lee. They took everything from me. I'm tainted. They threatened to hurt you if I said anything. I can't go to the police because Matt's uncle is a senior cop. Any chance of a future has vanished. I'm sorry … but I can't look in the mirror anymore. I have to leave you. Please … look after yourself.

Love you lots.

Tish

I felt cold all over. She took her own life. Those vile leeches sucked the will to live out of her. *Oh, fuck.* This is going to destroy Brad.

———

Brad

I found her watching the telly when I got home. I completely bombed the exam, but I was so happy to see her up and about that a smile cracked my face open. It felt weird but nice on my face. Like when you shave after having a beard for so long.

"Hey gorgeous." I leaned down to plant a kiss on her lips, and got a buzz when she stretched her neck to kiss me back.

She came back to me. Thank fuck.

"How was the exam?" She seemed twitchy. Chewing on her cheek as she jiggled her knees.

"It sucked." I shrugged. "How are you feeling?" I was distracted by Ruby coming to greet me, rubbing her nose on my knee, but my hearing was still tuned to Veronica. Soft sniffles wrenched my full attention back to her wet face.

"I'm so sorry."

"What for?" I reached my arm out, but she pushed me back.

"For everything. For losing it. For not being totally honest with you. For doing what I'm about to do." Panic choked its grip on my neck. "I'm going to tell you everything. Please bear with me."

Managing a nod, I sat still as she poured out the story of meeting my sister and the strange request to help me paint, which eventually led Veronica to Tish's diary. The unbelievable tale twisted my brain into a giant knot, until I felt like it was on the verge of an explosion.

I felt the weight of the diary as she placed it in my lap. Looking at it, I knew it could only be Tish's. Bright yellow and covered in daisies. I'd never seen it before.

"You've read this?"

She nodded in slow motion, mouth turned down, tears streaming down her cheeks.

The spine crackled as I lifted the cover, it easily fell to the last page of writing.

Sorry …

They took everything …

Tainted …

Vanished …

Have to leave …

Please … look after yourself.

"Please leave."

"Brad."

She reached for my arm, but I yanked it away violently before she could touch me.

"No, Veronica! Leave me alone!"

She jumped up and fled, with Ruby not far behind. The echo of the door slamming beat against my temples.

As I read, my grip on the book was crushing, just like the words spilled in ink.

Not an accident.

I could've saved her, and I didn't.

Heaving the contents of my gut into the toilet wasn't going to rid me of the sickening images running through my head, but I couldn't stop myself. I wanted to keep spewing it all up until I was empty, and then I wanted to find all those motherfuckers and slit their throats just like they'd done to mine.

She wrote down every detail. Everything she could remember about that horrifying act of evil. Everything she knew about those men. Her boyfriend and his father. Fucking dead men, I didn't care who they knew. But, I understood why she hadn't gone to the cops. And why she'd hidden the diary. It contained a lot of damning information.

The sound of my heaves bounced off the tile walls, smacking against my body to force more burning vomit out of it. Clenching my eyes shut, I turned to the sink to splash my face with cold water. It gushed down the drain as I gripped the bench, seething. It wasn't enough. I needed a shower. The tap squealed as I used too much force to wrench it shut. In the mirror, my eyes were blood shot, and surrounded by small, red spots where I'd broken the capillaries. Those fuckers were going to have black eyes and their balls shoved down their throats when I'd finished with them. I twisted the heels of my hands into my eye sockets. *Fuck me.* I had to get a grip.

The shower was scorching hot, pummelling my skin. The heat was supposed to loosen the tension, but I was stretched too tight. Time warped until the space inside my head, fuelled by anger and hurt, remembered an early morning bike ride down Mount Glorious. When I'd considered following my sister's fate. But I couldn't give in to desperation and lose control again … because of Veronica. She'd filled a space inside me that nothing could touch before. I had to find her, and apologise for going all ogre on her.

So many things made sense now. The nightmares. The way she'd freaked out in the city. My train of thought froze. That didn't make sense. I slapped my palm against the wall, spraying water everywhere. How did she know about that house if she only just found the diary? She hadn't told me everything. *Shit.* I ripped the curtain open, and choked on my own spit when I saw the mirror. Scrawled into the film of steam, in my sister's handwriting, was the message, 'They have her.'

My gut plummeted with the thought of losing her. Fear dried my mouth as I skidded through the house, throwing on clothes. The drive seemed to drag on for eternity. I made two calls on the way there.

Sometimes you need a little insurance.

———

Ronnie

I had nowhere to go.

Out of habit, I aimed the car towards St Lucia. Blindly driving through the quiet streets until I found where I used to run along the river. The sun hung low behind the thick trees, throwing long shadows over the river, and dropping the temperature to just chilly.

Ruby followed me along the path as I ran in my bare feet, jarring my ankles. The clicking of claws on concrete, and the friction of denim on denim added a soundtrack in the absence of music.

He hated me. I was the messenger who was damned to be shot every time. Who wanted to hear news like that? Who would believe a story like that? Now he knew I was a freak, he couldn't stand to be near me at all. I knew it would happen. A bitter laugh pinched my throat and I stopped running. It wasn't helping.

I lowered my body to sit cross-legged on the path, and Ruby plonked herself in my lap, panting heavily. She twisted her neck to lick my cheek, and we sat watching the flow of the water and the movement of breeze through the trees. The scene around us was totally peaceful, while inside I was fracturing. I ran my hand along Ruby's fur, drawing some solace from her presence and her innocence, and closed my eyes.

Concentrate on your breath. Clear your thoughts. Call on your guides to protect you, and let the messages come. Granny's lessons came back to me. I followed the steps, holding onto Ruby to keep me grounded, as my mind drifted to another place.

The dark room surrounded me. There was no source of light, other than a dull lamp in one corner beside a wall of shelves.

Concentrate on your breath. "Show me more."

The room appeared to spin, and I saw where the stairs descended into the room. A table sat in the centre. My arms tightened around Ruby and my breath quickened at the image in my mind. Felicity lay on the table, arms and legs tied to each corner with coarse ropes. She was half naked. Bloody welts covered her bare, motionless legs. I watched closely for the rise and fall of her chest, holding my own breath until I saw a slight movement.

My body slumped as the vision faded. *Whoa.* The darkening sky spun overhead as I slowly came back to awareness *How long was I out?* Ruby sniffed around my face, checking that I was okay. I was so far from okay. *Felicity's in trouble!*

"Let's go, Ruby." I jumped up, stumbling a few steps before dashing back to the car with the dog barking at my heels.

I needed a plan. My mind raced through all the information I'd learned from Tish and Felicity, as my fingers gripped the steering wheel. I couldn't break into the house. They would have tight security for sure.

The alleyway. I parked down a side street, debating whether or not to take the dog. I loathed the idea of leaving her here, but I didn't want to put her in danger either. And she'd give away our position if we needed to hide.

She also had sharp teeth. She's coming. I needed all the help I could get.

The sun had just dipped below the horizon, gracing the sky with a layer of orange under blue. It'd be dark in there.

The ropes. I searched through the glove box for my pocket knife, and slipped it in my back pocket, putting my phone in the other. That was all I had. It was no good calling the police. I couldn't exactly report having a vision. We were on our own.

I aimed for the alleyway. Ruby stuck to my side like glue. She was quiet, as if she knew we were heading into danger. I found the door, but it was locked with a padlock. *Damn.* The tension was so high I could hear the pulse in my temples.

I scanned the brick wall, looking for another entrance. There was nothing that I could see. We headed over to the industrial bin and checked behind it. *Bingo!* A broken window that'd been boarded over. Using my pocket knife, I jimmied it open, cringing when it clattered to the ground.

I switched on the torch app on my phone and shone it through the opening. The window belonged to a small, empty storeroom. It looked all clear. I backed out, putting my phone away, and held out my arms to Ruby. I released a squeak when she bypassed me and jumped straight through the window, waiting quietly inside for me to follow. I leaned down to give her a pat after dropping through after her. What a dog. She was incredible. I loved her to bits. If she got hurt in any way tonight, I'd never forgive myself.

I pulled out my phone again, and inspected the inside of the larger room. It was one big empty room with brick pillars staggered throughout. Shining the light towards the door, I saw a track worn into the dirt covered floor. We followed it to a staircase leading underground. As we descended, goose bumps pricked the skin of my arms and neck. I felt as though we were descending into the belly of the beast.

Isn't that exactly what we're doing?

Quietly, we moved through a dank tunnel lined with brick. It ended in a wooden panel. I couldn't see a handle anywhere. I started to fret, smoothing my hands over the surface to feel for a groove, a button, anything. It was one solid piece of wood.

Dropping my hands, I chewed on the flesh of my cheek and closed my eyes. The vision of the room came back to me, and I saw the wall of book shelves. My pulse jumped, my muscles tightened as I heaved all my weight onto the smooth surface. It budged easily, as if it was used to it.

Slipping into the basement was like slipping into my vision in 3D. I raced to the table, whipping out the pocketknife, and got to work on the ropes.

"Felicity," I whispered, feeling for a pulse in her wrist. Its thready beat put me further on edge, and I sawed harder at the rope. Ruby stood guard in the doorway, ears straight up on alert.

Felicity was unconscious. I'd have to carry her out of here. She'd wasted away to almost nothing. I wasn't worried about getting her up the stairs, it was getting her through the window that'd be a problem. Maybe we could find another exit.

The last rope gave way as Ruby began a vicious growl. I spun away from the table, holding out the knife towards the staircase that led into the house as a pair of black slacks came into view. Adrenaline rushed into my system. *Here we go.* I commanded my hand to grip the knife harder. If I lost that, I was fucked.

"Ronnie. Imagine my surprise when I saw you on the security monitor, ruining all our good work." Lindstrom rounded the table, stopping before he got too close to the dog.

He watched me with interest, as I backed up towards Ruby, putting myself in front of her.

"You value the dog's life more than your own? And you've come to save a woman who despises you. With a dog as a companion, and a pocketknife. I thought you were a smart woman, Ronnie." He pronounced each word with chilling precision.

My shoulders jerked when he slapped Felicity across the face. A moan escaped as her head snapped to the side.

"I was annoyed that Felicity wouldn't bring you to me. And then Matthew informed me that I couldn't use him as bait. I couldn't begin to tell you how furious that made me. Stupid boy. It made you all the more attractive, of course. The grand prize."

He casually placed his hands in his pockets, inspecting the frayed ropes now tangled on the concrete floor, tutting as he kicked one pile.

"Never mind. We have plenty more." He inclined his head towards the shelves and I followed his gaze.

Stupid move. He lunged for me, wrapping his firm grip around my wrists so I'd drop the knife, and kicked Ruby aside when she went for him. She hit the wall with a sickening thud, and slumped to the floor. I let out a scream of agony. She was all I had left. I fought against him as he pulled me closer, watching Ruby for a sign of life. She didn't move an inch. My blood boiled, I turned manic eyes on him as the adrenaline surged higher in my system. With every ounce of anger and hatred I felt for this beast, I threw my head forward, smashing my skull into his forehead. His hands slipped off as he staggered back.

I heard shuffling steps behind me, and spun around to find Felicity's father entering the room. I shook off the knock to the head and charged at him in offensive mode. His eyes grew wide, and his jaw dropped, caught off guard. At least he had the sense to look scared. That was his daughter, unconscious on a fucking table, and he was doing nothing to save her. Baring my teeth, I jumped and twisted, kicking my leg to the side, aiming directly for his weak spot. His legs. My foot connected with a crunch and he crumbled with a shout, like the dirt that he was.

My elbows were wrenched behind me, shooting pain through my shoulders and spine. I snapped my teeth shut to contain the cry. Lindstrom didn't deserve the satisfaction. Before I could catch my breath, he banded his arms around me and dragged me backwards towards the table. I pushed with my feet and slammed back against him, crashing into the table, and dragging it across the floor with a loud scrape.

Lindstrom's grunt whooshed past my ear and his arms went lax, freeing me. I jumped forward and turned to find

Felicity holding up the bloody pocketknife. At her feet, blood gushed from the back of the beast's neck as he lay in a lifeless heap on the floor.

She was so pale, swaying on her feet with a haunted look in her eyes. The knife clattered to the floor as she relaxed her hand and dropped it to her side.

"Can you get up the stairs on your own?" I asked as I rushed over to Ruby, gathering her in my arms. Relief flooded my veins, but we weren't out of danger yet. When I turned back, Felicity was already at the stairs, struggling to put on her skirt.

"You broke my legs, you bitch!" Mr. Stevens cursed across the room, grasping his legs, his face twisted in pain.

Felicity responded for me. "I hope it fucking hurts. She just helped me kill the man who's been blackmailing you. You should be thankful. Doesn't matter now, anyway. Everyone is going to know what you did." She sidestepped her father as he released a roar of frustration, and slowly climbed each step, one at a time, with a hand on my shoulder.

"Are there any others in the house?"

"Don't know," she croaked.

The appearance of a pair of legs in jeans as we reached the top of the stairs answered my question. I followed them up, and my heart sank at Twit's face scowling down at us.

"Ladies. You've made a mess. Can't say I'm sad to see him dead, though. You've done me a favour. Time to collect your reward."

His fist snapped out, catching Felicity on the temple, and she flopped backwards like a ragdoll down the stairs. The sickening crack of bone made my hair stand on end. I didn't move or look back, not willing to take my eyes off him. I'd learned my lesson from his father.

Ruby's chest pumped at a faster pace, like she knew the danger wasn't over despite her unconscious state. I held her tighter, pleading for her to come out of this alive and well. I needed to think, damn it. He had me blocked. I could try running down the stairs, but with my extra baggage, he'd have me in an instant.

Mr. Stevens' moans and groans echoed up the stairs. *Limp dick.* His daughter had been through worse and she hadn't complained. I couldn't hear or feel any movement from Felicity. My head conjured the worst kind of fate for her, but I couldn't turn and check for myself.

Twit bared his teeth in a smile I'd seen only moments before on his father's face. The moisture left my mouth like the receding tide before a tsunami.

He hooked his hand around the back of my neck, grabbing a handful of my hair. "I've been waiting for this moment for a long time, *bitch*. You should be more careful with that mouth of yours. I know exactly how it should be used."

I grunted as he tugged me forward so I tripped up the steps, taking the skin off my shins on the edge of the steps when I landed on my knees. I managed to place Ruby on the ground, as far away from his foot as I could, before my face was yanked in front of his crotch. I slammed my eyes shut and fought the urge to vomit.

The fucker was hard.

"I'm going to have so much fun with you." He sang the words like I was his favourite play toy.

I pulled back on my hair to reverse the tension, feeling like he was going to tear off my scalp. Tears leaked down my cheeks. I couldn't stop them. I knew this was how my life would end. Used for the amusement of a sick fuck and then discarded somewhere like my life had zero worth.

With my hair locked in his grip, he dragged me across the floor to another room, switching on the light to reveal a bedroom. From my position on the floor, I saw ropes dangling from the corners of the iron bed frame. Suspicious stains on the carpet didn't bode well. The room's musty, metallic smell seeped into my nostrils, coaxing a heave from my stomach.

"Bitch. I should make you lick that up, but I want you to lick me with a clean tongue."

He dragged me further into the room and opened another door. The bathroom.

Oh, shit. What is he going to do, drown me?

He pushed me up against the bath. Panic had my tears pouring out until I realised I preferred this ending than being tied to the bed and tortured. I've heard drowning was supposed to be peaceful. I'd get to see Granny again. Soon. That would be okay. I sniffed and wiped my face. Twit let me go so he could lock the door. I don't know why he bothered. Every bathroom door can be unlocked from the inside, and this one didn't look any different.

I fixed my attention on his back, watching him grab the liquid soap from the bench. He spun around, crouched in front of me and reefed my jaw open, squishing my cheeks in to keep my mouth open as he poured the soap in.

I'd never be able to smell lavender again.

"You've got a dirty mouth, bitch. We're gonna fix that."

I sealed the back of my throat with my tongue, but he threw the bottle down and gripped me around my neck with his other hand so I had to gag. Soap sprayed all over his face and neck, and he retaliated by cutting off my air flow and landing a heavy fist to my cheek. White spots peppered my vision.

"Fuck!" Twit let me go, standing over the sink to rinse out his eyes.

I spotted a can of deodorant on the bench and snatched it up while he was occupied, hiding it by my side as I coughed and spluttered. This was my chance to get away. And if I didn't succeed, I was going to nail that fucker in the eyes so he'd be blinded for life. He deserved to live in darkness.

He turned back to me, putting his face in front of mine so I could see his bloodshot eyes behind blinking lids. I raised the can and pushed down the nozzle as hard as I could, unleashing a chemical cloud offensive.

He screamed like a pig and stumbled backwards, hitting his back on the wall beside the door. Lurching forward, I pulled on the handle and sure enough, it gave way, setting me free. So I thought, until my head was yanked back, putting my neck at a painful angle. He'd gotten hold of the end of my hair. I cursed its long length.

Something rough knocked into my leg and my head snapped forward, suddenly released of its tether. A feral snarl ripped through the room from behind me, drawing out another scream from Twit.

"Fuck off. Dumb mutt. Aargh!"

I turned, unable to believe what I saw. My sweet Ruby was channelling her inner wolf and had her teeth locked onto Twit's leg, yanking and pulling until blood seeped through his jeans and he fell back on his butt. Every hair on my body stood on end, as if the room was as cold as an ice cave.

Ruby. She's okay. And she's saving my life, again.

Kicking out his leg, Twit pulled on her collar, but she switched her grip and latched on to his arm. He wrenched up so the dog was level with his face, her legs leaving the ground. She let go, falling into his lap. Her vicious barks amplified in the small tiled room, making it sound like he was being attacked by a pack, not a lone wolf.

My jaw hung wide, my eyes even wider. It all happened so fast, I couldn't keep up with her. She jumped at his face with her jaws ready to inflict severe damage. I spun and bolted for the door. I didn't need to have that imprinted on my brain so I could replay it in my dreams, and I needed a weapon so I could knock him out and get us out of here.

The growls and screams followed me down the hallway as my eyes scanned for a lamp, a vase, a bloody mug … anything! I didn't care. I just needed...

Why has everything gone quiet?

Ruby trotted up to my legs, her jowls coated and dripping with blood and bits of skin. She sat at my feet and cocked her head to the side as if to say, 'are you okay, mum?' I was sure all my blood had drained to my legs and my head had detached from my neck, leaving me numb as the room warped out of focus. I patted the rough fur behind her neck.

"Good girl. Let's go and see Felicity."

I stumbled back to the stairs, holding the walls for support, the bitter taste of soap still in my mouth. The sight of Felicity sprawled halfway down had me sitting on my arse and my skin pulling tight. I could just see Mr. Stevens' legs at the bottom of the descent.

Sliding down one step at a time, I reached a clammy hand for her neck to check if she had a pulse.

"Is she still alive?"

I jerked, shrieking at the noise from below and Ruby's piercing bark near my ear. I'd assumed that Felicity's father had passed out.

"Stay, Ruby."

The dog plonked her tail down beside me. I didn't have the stomach to watch more carnage and he was incapacitated, so I figured it was safe.

"Why do you even care, arsehole?"

A flutter of movement pressed against the pads of my fingers, flooding my body with relief. Rubbing my knuckles against her breast bone, I checked to see if she was responsive.

"I didn't want to hurt her. He made me do it. He was blackmailing all of us with the video footage. He made us do horrendous things while he watched." Stevens broke down, sobbing.

I had zero sympathy. He was only concerned about not getting caught.

Sick mother fucker.

Felicity's head lolled to the side. *Come on, Felicity. Snap out of it.*

"Why? What did he get out of it?"

"Power. Manipulation. He'd always been given anything he wanted. Could demand anything from anyone and they'd do it. Nobody said no to Derek Lindstrom or he would destroy them. It all became a game to see how far he could go. He wanted to claim the high-profile people as his puppets, because they had the most to lose and Derek could benefit from their power. He thrived on it."

"Why didn't you get evidence against him and take it to the police?"

"He would've killed me. Even with him dead, my life is still in danger. Evidence has a way of disappearing. There are too many people with a vested interest in keeping this quiet."

"Jesus."

Curling my hands around my legs, I rocked myself to calm the onslaught of anxiety driving my blood to a gallop and wracking my body with shivers. The man was an unstoppable force of evil, and my little pocket knife had taken him down. Thank God for my gift.

Felicity's gasp of air had my eyes popping wide and my arms flailing.

"Ron—" She couldn't get my name out. The look of horror on her face as she stared over my shoulder had me turning my head. Beside me, Ruby sprang up, her hackles on end, and ferocious barks deafening.

I jumped up at the sight of Matt Lindstrom at the top of the staircase, his face a bloody mess with one cheek ripped open, exposing the bottom of one eye socket. The barrel of his gun pointed between my eyes.

I only had time to grip the handrail before I began to fall. I remembered the sound of a gunshot and Ruby's high pitched yelp, and then... nothing.

———

Brad

The imposing house sat in benign darkness. No sign of what might be going on inside, except a sick feeling in my gut and an ever-present chill at the back of my shoulder. It tugged me forward, easing any doubts about my sanity that might've crept in. Writing on a mirror, for Christ's sake. It was insane. But I could feel my girls were here. All three of them.

Jumping the fence, I snuck around the side hoping to find an open window. These old houses had push out windows that were invariably painted shut last century. This one was no exception. Not that I was an expert in breaking and entering.

Picking up a rock, I was ready to smash it through a window when a copper shined his light in my face.

"Oi! What do you think you're doing?"

Throwing the rock back in the garden, I smiled, shielding my eyes. "Gardening?"

"Nice try, sunshine." He reached for his cuffs.

"Wait on. I was the one that rang. My girlfriend is in there. I heard screams. We need to get in there, now."

"A likely story. Turn around and put your hands on the wall, legs spread."

Shit. "No, seriously, I did hear screams."

I hadn't until the faint sound of barking and a hair-raising scream came from behind the weathered glass.

The cop shone the light through the window and I followed the sound to the front of the house, pushed on by an icy hand on my shoulder and the crushing need to save my girls.

"Stay there." My shadow fell before me as he whipped his torch around, putting me back in the spotlight.

I ignored the order and ran to the front door, scooping up another rock on the way.

"I'm breaking in."

He yanked me back by the shirt. "No, you're not."

The unmistakeable explosion of a gunshot rang out from inside, and we both tensed, eyeing each other like we'd just gone from being opponents to being comrades, ready to do battle together.

He used his baton to smash through the stained, glass window, and radioed for back up as he reached in to unlock the door.

"I'll need you to stay back. This is police business."

"Fuck that."

I pushed past him, bolting down the hallway, and skidded to a stop in the kitchen.

"We're down here!"

Veronica.

Her cries were muffled, coming from within the pantry where a hidden door stood open in the back. Bumping elbows with the cop as he passed me, gun drawn, we followed her voice, nearly tripping over the sprawled body of a man whose face looked like it had been through a meat grinder. Blood gushed from a hole in his leg and a gun sat discarded by his foot. The policeman crouched down, putting pressure on the wound, and barking into his radio.

I looked away before my stomach added to the mess. Veronica sat huddled on one of the steps further down, with Ruby cradled in her lap, and a blonde woman lying at an awkward angle by Veronica's feet. Ruby wasn't moving. I shook my head, wanting this to be some sort of bad dream that I could wake up from.

"Veronica!" She had that glazed look in her eyes and the colour had drained from her face. Her body rocked gently back and forth as she stared blankly back at me.

Haunted. She looked haunted.

I wanted to know what happened. I wanted to snatch my girls away to safety and leave the cop to deal with all the other shit.

My foot hit the top step and a hand gripped my ankle. "Sir, this is a crime scene. You need to back up. Even better, go outside and wait. We need to question you. And before you even think of taking off, you should know I took down all the plate numbers of the cars in the area. Be a good boy and wait outside."

Opening my mouth to argue, the sound of approaching sirens had me snapping it shut. I let my shoulders drop with a gust of expelled breath and walked backwards, watching those haunted black eyes take in my retreat and feeling like a piece of shit for leaving her there, knowing... knowing deep in my soul that I'd seen that look once before.

On my sister's face, a week before she died.

And I'd ignored it.

————

After questioning me for fucking ever, they still wouldn't let me go back in the house to find her. Holding the back of my neck in my hands, I fixed my stare on the open door, wishing I had x-ray vision. A quake of fear shot shockwaves through my body. I rocked on my heels, trying to absorb the impact, as my life collapsed around me for the third time. *Please ... let her be okay.*

Flashes of red and blue lights swept the scene, and this time, I was ecstatic that they were here. I told them Veronica called me in distress. They sent one car. The news crew had their cameras aimed at the door, alerted by my tip of a possible hostage situation. I'd told the journalist about the diary, but I wasn't prepared to hand it over until I knew I could trust her. Anybody could be a pawn in this game.

Nothing was happening. Why wasn't anybody coming out? The wait was unbearable.

A chorus of sirens arrived together, three ambulances and two more cop cars. I paced back and forth across the footpath, while a small crowd of gawkers gathered to watch the spectacle.

I watched in horror as four stretchers were ushered through the door by a parade of ambulance officers. Minutes later, the first one emerged with the blonde woman strapped to it. Veronica walked by her side, holding Ruby.

I moaned as my arms fell to my side. *She's okay. They're okay.*

"Veronica!" I bolted past the cops, their shouts following behind me.

She seemed startled when I reached her side, before a mask of determination set her face. "Take Ruby to the emergency vet. I fell on her, and she was kicked and knocked unconscious for more than five minutes."

Oh shit. As I collected the warm ball of fur in my arms, she licked my face in greeting. The lump in my throat shrank away.

"Okay, but are you all right? Where are you going?"

"I'm going to the hospital with Felicity."

"Sir, you need to step back behind the tape." The officer tapped me on the arm.

I searched those beautiful, brown eyes, ignoring the officer's request. "*The* Felicity from the diary?"

"Yes. And my ex-flatmate."

Turning away, she climbed into the back of the ambulance with the stretcher. The doors slammed shut, and moments later, she was gone. Taking my heart with her.

"Sir, please step away from the crime scene." I snapped my gaze to him before dropping my eyes to Ruby, her whines breaking through my daze. Concern got my feet jogging back to the car.

I was going to look after my girl. One of them, at least.

Chapter
23

Ronnie

Felicity asked me to stay with her while she recovered from her physical injuries. She was lucky to get away with broken ribs, lacerations, and a concussion. The mental scars were too many to list. I didn't hesitate in saying yes. I felt a new bond with her. I hadn't understood why Lindstrom had tried to kill her when she'd known what he'd been doing for some time, and hadn't dobbed him in. It all became clear when she told me she'd stolen the video files from his computer, intending to send copies to the media so the police couldn't make them disappear. She had the balls to try and take him down, and in the end, she did it with a pocket knife and irrefutable evidence of the corruption that festered within high places. Every one of those sick bastards was going to rot in jail, or hell.

I guess if you experienced something like that with someone, it broke down all sorts of barriers. She spent a lot of time in bed or on the couch … who could blame her? It was a different experience this time, actually sharing the same space as her. Her face hadn't seen a drop of make-up since before the incident, and her designer labels were gathering dust in the wardrobe. I was worried, but she was seeing a psychologist, and I made sure she took her medications every morning.

She moved around the room, putting up photos of her loved ones. Adding splashes of colour to the greyscale room. I grabbed a couple out of the box to help.

"You want these on the bookshelf?"

"That's fine."

Placing a photo of her and an older woman on the shelf, I did a double take, picking it up again. Tiny, blonde, and wearing togs, Felicity beamed at the camera while pointing to a sand castle. A woman kneeled beside her, smiling from under a wide brimmed hat.

"This is you and your mum?"

She threw a glance at the frame. "Mm. On the Gold Coast."

It was her. The woman from the nightmare. Candace.

"Was her name Candace?"

"Yes … You said 'was'."

"Mm hmm. I know she's gone. She visited me a few times. She was there that day under the tree. Did Lindstrom …"

"No. My father killed her. She was becoming a liability. My father did all the killing under Lindstrom's instruction. That was what they were blackmailing him for. At first, Lindstrom threatened to expose my father for tampering with evidence to get his clients off the hook. He made him do horrible things, but I think my father liked it. He tortured me. They're both insane."

"That's FUBAR. I'm so sorry." I walked over to spread my arms around her frail frame, feeling awkward about my attempt at friendly affection. She let me hug her, but didn't return it. Shards of dark pain lanced through my chest at the contact, and I quickly broke free, smothering a gasp.

Felicity checked the peephole when we heard a knock. The last few days were filled with a stream of journalists, and police bombarding us with questions. The sound of knocking set us both on alert.

"It's your boyfriend."

"Don't let him in." Not budging from my position on the couch, I ignored the stab of pain through my heart. Brad was on the other side of that door, but in reality, so out of my reach. I heard the locks click open. I twisted my head in annoyance, but at the same time, I anticipated the sight of him.

"Felicity … I'm Brad, Letitia's brother … You were her friend."

"Don't get too excited. I was the reason she met Matt. You don't want to thank me for being her friend." She stepped back, opening the door wider. "She's on the couch." Felicity quickly made herself scarce, disappearing to her room.

I sat forward, joy rushing through me as a fuzzy head poked into the room.

"Ruby!" She skidded on the slippery tiles in her excitement to see me, slamming into my legs. "Hey, baby. I missed you so much. Are you okay?" She thrashed her head around, pushing into my hands as I rubbed her head and neck. Her whole body wagged with her tail, and little grunting, sniffling noises escaped her throat. "What did the vet say?" I found Brad smiling at us when I raised my eyes. Hands hidden in the pockets of his jeans, he turned the power of that steely gaze on me. I felt it pulling me in, urging my heart to embrace him. I yanked my eyes back to Ruby.

"She had bruised ribs and a knock on her head. No permanent damage. She's on pain meds for a few days, but she'll be fine."

My fingers encircled her ears as I rested my forehead to hers. "Thank goodness. I'm so sorry, Rubes," I whispered. She snorted in my face, making me giggle.

"Are you all right?"

No. "Yeah. I'm fine. Thanks for bringing her to me."

I couldn't look at him. It tore at me, recalling the look in his eyes as he ordered me to leave. I love him with every part of me, but he'd never love all of me back. Not now that he knew.

"Are you coming home?" The last word broke from his throat.

"I'm living here for now, until the sale of Granny's place goes through, and I can find a place of my own."

"What? No, Veronica." His eyebrows lowered, mouth drawing in a tight line. "I didn't want you to leave forever. I just needed some space to deal with the bombshell you dumped in my lap."

"Oh, I dumped it there, huh? I never asked for any of this." My arm swept between us.

"That's not what I meant!"

"Look, Brad, you don't want me. Not really. You'll look at me and see all the bad shit that's happened. You'll see your dead sister. You'll always be dealing with me spacing out and having bad dreams. It's best if we just called it quits." I chewed the side of my mouth and swallowed back tears.

"I look at you and I see the future, not the past."

Oh, Jesus. I wished I could believe him, but I'd been burned so many times.

"I can't do this." I shook my head. "I can't. Please … just go." Gripping onto Ruby's collar, I watched as he scrubbed the back of his head, his chest rising and falling in a harsh movement. He left, clicking the door quietly behind him.

I kept my composure enough to get Ruby a bowl of water and settle back on the couch. And then, I let go. Breaking into wracking sobs as my heart bled out for what would never be.

———

Brad

Alcohol hummed through my blood, muffling my senses. The couch held my weight, something I'd find challenging if I had to do it on my own right now. I switched on the TV for a distraction.

"… where it has been alleged that the office of high profile lawyers, Lindstrom and Associates, also acted as the base for an exclusive underground club where women were subjected to sexual exploitation and untold horrors. Forensics are seizing evidence as we speak. The investigation is expected to be ongoing for months to come. Perhaps most disturbing are the allegations that several high-profile members of the courts and the police may be involved. Back to you, Jim."

I almost punched my finger through the red button on the remote. I didn't want to hear that shit.

I wished I could go back in time and tell myself to stay in Rocky. Tell my parents not to get on the plane. Or sell Gran's house and move to Sydney. Why didn't I do that? I took another swig of beer, flopping back to fiddle with my phone, until the screen went fuzzy and my eyelids drooped closed.

Bang, bang, bang.

My sticky eyes eased open. The effort required was too much. I grunted when someone pounded on the door, as a headache pounded inside my skull.

"Fuck!" I shoved my head in my hands, and silently cursed myself for speaking.

"Open up! I know you're in there."

Ben. Shit. He wouldn't stop banging until I let him in. I heaved to the side, rolling off the couch to my hands and knees so I could crawl to the door. My arm stretched up to twist the lock, draining the last of my energy. I flopped back against the hallway wall, legs outstretched so he had to step over me to get in.

"Mate." He pinched his nose as he shut the door. "Ever heard of a shower?"

"Sprays water at you. Dirt goes down the drain?" I slapped a hand over my eyes when he flicked on the light, and then cursed again because that fucking hurt.

"That's the one."

"It's down the hall. Help yourself."

"Throw yourself in there, dickhead. You smell like a locker room in a brewery."

"Mm. Maybe in the morning." I let my shoulders slide sideways so I could go back to sleep on the floor.

"Nuh uh. Get up." Pain lanced through my head as he gripped me under the arms and dragged me up.

"Fuck! My head!" Leaning back on the wall, I wrapped my fingers over my face. "What're you doing here, anyway?"

His voice drifted from the direction of the kitchen. "You called me."

Bad decision.

I felt a tap on my wrist, and dropped my hands.

"Here, take these." His hands offered up a glass of water in one, and a blister pack of paracetamol in the other.

Taking the water, I gulped down half the glass. He popped out two capsules and dropped them in my palm. "Thanks, mate."

"You're welcome, wanker," he said, scowling at me.

"What's with the agro?"

"What the fuck do you think you're doing?"

"Talking to my cranky friend. What're you doing?" I smirked at him, even though it hurt my face.

"You called me, whining about how Ronnie wouldn't talk to you, and that you fucked it all up ... She's been going through hell. Can you imagine what it's been like for her? Your dead sister basically harassed her into telling you the horrible truth, and you snapped her head off. She put herself in danger to save her friend, and catch that psychopath and his frat boys. She would've been next. She couldn't tell anybody how she knew about it, either. Come on, man. You're Andrea's friend. You should've been more understanding."

Shit. I didn't think about how she was going to explain it to the cops. She must've thought I didn't believe her. I did. Even before I saw the writing on the mirror. I did believe her … because I've been feeling another presence in the house. And those cold patches that followed me everywhere I went? That must've been Tish.

Ben aimed his blue stare at me. "How are you gonna fix it?"

"She won't see me, let alone talk to me." I shoved the glass back to him.

He shook his head. "Drink the rest." He waited while I swallowed it down. "So, what else have ya got?"

"Huh?" I frowned. My pickled brain wasn't getting his drift.

"How. Are. You..." He poked a thick finger into my chest with each word, "… Going to. Get. Around..." He twirled his finger in the air, "… The problem?"

Shuffling back to the lounge, I lowered into the cushy seat. Ben took a seat on the coffee table, resting his elbows on his knees. I looked at him blankly as my head slowly whirred back into gear, thanks to the painkillers. A smile turned the corners of my mouth up, and Ben raised his eyebrows.

"I still have an ace up my sleeve."

Ben slapped me on the shoulder. *Ow.* "Good. Welcome back."

————

Ronnie

Sunday morning, Felicity decided she wanted to watch cartoons. Instead of stirring up those memories, I burrowed my head in a book, and pumped heavy rock directly into my ears.

I felt a whack on my leg and looked up to see Marissa and her sister … my sisters, looking down on me. Ripping out the earbuds, I jolted upright, leaving my jaw on the couch. The girls blinked at me and I blinked back at them. We all had the same long, curly, brown hair. The only thing their mother gave me that I didn't hate. None of us knew what to say.

Marissa broke the silence. "Hi, Veronica."

"Marissa. Hi."

They both shared the same blue eyes. She gestured to her older sister. "This is Penelope."

I held out my hand, and she took it while studying me silently.

"Hello … How did you find me?" The need to know burned inside me. This was so unexpected. A miracle.

Marissa piped in again. "Brad."

My pulse stopped, my eyes pricking at the mention of his name.

"He kept coming back to the café until he saw us again."

Oh, my God. Adorable Brad.

"Luckily, it was just me and Pen walking Casper. Mum gets a bit psycho if we mention you. Well, I only did it once, when I found your photo in a box. She yelled at me, and threw it in the bin."

Of course she did.

"Shut up, Marissa. She doesn't need to hear that."

"Sorry," she said, biting her lip.

"It's okay, I know how your mum feels about me. Believe me."

"I fished it out and showed it to Pen. We noticed your hair. It took a bit of coaxing, but we found out we had another sister. She told us you were sick."

"Humph. That's what she believes." I scooted over to the side and invited them to sit. "I don't know if you should really be here. Your mum will be so angry if she finds out. I don't want to badmouth her, but there's no love between us. She's not my mother. It's … difficult to think about her."

"Do you want us to leave?" Penelope's brow creased over narrowed eyes.

"No. I don't want you to get in trouble. I know what that's like."

"It's fine. Dad knows we're here. He's on our side." Penelope shrugged and pulled her hair to rest over her chest so she could lean back, crossing her legs. "Brad told us a lot about you. He seems cool."

"She thinks he's hot."

"Marissa!" Penelope bared her teeth at our youngest.

"Sorry!" She bit her lip again, hunching her shoulders.

I laughed. I let out a deep, raucous belly laugh because I was sitting here with my sisters, and they were doing that sibling thing I'd only heard about, and finally … finally, I was a part of it.

"He is hot."

"And sweet. I thought it was romantic that he wanted to surprise you. He looked for weeks." Marissa sighed dreamily, her eyes glazing over. What went on in her imagination, I could only guess.

Weeks?

"How old are you?"

"I'm nearly thirteen. Pen is seventeen. How old are you?"

"Twenty-four, nearly twenty-five." I smiled, suddenly feeling geriatric.

"Cool." She turned to Penelope. "Hey, Pen? She can get you into the clubs."

"Oh, my God. You're so embarrassing." Penelope slapped her on the arm. I couldn't stop grinning. These two were quite a pair.

"That's something I wouldn't be able to do. Sorry, I don't do crowds."

"Why?" Their questioning gazes locked onto me.

Should I tell them? "I … don't like touching other people because I can sense their emotions or vibe. It drains me. And I stay away from people, because they treat me like a leper when they find out I can see and talk to the dead."

"Yeah, Brad told us. Only after we told him about what mum said. Don't get mad. He wanted us to be cool. So … what's it like?"

All that registered in my mind was Brad. Ever since we met, all he ever did was try to get close to me. When I told him about my curse, he still didn't let go. He really did accept all of me. He came to my rescue. He took care of my dog. He brought me a family.

I have to go and see him.

———

I let Ruby through the side gate and took the back stairs to the deck, two at a time. Ruby tore around the yard, yipping as she weaved through the plants, chasing an invisible cat. She leaped over the pond and froze on the spot, panting heavily with her tongue lolling out the side of her mouth. She'd missed this place, too.

When I reached the deck, a turbulent, grey-blue gaze hit me with the force of lightning. He was waiting near the table. His eyes took in every inch of me, and my body quivered under the weight of his longing. I could hardly contain the force of my love for this man.

He twisted to drop a pencil near the sketchpad on the table. I didn't notice it before. I stepped closer to have a look. A gasp broke free. He'd drawn me and Ruby as we were when he brought her to Felicity's house. I turned around to look at him, letting all my emotions play across my face.

Thank you. I missed you. I'm sorry. I love you.

Lovable Brad.

"Are you staying?" His hands flexed by his side.

Leaning up on my toes, I cupped his face in my palms, feeling the soft beard he'd grown in the last week, and kissed my answer onto his lips.

He embraced me in a tight hug, lifting me off my feet, and nibbled on my mouth.

"You're staying."

"Yes." As my answer squeezed past my strangled throat, I allowed the tears to fall. "I'm sorry. I'm sorry."

"Me, too." He brushed his thumbs across my cheeks, soothing me with his touch.

"I love you," I breathed the words looking deep into his eyes, catching every fleck of blue in the storm of grey. They crinkled at the corners, his white teeth flashing as my words registered.

"Yeah, I know."

Epilogue

Ronnie—Six Months Later

Sucking in my cheeks, I dragged my tongue along the underside of Brad's cock as the shower sprayed a river of water down his chest. He aimed his moans at the ceiling, tilting his head back and holding on to my hair with one hand. Firm butt cheeks filled my hands as I gripped them tightly.

We were supposed to be getting ready to go into the city for a stroll around the night markets. He wanted to conserve water. All we were managing to do was waste hundreds of litres of the stuff.

"Ah, stop." Pulling his hips back, he reached for my arms, lifting to pin me against the cold, tile wall. "My turn." He grinned and sank to his knees, hooking one of my legs over his shoulder.

I think we might be late.

His hot tongue made contact with my centre. The echo of my mewls encouraged him to lick with more enthusiasm. Diving his tongue in deep, he drew it out to circle against my clit before repeating the action. My head spun as he took me to places I only dreamed of. I couldn't think. I'm not sure I was thinking at all. I was one mass of need.

Waves of bliss shot me higher, making me aware of every part of my body … especially where he touched me. My leg slipped off his broad shoulder, as he stood and spun me. Guiding my hands to the wall, he let go to trap my hips in his grasp. The rip of a wrapper sounded and seconds later he was slamming into me, thrusting his hips and yanking mine back to meet his. The drag of his erection along my slick walls made my muscles clench, anticipating my release.

"You feel amazing. I can't stop thinking about how you feel, how you smell." He leaned his mouth against my ear. "How you taste."

I reached back to grip his thigh, pulling him harder against me as he took me to the edge and followed me over.

———

Lots of people. Why did I agree to this? Oh, right. The shower.

I clung tightly to Brad's arm as he guided me through, trying to distract me by pointing out trinkets and art works.

"Ronnie?" Looking back, I spotted Beverly and John, adorable in matching jeans and T-shirts.

"Beverly!" She returned my smile and my embrace. I felt a warmth spread over me, and immediately sensed that she was okay. Fabulous, in fact.

She stepped back, and John wrapped a protective arm around her back. "It's so good to see you out and about, sweetheart."

"He persuaded me to come." I swung a hand at Brad's chest and he caught it in his grip, pulling it down to his side, and threading his fingers with mine.

"John and I are out on a date, too. It's becoming a regular Friday night thing. I feel like we've just met." She kissed her husband on the cheek, and he responded by grabbing her face and planting one on her lips.

Turning back to me with a pink blush rising on her beaming face, she cleared her throat. "Well, we'll leave you to it. Have a nice night."

"Thank you, we will. You too."

Brad led me out of the crowd and towards the river, finding a bench for us to sit on.

"Beverly looks well, doesn't she?"

I'd taken Brad to meet her once she was recovered and back to work. "Yeah. She's in remission. John's ecstatic to have her back, by the looks of it."

"Date night. Hm. We might have to do that when we have kids," he teased, smiling his cheeky smile.

Kids. Huh.

"This is where I was sitting when I first saw you," he continued, sounding pensive all of a sudden. "Life has changed so much. For the better." He lifted my hand to his lips, letting them linger on my skin before resting it on his thigh.

I turned to watch his profile. Strong brows, straight nose, bold chin. Freckled face. I'd never get sick of that view.

"Yes, it has. I'm so glad you broke my tailbone."

His deep laugh rumbled. *Life is fucking fantastic.*

"Hello."

I frowned at the tiny woman watching us from the path. Long, blonde hair with pale pink highlights twisted in a pile on her head, topped a gorgeous face. She was dressed to grace the runway. High heeled boots, beautiful long jacket over a bright, funky dress. The combination worked well and it was unique.

"Are you going to answer me, or have you forgotten me already?" I recognised that snark.

"Felicity?" *God.* I hadn't seen her in months.

"Finally!" She rolled her eyes. "You two are disgusting in public, by the way."

"Look away." I laughed. "How are you?"

"I'm great. I'm off to the US to live with my brother. Chris has been really supportive. He came to stay with me for a while after … you know. I just needed to get away. Start fresh." She dropped her eyes to her boots as she scuffed them along the pavement.

"I think that's a great idea. Good luck with everything. I'd like to stay in touch, if you want?"

"I'd like that. Thanks. Good luck to you too." She started to turn away, but she twisted back to face me. "Thank you, Ronnie."

I nodded before she glided off on her heels to her new life.

"Wanna come home with me?" Brad ran a finger down my cheek to catch a tear.

"Is that a proposition?"

"Always. Everything I say to you has a dirty thought behind it. You should know this by now."

"Pfft. Incorrigible."

He pulled me up and started jogging, pulling me behind.

"What are you doing?"

"Thinking dirty thoughts!"

Huh. Of course, he was. Thank God.

I saw a flash of yellow as we ran along the river. Tish with her thumbs up and a brilliant glow around her. *She's saying goodbye.* I nodded, mouthing 'thank you,' before she vanished.

Gift or curse?

Gift, definitely gift.

Acknowledgements

As always, thanks to my wonderful, beautiful family. I love you guys to the ends of the Earth. I hope you know that. Sorry for all my absent/ zombie moments. Sorry for the toasted sandwich dinners and the weekends we can't do family outings because I'm working to a deadline. Kids, I hope when you're older you can understand why I do this and find something of your own that drives you and fulfils you. (What are you doing reading this? Put the book down!)

This book took years to come to fruition. During that time, I suffered several life changing blows and some wonderful surprises, too. This book was definitely an emotional journey in itself. I probably poured too much of what I was feeling onto these pages, and gave my editor a hell of a job. To my exceptional editor, Eeva, thank you. Thank you. Thanks for talking me down from the ceiling and up from the floor. Thanks for being tough and honest. Thanks for not sleeping so you could finish editing this beast. Mostly, just thanks for being there.

My friends, you know who you are, you're so patient and understanding with my frazzled self. I thank you for lending your ears, your shoulders, your support, and your love. I apologise for the sparse communications. Know that I think of you and only wish the best for you, and that your support means so, so much to me. I should tell people that I come with a bad friend warning—goes months without communication. Will dance on the fringes of your life, but will jump in when you need me. Massive hugs to you all!

Mum and Dad. Sorry for the shock. I hope your Kindle recovers. Thanks for being proud.

Jennifer at More Than Words Promotions. You're a gem. A talented gem. I'm so glad that I found you.

To the ladies from the USQ library, thank you for your invaluable information and assistance.

To all the awesome bloggers. What a fantastic community, I'm so proud to be a part of it. I've said it before, but I didn't truly understand it until I published my own work. What you contribute to this industry makes a massive difference. And you do it tirelessly, and often thanklessly. Please know that you are appreciated so much. The word ginormous isn't even big enough to describe the magnitude of thanks you deserve.

To my lovely readers. This is for you. It's all for you. I sincerely hope you've managed to escape for a while. I can't thank you enough for choosing to read my story out of a sea of others just as worthy, if not more worthy of your attention. If you loved it, let me know. I'd love to hear from you.

———

Read on for an excerpt from *Convincing You*.

Excerpt from Convincing You

Andrea

Brisbane, Australia

19th December, 2016

A cracker loaded with brie and quince paste was passed in front of my face as Lee handed it to Ronnie.

Brie. Sweet, sweet, unpasteurised, soft, bacteria-ridden cheese. *Oh, how I've missed you.*

I licked my lips, sucking in the smell as my nose followed the delicacy.

"Are you sniffing my food?" Wrinkles carved grooves into Ronnie's cheeks.

"It has been nine months. *Nine. Months.* Yes, I'm sniffing the brie. I *miss* it." My statement came out as a whimper.

Ronnie took a small bite before asking, "Can you still have soft cheese if you're breastfeeding?"

"I don't think so," Lee answered, scrubbing the back of his freckled neck.

I arched my sore back. "What? Of course I can. Don't tell me that."

Ben wrapped his fingers around my ponytail and stroked its length. "I dunno. I think it might be too risky for the baby."

I twisted to look at him. "Bullshit. You're wrong." I searched his serious expression for any hint of a joke. A twitch in the corner of his mouth. A change in his eyes. Nothing. He was stone-cold sober. "Don't tell me I can't eat the cheese. I want the cheese. Babe, you know I can't do without the cheese."

Ronnie rested her forearms on the table and leaned forward, her gaze glued to mine. "I read an article last week about this woman who did all the right things during the pregnancy and as soon as the baby was born, she gorged on all the cheese. Brie, camembert, blue vein—she went to town. She fed the baby a couple of hours later. The poor thing ended up in hospital with a nasty infection."

"Are you shitting me?" I dropped my chin, mouth agape. If this was a joke, she was no longer my friend.

"Yes. Yes, Andy, we're shitting you." She leaned back with a huge grin on her face as Lee and Ben sniggered. "It's way too easy."

"I hate you."

"Not true."

Ben tried to tuck me under his arm. I pouted and inched away. "You're so mean to me in my vulnerable state. You know it's my due date and I'm still fecking preggers."

"He'll be here soon. He's just way too comfortable inside there." Ben nuzzled my neck, whispering in my ear, "I don't blame him. I wanna be inside you right now."

I wriggled in my seat as a choking noise came from across the table. "Jesus, I heard that." Ronnie scrubbed her hands over her ears, masses of dark curls bouncing as she did.

I didn't give a shit that she'd heard what Ben said. I loved that he still found me desirable despite the fact that I'd swelled to twice my normal size and couldn't see my toes, let alone touch them.

The loud clap of Lee's hands made me jump. "Who wants prawns? Not you, Andy. I did a rolled turkey roast for you. Sorry."

Prawns. Another thing I couldn't eat. *Yet.* After this kid was out, I was going to fill myself with all the pre-prepped salad, shellfish, soft cheese, and wine I could get my hands on.

Lee dragged his chair back as Ronnie jumped to help him.

I rested a hand on Ben's thigh. The delicious smell of our early Christmas dinner wafted from the kitchen. "Do you mind if we exchange gifts first? I can't wait. We might have to run off to hospital at any moment."

"You can't hold off for another half an hour?"

"Nope."

Ben pushed his chair back.

"Babe, can you grab the presents for me please?"

"Already on it."

He was the best.

Lee stood behind Ronnie with his arms around her teeny tiny waist, one palm spread over her stomach. They presented such a contrast. Her with sultry, dark features and caramel skin, and Lee with freckles and auburn locks. He was only just taller than her. She and Ben were eye to eye, but he was twice her girth, although they were both solid muscle. All three of my dinner companions could've done a Nike ad, while I was the Oompa Loompa in the background.

Not for much longer hey, baby boy?

Our hosts watched me from the kitchen. Something silently passed between them, evident from the way they held each other.

"Are you coming over here, or are you going to make me get up?" I raised a brow.

They returned to their seats with matching smirks.

Ben slid in beside me, placing down an envelope and a box wrapped with multi-coloured braided ribbons and topped with a pretty bow.

"Thanks." I handed the envelope to Ronnie. "Merry Christmas!"

Lee had given Ronnie tickets to Sydney for her birthday two weeks ago. They were going before uni started back in March. As soon as I found out what he'd planned, I'd known what I wanted to give her for Christmas.

A smile tilted her mouth at one corner as her eyes flitted around the table. She ducked her chin and used her knife to open the present. Slipping out a piece of paper, her eyebrows scrunched before popping high. "A private ghost tour of Sydney." Her shoulders kissed her earlobes. "I'm shitting myself. Thanks."

"All the oldest buildings are haunted, but you already know that. I figured you could kill two birds with one stone. Face down your fear of spirits and get an inside view of some beautiful old buildings."

"You'll be with me. I'll protect you, babe." Lee kissed her cheek and she responded with a roll of her eyes.

He knew damn well she didn't need protection. They were cute together. It was nice to see them both happy after the fucked-up shit that had gone down earlier in the year. She'd nearly died trying to save her friend from an underground sex cult. Nothing would ever clear those images from their heads, but they could create new memories—happy Polaroid moments, shining light into the darkest corners of their minds. Not that ghosts would provide particularly happy snaps necessarily, but Ronnie could handle anything that was thrown at her now. She was a badass.

"Your turn." Ben pushed the box across the table to his mate.

"Did you wrap this?" Lee tried to hide a smirk.

"That's all my handiwork, mofo. You know I'm good with plaits."

My eye twitched as Lee fiddled with the ribbons, trying to delicately untie the bow. "Just rip it."

"You sure?"

"Yes! Jesus." I almost dragged my hands down my face.

He yanked at the paper, tossing bits on the table. "Do you know what you're gonna call Benny junior?"

"Sebastian." I answered without thinking.

"Hell, no." Ben frowned.

"Why not?" I thought we'd discussed this already, but maybe that had all been in my head.

His blue eyes pierced mine. "Sebastians don't play rugby."

I wracked my brain trying to remember if there'd been any players named Sebastian. Surely there were. I shook my head. "What if he doesn't wanna play?"

Ben paused, his Adam's apple bobbing as he blinked at me.

"Are you going to make him?" I asked.

"No?" It sounded like a question.

I took it as a definitive answer, rubbing my belly. "I'm relieved to hear it."

"Is Stewart gonna make him play league?" Ben narrowed his eyes.

"Not if he knows what's good for him." My brother wouldn't dare. I'd slap him if he tried to influence my child in any way.

He scoffed. "He has never known what's good for him. I still can't believe they let him into the police force."

I couldn't get over that one myself.

"Why Sebastian?" Ben frowned.

"I don't know. I just have a feeling." The moniker had been rolling around in my thoughts more and more lately. There was something attached to it, tangled strings that needed unknotting. Unfinished business. I'd never known anyone with that name, but it wouldn't leave me alone. Our son *had* to be called Sebastian—I knew that much. I just didn't know why. "It'll grow on you. Trust me on this one, okay?"

Ben pushed a breath through flared nostrils. "Do I get to pick the middle name?"

"Absolutely ... as long as it's Ben." I smiled with all my pearly whites on show.

His lip quirked. "Sebastian Ben Locke." Running his tongue along his teeth, he looked at me. "Seb for short. That's okay."

"Cute." Lee added. "And he's going to play league. Is anyone interested in my critique of my present?"

Ben and I twisted our heads and found that Lee had opened the box and was wearing his present on his head. A fluffy wallaby with a baby in her pouch sat atop the brim of his Australian national rugby union official team cap. I'd made the alterations myself.

Ronnie gave him the side-eye while leaning away.

"I love it." Lee grinned.

I snorted. I couldn't help it. He looked ridiculous.

Ben, Lee, and I were laughing so hard I didn't realise at first that we were the only ones. Ronnie had a smile on her lips, but her worried eyes were on my stomach. She almost appeared sick. Or spooked.

Sebastian rolled. I shifted in my seat, holding my side. Her gaze tracked my hand. She grimaced before turning away.

What is that all about?

The only answer I got was a sinking feeling in my gut that had nothing to do with Seb's movements and everything to do with the way Ronnie stared at my baby bump.

I take it back. I don't want to know.

About the Author

Author of smart, sexy characters, J.M. Adele loves to flit between the dark and light sides of romance. Somewhere along the way an almost constant procession of imaginary characters settled into her thoughts and she picked up a pen to share their stories.

She lives in Queensland with her three greatest loves, her children. When she's not writing or being a mum, you might find her hiking up a mountain, singing in the car when nobody is looking, or curled up with a good book.

Follow J.M.

 www.jmadele.org

 www.facebook.com/authorjmadele

 @JMAdeleBooks

 @j.m.adele